SWORD OF DEATHS

The Scythe Wielder's Secret: Book Two

Christopher Mannino

MuseItUp Publishing
Canada

MuseItUp Publishing
14878 James, Pierrefonds, Quebec, Canada, H9H 1P5

Layout and Book Production by Lea Schizas
Print ISBN: 978-1-77127-739-6
eBook ISBN: 978-1-77127-738-9
First eBook Edition *August 2015

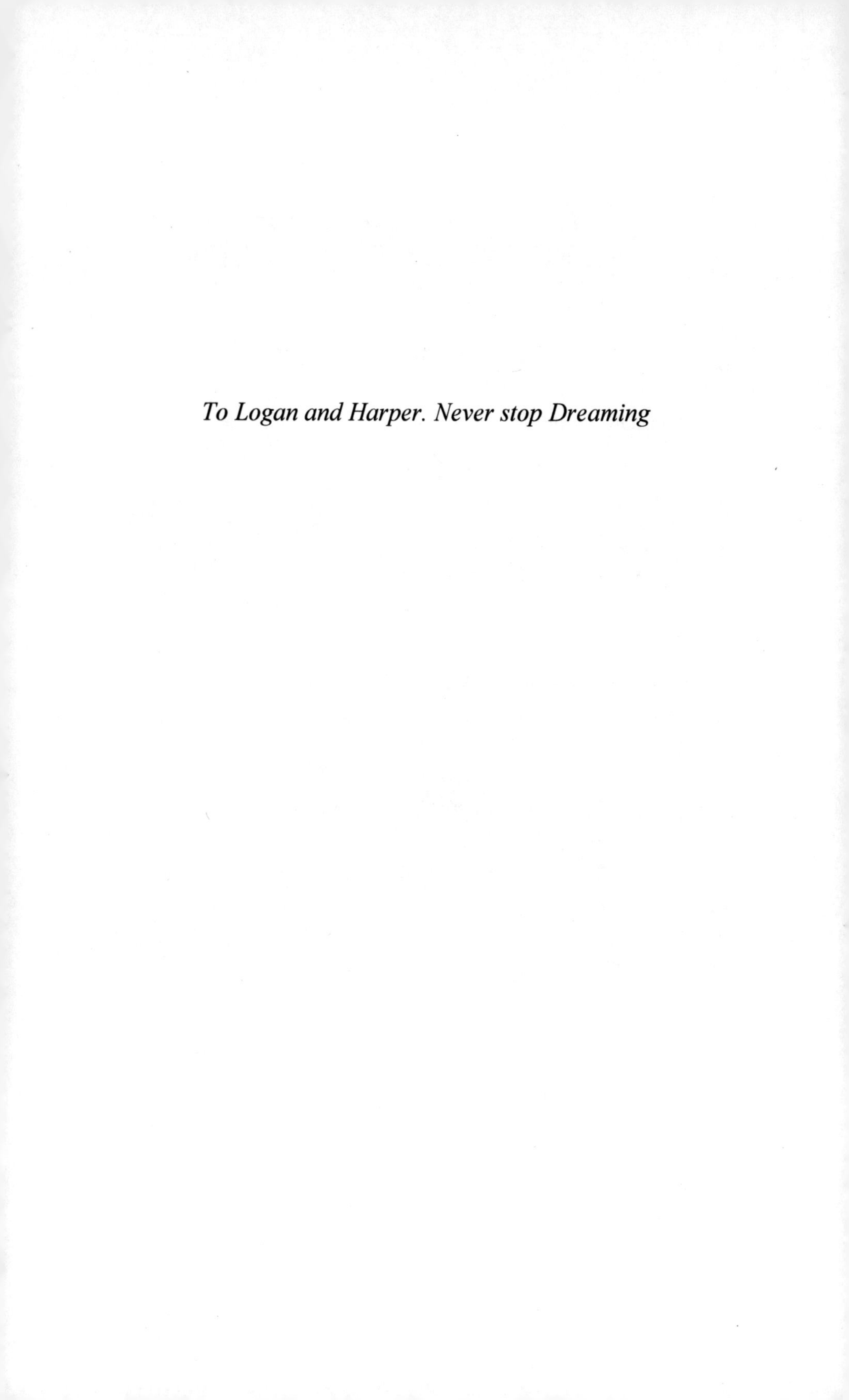

To Logan and Harper. Never stop Dreaming

Praise for ***School of Deaths***:
The Scythe Wielder's Secret: Book One

"Amazing Story! I found myself immersed in the story from the first page!"

—NerdGirl Reviews

"Not just a book for young adults, but an imaginative read for everyone who likes something a little bit different. 5 Stars!"

—Reader's Favorite

"Wonderful! Addictive! Two thumbs up! The plot itself was beyond intriguing. It definitely took me for a spin. I wasn't expecting the story to take me where it did, and it definitely kept me guessing all the way toward the end. The author did a wonderful job at keeping me both entertained and fascinated by the world he created. Would recommend School of Deaths to YA lovers everywhere."

—Kristy Centeno, author of *The Keeper Witches* series and the *Secrets of the Moon* series.

CHAPTER ONE: SUZIE

A Female Death

The Death laughed. He waved his scythe and the world behind her vanished. Two immense eyes rose behind him, surrounded by leathery skin. She heard the beating of wings.

"You are weak," said the Death. "You're nothing at all, Suzie. Just a girl." He laughed again.

"Leave me alone!" Suzie walked forward but stopped as a sharp, shooting pain coursed through her.

"So weak, so worthless."

"Go away! Leave me alone!"

The man, the strange eyes, and the entire world shattered, splitting into fragments of glass. Shards flew toward her, burrowing beneath skin. So much pain.

She looked down. The glass was gone. Markings covered each hand. The marks crawled upwards, moving onto Suzie's neck—strangling her.

Something clawed at her throat, pulling her down, ripping her apart. She gasped for air.

She exploded into a burst of light.

* * * *

Suzie Sarnio opened her eyes as sunlight poured into the small bedroom in Eagle Two, Room Five. Wiping sweat from her face, she looked around the room. This was home now. Not just for a time, but forever. She'd failed the test. Now she could never return to the Living World.

Suzie Sarnio was a Death.

She heard her housemate Billy moving chairs in the kitchen. He was probably planning some surprise for her fourteenth birthday today.

The past year ran through her mind in a blur. She'd been a normal girl in Maryland, with normal friends, and a normal life. Then a stranger named Cronk, a hooded man waving a scythe, showed up, explaining she was a Death. Now here she was in the College of Deaths. She'd Reaped a soul, and helped overthrow the Headmaster of the College. Every new Death was given one chance to return home, a test at the end of their first year. Yesterday, she'd taken hers and failed.

"Is she awake yet?" she heard her friend Frank say.

"Haven't seen her," said Billy.

She pulled herself up and swung her legs to the floor. Putting on a pair of shorts and a tee-shirt, she yawned while opening the curtains. West Tower shot into the clouds in front of her, a gnarled mountain of stone writhing a hundred stories high, like an enormous stalagmite. On the far side of campus, she saw its twin East Tower, looming over the campus. Earthen mounds stretched between the two in a massive canyon-like labyrinth. She remembered her time in East Tower, and how she'd discovered Headmaster Sindril's plan.

The Dragons need you alive, he'd told her. He'd confessed to plotting her abduction, and had re-written her final test, so the only way to pass would be to kill Cronk. She'd refused. She wasn't a murderer. By refusing to kill, however, she'd ensured that she'd remain a Death eternally.

"You are weak," said the Death. "You're nothing at all, Suzie. Just a girl." Sindril laughed again.

It was only a dream. Sindril was gone now. Probably fled to his Dragon friends.

So much had happened in a year, and now, here she was in the World of the Dead. Her home *forever*.

The only female Death.

She sighed and opened her door.

"You're up," said Billy. A crudely painted banner read "Happy Birthday Suzy." Three large boxes wrapped in colored paper sat on the kitchen table.

"I-E," she said.

"What?" asked Billy.

"I spell Suzie Z-I-E, no Y."

"Guess I've never seen you write it." Billy laughed. He hurried to the stove and brought a plate of warm pancakes.

"You guys shouldn't have—" she started.

"This is a celebration," said Frank. "Summer vacation. Three months off from school, and no more Sindril! Now maybe the 'Mentals will get the respect they deserve."

"We don't know what will happen, or who will take over." Billy shook his head.

"It's true," said Suzie. "Frank, I don't think you should tell anyone that you're—"

"I won't. I need you both to promise that you won't let anyone know."

"It's our secret," said Billy.

"You're a Death." Suzie nodded.

It wasn't true. Frank was an Elemental in disguise. The situation with the 'Mentals was complex, but she hoped with Sindril gone, things would improve. Under Sindril's leadership, the 'Mentals had been slaves to the Deaths. She'd enlisted their support to help overthrow him. Sneaking into his office during a 'Mental attack, she found proof that Sindril had allied with Dragons, the historic enemies of Deaths. The 'Mentals then helped her broadcast the proof to every Death at the College, ensuring Sindril's downfall. However, even with new leadership, centuries of prejudice wouldn't vanish overnight. Frank was better off if no one knew what he truly was.

"Thanks," said Frank.

"Are you guys eating?" she asked.

"Already ate, sorry," said Billy.

"Me too," said Frank. "Grabbed a gorger before I got here."

The pancakes were doughy and undercooked, but she loved them. Usually she just ate gorgers, the food that took whatever flavor you wanted. It was nice to have something cooked for once.

"I don't know whether I should feel happy or not. I still feel torn about failing the test yesterday."

Billy put his hand on hers. She felt a slight blush rising to her cheeks, the feeling she always got when he touched her.

"I was upset too," he said. "When I didn't take the test last year, a part of me felt like I'd made the biggest mistake of my life. I'd blown any chance I'd ever have of leading a normal life, but here we are, Suzie. I'm thrilled to be here with you. This is my home now. It's yours too."

She nodded and smiled, taking another bite of pancake.

"Why don't you open your gifts," said Frank.

"There's three here," she said. "Jason didn't—"

"No," interrupted Billy. "It wasn't him." Jason had been their housemate last year.He had been their friend. Now he was gone, one of only two first-year Deaths who actually passed their test. The other, Luc, had bullied Suzie more than anyone. She was, after all, the only female Death in the entire world. Strange to think both Luc and Jason were back in the Mortal World with no recollection of their year as Deaths.

"Someone left this one at the door," said Frank. "I saw it on my way in. Why don't you open it first?" He handed her what looked like a shoebox wrapped in yellow and red paper. She opened the card.

"It's from Cronk. It says: To the bravest girl I know. Happy Birthday, and Thank You."

"You did save his life," reminded Billy.

"A part of me just wanted to go home." She sighed. "To forget all this, and see my family, but I couldn't kill him. Sindril didn't give me a choice."

"That's not true." Frank grinned. "You always have a choice, and you made the right one. You're a strong person, Suzie. What did Cronk give you?"

She laughed while opening the box and found a set of paintbrushes and a pad of paper.

"He knows you love art," said Billy.

"I do." Suzie smiled, taking another bite of pancake.

"Open mine next," said Frank. He passed her a small box in brown paper, tied with twine. A small card on the front said: *To the best friend I've ever had.*

She opened it carefully, untying the twine and removing the paper without ripping it.

"What is it?" she asked, pulling out a worn book with an unmarked cover.

"Careful," he said. "The 'Mentals may have preserved it, but it's very delicate. That book's a million years old."

"That's impossible," said Billy. "It'd be dust now."

"Difficult, but not impossible. Though I wouldn't try to read the book, or even open it. I thought you should have it, as a keepsake. This belonged to Lovethar. Some say it was her diary."

Lovethar's diary. Lovethar, the only other female Death, who'd lived a million years ago.

"That's amazing," said Suzie. "Thank you so much." She rose and hugged him. Tears pooled and streamed down her cheeks. How could she ever think of leaving? These were the closest friends she'd ever had. This was home.

"I guess that leaves mine," said Billy. "It's nothing much."

She pulled the gift toward her, nervous to read the card. Did Billy like her as much as she liked him? They'd kissed, but maybe he just wanted to be friends. Would Frank be jealous if he knew how she felt?

She opened the card. "I'm glad you're here with us. Happy Birthday." She opened the box and pulled out a framed picture. At first she didn't recognize the fierce woman holding the scythe. She thought it might be Lovethar, but when she looked harder, she noticed her freckles and that curl that never seemed to stay. The pale girl with long, black hair had to be her. Three other Deaths stood behind her in the image: Billy, with his disheveled sandy hair, icy blue eyes, and long scar across his right cheek; Frank, with his dark brown eyes, hiding their true green color; and Jason, with his glasses and awkward expression. The painting was amazing, and the faces looked very real.

"Jason helped me a bit, before he left," said Billy, "but I've been drawing for a while. Never took Art or anything, and it isn't much. I was going to give it to you before your test, but with everything going on, I sort of forgot. Guess I lucked out."

"It's perfect," she said. She stood and kissed him on the cheek.

"So, birthday girl," said Frank. "What's the plan today? It's summer break now, we can do whatever you want. Did you want to hang around the campus, or go somewhere else?"

"I want to go somewhere I've never been," said Suzie. "Nothing on campus, but not Silver Lake or the library either. I want to see something new."

Billy laughed. "You're a real explorer. I thought you'd had enough of that, especially after you and I found that 'Mental village, but nope, always want to explore more."

"It's my birthday, and that's what I feel like doing."

"All right, all right," said Billy. "How about Mors? I've only been once, but it's pretty amazing."

"Mors?" she asked. "Where's that?"

"It's on the sea," said Frank. "The capital of the Deaths, and the great port. Where Deaths get most of their supplies. I've heard of it, but have never been."

"Mors it is," said Suzie.

"Pack your bag," said Billy. "It'll take a day just to get there. We'll take the canal."

* * * *

Suzie sat on her bed, remembering her first trip to the sea.

"Shut up, Joe. Mom, he's being annoying."

"Joe, leave your sister alone."

Suzie turned away from her stupid brother, looking at the traffic.

"I told you we should have left an hour earlier," said Dad.

"We'll still make it to the rental on time. Don't worry, honey."

The packed SUV crawled up the long, sloping ramp leading to the Chesapeake Bay Bridge. Within minutes, they'd climbed high above the water below. Most of her friends had been to the Eastern Shore, but she'd never crossed the Bay. The lab they'd done last year, in second grade, really showed how endangered the crabs are.

To her right, she saw a moving cloud of black smoke.

"Daddy, there's a boat on fire," she said, pointing.

"Don't be dumb," said Joe. "It's just a tanker. That's its engine."

Suzie grimaced. "Don't call me dumb, idiot."

"You two, knock it off," said Dad. "I'll turn this car around."

"On a bridge?" asked Joe.

"Well, at least after we've crossed."

Suzie caught Dad's smile in the rear-view mirror. He scratched his moustache, and adjusted his sunglasses. Mom turned the page in her magazine. Suzie tried reading in the car once, but it made her sick.

Two hours later, the car pulled into a small town in Delaware.

"We're here," said Dad, turning right at a strange totem pole. "I haven't been to Bethany Beach since I was a kid."

They drove a mile more, and then entered the driveway of a single story house with wide porches and immense windows.

"This place is huge," said Suzie.

"Well it's ours for the weekend," said Dad. "I'm going out to pick up some dinner. Why don't you kids head to the beach? You can see it through the window there."

Behind the rental, a tall sand dune blocked their view of a semi-private beach. Suzie ran to the bathroom and changed into her new suit. Excitement bubbled in her heart. Would she see Africa on the other side, or would the water just go to the horizon? On TV, the ocean seemed endless.

She adjusted the straps of her bathing suit, joined Joe and Mom at the back door, and then sprinted towards the dune. At the sand's edge she kicked off her flip-flops, and walked bare foot over the hill. The sand felt warm and gritty. Tiny twigs and shell shards prodded her toes.

A seagull cawed loudly, sailing gently on a breeze. In front of her, a line of grayish water struck the beach with a frothy white crash. The wave receded, drifting away into the ocean.

"It goes on forever," she said, staring at the boundless expanse.

"What'd you expect, dummy?" asked Joe.

I'll never see Mom, Dad, or Joe again. It was my choice, and I chose to stay. Unlike Sindril, I'm not a murderer. I could never kill someone.

Despite her nostalgia, she smiled at the irony.

I couldn't kill, but I am a Death.

* * * *

Billy brought them through the campus of the College of Deaths. Earthen ridges and mounds formed an elaborate reddish maze. East and West Towers shot for hundreds of feet above the rest of the campus: two towers of twisted stone. A glimmer of metal told Suzie they were near the Ring of Scythes, which surrounded the College.

They walked to a long mound with rows of arched windows. Billy led them through the open door, and Suzie was surprised to see long piers, and hundreds of small boats. The building smelled like the sea.

"There are boats here on campus?" She'd been here a year but had never seen this place.

"It's the end of the Lethe, the canal that connects Mors to the College," said Billy.He pointed to the rear wall, which was open. A series of small canals led away from the piers beneath arches of metal a few yards away.

"Most supplies are shipped in," he continued. "I figured we'd take a boat out. We're actually right next to the Ring of Scythes. You'll see it clearer from the boat."

Billy bought them each a ticket and they climbed onto a low barge with skulls carved near the bow. A tall Death with dark skin and long, braided hair helped her aboard.

"You're the girl," said the Death. "I've heard of you. Is it true you killed Headmaster Sindril?"

"No," said Suzie. "What are you talking about?"

The Death shrugged and helped Frank into the boat.

"Doesn't matter to me," he said, "but there's many talking about you."

"We don't want any trouble," said Billy.

"Of course," said the Death.

He untied the boat and they bobbed on the gentle canal water. Four Deaths with oars pulled. There were a few other passengers, and a large pile of boxes in the center of the barge. It swung away from the pier and Suzie stumbled.

"Let's sit down," said Billy. "It'll take a while to get there."

He and Suzie sat near the bow, with Frank behind them. The boat slid past the outer rocky wall of the building, and they were outside again. An enormous arch, bigger than any she'd seen in the Ring of Scythes loomed in front of them. The Ring was formed from massively oversized scythes, which stretched into the air, connecting to form arches. Only Deaths and 'Mentals could pass through the Ring, which could be sealed. She'd learned that the hard way, when Sindril sealed her out. Why did she keep thinking about him? He was gone now, nothing to worry about. He'd fled the College, returning to his friends the Dragons.

Where the Lethe Canal passed beneath the Ring of Scythes, two scythes stretched into the sky, forming an archway of solid metal thirty feet high. The long-haired Death stepped behind her.

"Left over from the Great War," he said. "All the scythes in the Ring are, but those two were the greatest of all."

"Were they?" asked Suzie, looking back toward the College. East Tower was directly behind the boat; West Tower had vanished behind its twin.

"My name is Eshue," said the Death. "Esh-oo-ay." His accent was African, and he moved in a strange, dancelike manner. "My father is captain of this boat. Welcome."

"I'm Billy."

"Frank."

"You know who I am," said Suzie.

"The female Death," said Eshue. "Susan." He nodded and gestured to the scythes again. The boat passed under them. Beneath the enormous blades, Suzie's skin tingled.

"A wonderful use of mortamant, don't you think?" Eshue chuckled. "The scythe can slice through anything. Light and dark, life and death, truth and lies. You know that already, though. Have you been on the Lethe before?"

"No," said Suzie.

"This is the canal that feeds the College, the vein that connects mouth and heart, heart and body, in the World of the Dead."

Frank gave her a look and rolled his eyes. She sighed. This was going to be a long trip. They passed beneath a long bridge, and civilization faded. The crowded College, its mountainous towers, and its glimmering Ring of Scythe grew smaller. Open fields and scattered trees stretched around the canal. Dense forest spread across the horizon on either side. She stood and walked to the side of the boat. The canal's still waters rippled behind the oars. Another barge carrying enormous boxes passed in the opposite direction. She leaned down and reached toward the water.

"Don't," said Eshue, grabbing her hand. "Don't touch the water. It is bad luck. The Lethe is cursed. They say the souls of Deaths who *cease* go here, forever forgotten. They drift the currents, trapped between the city and the College, never able to reach the sea."

"That sounds like a superstitious old tale," said Billy.

"Maybe so," said Eshue, "but on my father's boat, please do not touch the water. I don't want bad luck."

Suzie sat down again and Eshue walked away.

"Why do Deaths *cease*?" she asked Billy. "I know that if we're killed in this World, we get erased from everything. But why?"

"Next she's going to ask what happens in the Hereafter," said Frank.

"He's right," said Billy. "There's no answer to that. It just is."

"So if I'd killed Cronk—"

"You'd be in the Living World now," said Billy, "and none of us would remember his name. Suzie, you can't spend the rest of the year obsessing about the choice you made. It'll drive you crazy. You're here now, that's all there is to it. Yesterday you said you were glad to stay."

"I am," she said. "It's just—"

"I understand," he said. "Believe me, I do."

"What is there to do in Mors?" she asked, changing the subject.

"I only went once myself. Last summer, a few of my friends went for a few days. We looked around, went to the port and the beach, and of course there's Silver Fair. You'll love that."

"Silver Fair?"

"It's like an amusement park. Well, sort of. Don't forget that Deaths are taken when they're kids, so plenty of them are our age. Silver Fair is great."

"An amusement park. Never thought they'd have one of those." Suzie smiled and watched a cloud drift by. She tried to imagine what an amusement park for Deaths might look like.

CHAPTER TWO: FRANK

Mors

Frank watched the clouds overhead. The boat continued floating down the Lethe.

Plamen.

Glancing at Suzie, he frowned. He'd lied to her every day for months. No wonder she was obsessed with Billy now.

Plamen.

His name stuck in the back of his throat. The name he'd abandoned last year. The name of a 'Mental.

I am Plamen.

The boat rounded a bend, and a row of buildings emerged on the horizon. He watched them, feeling a growing sense of his power. It throbbed behind his eyes, trying to break into his thoughts.

Fire and blood.

Fear and pain.

Jumbled images surrounded him. He clutched the side of the boat, trying to steady himself. The visions passed through his mind, tearing into his thoughts. Hundreds of pictures, the past and present, collided in his thoughts and vanished in a smoky haze.

He took a deep breath, staring at the outline of Mors. Suzie hadn't noticed—too busy gazing at Billy again. The flashes were getting worse. He closed his eyes, desperate to sort through the jumble of images. Was something about to happen, or had something happened long ago?

One day, he'd be a seer, like his parents. One day he'd master these abilities. However, that day was far in the future.

He turned to Suzie again. Her black hair caught in the wind, blowing behind her freckled face. The beautiful girl turned and smiled at him.

"You have a far-off look," she said.

"So do you."

"I was just thinking about the Living World. There has to be another way back."

"There isn't."

They looked at each other in silence. The boat swam on.

Fire and blood.

He sighed, trying to separate past from future, but the blur remained. Pushing all thoughts of the vision aside, Frank watched the only female Death.

Girls.

The only girl he'd spent time with for a year now smiled at him. Michi and the other 'Mental girls seemed a lifetime ago.

"With Jason gone," said Suzie, "we have space for a new housemate. Maybe you should join Billy and me in Eagle Two."

Frank choked back his surprise. Move in with Suzie?

"You're around all the time anyway," said Billy. Of course he'd be there.

"Let's see if they'll let us," said Frank. "It depends on who they pick for Headmaster. I hope it's Rayn. For a Death, he at least understands 'Mentals. He'd help things cool down."

"We hope things will be better," said Billy, lowering his voice to a whisper. "Don't forget there were two attacks last year. I doubt the Deaths have forgotten that. For all we know, things might get worse now."

"Sindril's gone," said Frank. "He was one of the worst, a true 'Mental-hater. No, I think things will improve."

Would they?

Fire and blood.

He'd seen enough this past year. He'd *caused* enough himself. No more.

"Is that Mors?" asked Suzie.

"That's it," said Billy. A dozen narrow towers rose from the horizon. Then a large blue and gold dome emerged from behind the tree line. The boat sped up and the canal widened.

"Finest city in this world," said Eshue. "The great City on the Sea, and the first city founded by Deaths alone. The first Deaths crossed the ocean to attack the Dragons. They built a town where they landed." He gestured toward the city. "The magnificent city of Mors."

It looked less impressive when they drew closer. Unlike the natural-looking canyons and immense mountain towers of the College, Mors was a jumble of mismatched buildings, many in disrepair. A nearby white tower with a broken top leaned against a half-finished brick structure. The College had been built by 'Mentals, Frank's own people, the most skilled laborers in the world. Mors had clearly been built by Deaths.

The boat hit the dock and shuddered.

"We've arrived." Eshue gestured. "Enjoy your stay."

Frank didn't like the way he grimaced at Suzie. The dark boy reminded him of Frenchie and the other bullies who'd given Suzie a terrible time last year.

"Thanks for the ride."

"Let's find an inn, then head into town," said Billy.

"Sounds good." Frank frowned when Billy's scar caught his eye. The disfigurement was Frank's fault. A sense of guilt lingered, but lessened every time Suzie gave Billy a longing look.

They glanced around. The Lethe Canal continued past the docks, heading straight into Mors. Here, the canal stretched about a hundred feet across, with dozens of small piers crammed against either bank. The tall, broken white tower stood in front of him. Beneath it, multicolored stalls of red, blue, black, and every other color spread in either direction. A tall pyramid of black and yellow stone rose behind the white tower. A large white and blue dome sat on the edge of the horizon. Something glinted at its crest.

"This place is very different from the College," whispered Suzie.

"It's a mess," replied Frank.

"I like it," said Billy. "The city has a *life* to it."

"Funny statement coming from a Death," muttered Suzie.

Billy led them away from the piers. "This is the Wharf," he said, waving his hands at the jumbled buildings. "The Lethe continues, joining the sea on the other side of the city. The Wharf is for passengers. It's the entrance to Mors."

Far to his right, Frank watched a line of Deaths ride toward the city on horseback.

They turned a corner and joined a small crowd of Deaths. Some gave them long, lingering looks. There was only one female Death, and she drew attention.

You are strong. He'd whispered it into her mind so many times, the phrase echoed in his head each time he looked at her. Was Frank talking to her, or to himself? At first, it'd been so simple, encouraging a change to help the 'Mentals. Now, with Suzie's beautiful face smiling at him so often, things were confused.

"Western Park, and that's the Capital." Billy pointed to the blue and white domed building ahead.

"I thought the Council met in the College," said Suzie. "When I went to Sindril's office, they told me it was right beneath the Council Chambers."

"They have an office in East Tower, but this is where they meet normally," said Billy. "Eleven of the Twelve live in the Capital Building, and Lord Coran lives in a private mansion on the Sea. Only the Headmaster lives at the College."

"Not any more," said Frank. "Sindril's gone. Fled."

"The new Headmaster will live at the College," said Billy. "The other members of the Council of Twelve will continue to live here."

They continued walking toward the dome, passing through a field dotted with trees. To his left, fountain water leaped into the air; to his right, a series of strange arches stood behind a row of houses.

"A roller coaster," said Suzie.

"What's that?" he asked. A series of carts snaked across the arches, slowing on each hill before falling quickly. Deaths riding in the carts yelled, but sounded happy.

"It's something from the Mortal World," she answered. "A ride."

"The amusement park is down there," said Billy, following his gaze. "We'll go soon."

They continued through Western Park until they reached the Capital: a marble palace crowned with a sapphire and ivory dome. A shimmer of gold gleamed at its peak. Massive carved figures covered the outer walls of the Capital: thirty-foot tall Deaths using their scythes to carve a city.

They walked around the building where a flight of steps led to a busy street. Deaths rode by on horses, some pulling wagons. Rows of colored houses led steeply downhill, toward a shimmer of blue by the horizon.

Billy led them through street after street, past buildings of every shape and size. They hurried through an open-air bazaar filled with smells, sights, and stares. They passed through an alley, and Frank let out a sigh.

The Sea. Mors stretched to either side of the coast for miles, but the Sea extended beyond the horizon. Seagulls cawed overhead, and the salty sea air filled his lungs. 'Mentals lived in the forests, the deep roots of the trees energized them. Yet, there was a different life here, an invigoration he hadn't felt in the World of Deaths before.

In front of them, the beach widened. An enormous plaza of red bricks stretched for over a hundred feet in front of him, surrounded by a circle of benches.

"I remember this," said Billy. "It's a map of the Mortal World. You guys wait here, I'll get us a room. I stayed at the Donkar Inn last time I came, it's not too bad." He walked away.

Frank and Suzie walked between two benches and looked down. At the center of the circle was the largest map Frank had ever seen.

"It's Earth," said Suzie. "It looks like a photograph."

“There’s ‘Mental power at work here,” said Frank. “That’s no ordinary map.”

Clouds below them drifted over images of land. The entire map moved. Continents drifted away from him and oceans shimmered. He tugged on his power, rooted at the base of his thoughts. Would he sense individuals there? Did he even want to?

To his right, Frank saw a small plaque engraved on the ground beneath the map.

“Says it’s a live image of the sunlit side of the Mortal World,” he said.

“It’s so far away,” said Suzie.

“You miss it, don’t you?”

“It doesn’t matter. I made my choice. This is home now.”

* * * *

Frank inhaled the muddled air. A blend of confused smells accosted him. Metal, smoke, and wood filled his nostrils, mixed with the unpleasant aroma of grease and Death foods. Beneath it all, the gentle, enticing salty air of the sea lingered.

“I never dreamed they’d have an amusement park in this world,” said Suzie. They stood on a line by the main entrance. Roller coasters snaked overhead, and yells and shouts punctured the air every few seconds. Deaths thought the ’Mentals were strange, yet this place outstripped any odd behavior he’d seen. Once inside, they came to an open field. A dozen Deaths demonstrated how to use boskery blades.

“Hey, it’s Billy and Frank, from the Gray Knights,” yelled a voice in the crowd. “Show us some moves, guys.”

Frank picked up the double-bladed boskery scythe and whirled it into a circle of steel, spinning the blades faster and faster. Billy did the same, and Frank approached him. The two exchanged a few light blows, and the crowd cheered.

“Come on,” said Suzie, “I want to ride a roller coaster.”

Frank handed his blade to another Death and joined Suzie in a line for the *Silver Scythe*, a rickety, dangerous-looking wooden contraption.

Frank climbed into one of the carts, with Billy and Suzie in the cart in front. With a shudder, the cart lurched forward.

"You'll like this," said Suzie, turning around. Were they holding hands?

The cart shook violently, stumbling its way along the track. It turned, and then climbed upward. Frank looked over the city, peering for miles. The coaster rose high above the fair. The sea swam on one side of sight and the distant forest stood to the other. He smiled. This jealousy over Suzie was so—

His thoughts broke off, and his heart pulled its way out of his chest into his throat, as the coaster suddenly dove. Suzie screamed. He fought the urge to vomit. The coaster veered to the left, and dove a second time. Suzie turned around, a massive smile plastered across her face. His fingers tightened on the sides of the cart, and the coaster climbed again. Deaths *liked* this?

An agonizing five minutes later, he staggered off the ride. Suzie and Billy walked to a food stand and bought a lump of spun sugar, called cotton candy, though Frank couldn't see any cotton in it.

"Come in, come in," shouted a Death with long blond hair. He waved toward an assortment of scythes in the back of a tent.

"Finest scythes in Mors," he said. "Made with the purest mortamant, and able to cut a soul in half."

"No," shouted another Death, this one with an eye patch. "Look at these scythes. One look at mine, and your thoughts will slice in two. Finest blades this side of the Sea."

They walked past tent after tent and stopped at a large field. Wooden signs painted like cartoonish dragons stood in a row. Each dragon had a large bull's eye in its center.

Frank jumped when a bang rang out across the field. Nearby Deaths pointed long rifles toward the targets.

"Deaths young and old," shouted a man behind them. "Behold the only firearms allowed in this world for recreational purposes. Stolen from the Mortal World, and now used for your pleasure! Step right up, step right up. Only ten tickets and you can blast the hearts out of our army of Dragons!"

"Army of Dragons," laughed Frank. "They're just wooden targets."

"Ah, that may be true," said the man. He stepped into a view: a tall, chubby Death with a bright red coat and a moustache two times too large for his face. "Where is the challenge in shooting wooden targets, you ask? Well, have no fear, young sir. The Range isn't the most popular attraction at Silver Fair for nothing! Just watch."

He waved to a group of Deaths holding rifles. They aimed at the targets. Then, a half-naked man with bright purple hair ran into the field.

Frank's stomach clenched. *A 'Mental*.

"Stop!" shouted Suzie. "They'll shoot him."

The Deaths fired and the purple-haired man stretched out a hand. A wall of ice appeared in front of him. Two of the Dragon targets shook when bullets hit them, but the man seemed unhurt.

"This is awful," said Frank. "They're making him defend himself for their amusement."

"Isn't it wonderful," said the red-coated Death. "If they can't block the guns, they die." He laughed. Frank stared at him, fighting the urge to use his power and rip apart the Death's mind.

"That's horrid," said Suzie.

"We need to stop this," said Frank. He jumped over the fence and ran out onto the Range.

"What do you think you're doing?" shouted the ringleader. "Get out of there."

The purple-haired 'Mental turned to Frank with a frightened expression. His feet were chained to the ground.

Frank tugged on the power lurking behind thoughts, and reached for the other 'Mental's mind.

I will help you.

The stranger just stared, tears glistening in the corners of his eye.

Two large Deaths ran onto the field and grabbed Frank, hauling him back to the side.

"You and your friends aren't welcome here," said the ringleader. "What are you, some sort of 'Mental-lover?"

"Let him go," said Frank. "He has rights."

"I have rights," said the Death, rubbing his long moustache. "It's within my rights to escort you out of Silver Fair. You can leave on your own now, or I can have security bring you out."

He could split this Death's mind in half. His power continued to grow. Like an angry wolf lurking in the shadows, the power growled with dangerous temptation. A single thought and he could help this poor soul.

Billy caught his eye and shook his head. Too many Deaths around, and Frank couldn't risk discovery. Frank wrestled back the darkness, the frightening force he dared not wield.

"Let's get out of here," muttered Frank, looking at the growing throng. Even the 'Mental looked confused. Eshue appeared in the crowd, glowering.

"It's the girl Death," said a voice. "What's she trying to mess up now?"

"This isn't the time to pick a fight," said Billy. "Come on." He led Suzie and Frank away from the Range. Eshue followed them, but kept back a few feet.

They stopped at the Lethe, which ran through the heart of the city, toward the Port. A large bridge spanned the river. Eshue paused at the bank.

"Enjoying the city?" asked the dreadlocked Death. His breath stank of fish.

"How could you just stand there?" demanded Frank through clenched teeth. "They'd kill that 'Mental if he hadn't defended himself."

"The Range at Silver Fair? Amusing isn't it?"asked Eshue.

"I don't think anyone should be treated like that," said Frank.

"It was just some 'Mental," said Eshue. "He probably liked it."

Liked it?

"He was a slave, chained to the ground," said Suzie.

"He was only there to entertain," said Eshue. "What do you know? You're just a girl."

"Don't you dare talk to her like that." said Frank.

"What are you going to do about it?" asked Eshue.

"Leave it," said Suzie, stepping between them.

"You need to back off," said Eshue. "A girl and a 'Mental-lover, you don't belong here. You two belong on the Range as target practice."

Suzie spun around and punched Eshue in the face. The Death staggered backward, a trickle of blood streaming from his nose. He stumbled, tumbling backward into the Lethe.

"Suzie—"

"I'm sick of being pushed around," she said.

Eshue screamed in the water. He climbed onto the bank with a horrified expression.

"She didn't hurt you that much," said Billy.

"You don't know what you've done. I touched the *Lethe*! The water is cursed. You pushed me into it, you bitch. This is very, very bad. You and your 'Mental-loving friends aren't welcome on my boat. You won't ride back with us. I don't want to see you again."

A crowd of Deaths ran across the bridge pointing and yelling. Were more people going to criticize them for touching some water? It was Eshue's fault for being so thick-headed.

"What's going on over there?" asked Billy.

The throng grew, moving toward the Sea with raised voices.

"Let's find out," said Frank.

Suzie, Billy, and Frank joined the crowd. They lost sight of Eshue, then saw him behind them. The city poured toward the Port.

"Never seen anything like it," said a voice.

"Just there on the water?"

"You can see it now."

"How could this happen?"

So many shouts, so much noise. Frank could hardly make out the sentences, but sensed the anxiety.

Fire and blood. With a pang, the image returned to his mind. The jumbles dissolved into a single image of fire on water. Past and future collided to form a single warning for the present.

They rounded a bend and the endless sea emerged before them.

It was on fire.

No, not the sea. A massive plume of smoke billowed toward Mors. Beneath it, a large boat floated toward the Port. Flames soared up from the sides of the ship. It limped through the waters, listing violently to one side. Enormous tongues of red and gold flame licked the sky. Frank's eyes watered from blowing smoke.

"That's a mortamant ship," said a Death near him.

"How could this happen?" said another.

"I've never seen anything like it."

"It must be the 'Mentals," said another.

Smaller vessels circled the massive craft, but the Deaths seemed unable to do anything. The large ship hit the side of a long pier. With a crash louder than thunder, half of the burning ship fell into the sea.

The Deaths around him surged forward.

"Fire!" shouted a voice. "'Mentals did this. 'Mentals!"

Even if 'Mentals had done this, the Deaths deserved it. Yet, the fire seemed wrong. Why would his people target a boat?

The angry chants grew louder. A hand grabbed Frank and spun him around.

"You see what happens when you touch the Lethe," said Eshue. He glared with wild eyes, then spun away and darted into the throng of Deaths.

"We should get back to the College," said Billy.

"How," replied Frank. "If Eshue blames us for touching the water, will the other captains give us passage?"

Billy, Suzie, and Frank ran through the crowds. They halted at the large globe on the beach.

"What's happening?" asked Suzie. "Why is everyone panicking? I know the boat was attacked, but shouldn't people be trying to help?"

"That ship was carrying mortamant," said Billy. "The metal for scythes. If they've lost a shipment that large, the entire World of the Dead will be affected."

"Maybe it was an accident," said Frank.

"Accident or not, they seem to think it was a 'Mental attack. This city's going to turn ugly fast," said Billy. "If they were using 'Mentals to stop bullets *before* this happened, I don't want to see what they'll do now."

The implication hit home. They blamed the 'Mentals. Whether justified or not, if the Deaths learned he was a 'Mental in disguise there'd be problems.

"Let's get our stuff and get out of here," said Billy.

"Eshue said we can't use the boat," said Suzie.

"We'll find something else."

* * * *

Frank let the beautiful creature do the work. The sleek, white horses were calm and graceful. He'd never ridden before. Turning in the saddle, he saw Suzie clutching Billy's waist. Of course they'd ride together, while Frank rode alone.

"Hurry up!" shouted a horseman in front of them. They'd spent the rest of their money to secure the two horses, and rode with a larger group. The land route to the College would take an extra two days. None of the other Deaths said a word to them.

Behind him, against the sinking sun, the city of Mors seemed calm. Yet, the Deaths buzzed with anger.

None had survived the ship's attack. A huge amount of mortamant was lost. Everyone blamed the 'Mentals. In every street, he'd heard whispers of war.

Whatever progress they'd made by defeating Sindril, seemed lost now.

The visions were true; they always were. This was just the beginning.

CHAPTER THREE: SUZIE

New Beginnings

"Sit please!" shouted a Death.

Suzie fidgeted in the seat. Billy's fingers slipped around hers, and his grip tightened.

Lower Hall quieted, and the Deaths sat. Suzie looked at Frank, sitting across the table. His lip twitched and he glanced away. It'd been a tense two months since Mors. The 'Mentals serving at the College never spoke anymore, and anger hung in the air. Frank seemed on the verge of an explosion.

A white-haired Death, his face a mass of wrinkles, stood, leaning heavily on a cane.

"It is past time that we addressed this," said Lord Coran, leader of the Deaths. "New students arrive tomorrow, and the next semester starts Monday. Before I announce the new Headmaster, I want to mention the current *tension*."

She watched Frank clutch the table. This must be hardest for him, a 'Mental disguised as a Death, when the Deaths were increasingly suspicious of 'Mentals.

"All of you probably know by now, there was an incident two months ago, at the City of Mors. Three ships carrying mortamant were attacked, and their cargo was lost."

Three? Suzie had only known about the one she'd seen. She'd heard rumors of others, but hadn't believed.

"We do *not* yet know who is responsible."

"'Mentals!" shouted a Death near the front of the Hall. Others murmured their assent.

"Silence!" shouted Coran, in a surprisingly strong voice. "I repeat, we do *not* know who is responsible. We are conducting a thorough investigation. These incidents did keep us from choosing a Headmaster sooner. He is here now, and I am proud to introduce him to you. Deaths, I give you the new Headmaster of the Upper and Lower Colleges, and the newest member of the Council of Twelve: Simon Hann."

Hann stood while the Deaths cheered. Hann, her toughest teacher last year. Hann, who'd threatened to fail her. Hann, who looked more like a Grim Reaper than any other Death she'd seen. He looked even leaner this year, and his scowl filled the Hall. He had an ominous power in his walk. He'd shaved his goatee, giving his face a mean and sinewy look. Yet, all the same, he was a good choice. Hann was a tough man, but he was fair.

"Thank you," said Hann, raising his hands for silence. "Thank you, Lord Coran, and thank you young Deaths. This is an historic opportunity, a new beginning for many. With the new year, a fresh group of boys shall take their place among your ranks, becoming future Deaths. I look to you to set an example.

"This will not be an easy year. It is a year of transition, yet also a year of tension. For the first time in this College's history, there is a shortage of mortamant. All of you know, mortamant is the heart of the Deaths' world, and the metal used in our scythes. We have enough scythes to complete our normal course of study, but we must be careful. If any scythes are lost or misused, we will not be able to replace them. We will also limit the number of student Reapings. That is why I need each of you to help the new Deaths understand how valuable our scythes are."

He looked over the crowd, and for a moment Suzie met his beady eyes. Even across the room, she sensed something there. Was it doubt? Or perhaps fear?

"More ships are coming, and an investigation into the attacks is underway. Do *not* jump to conclusions. Early information leads me to believe that 'Mentals were not necessarily involved. With a new

Headmaster, we have a new opportunity to look at 'Mentals. They're not servants, but rather our *friends* in this world. This is one of the things I wish to highlight this year. To that end, I have named Rayn to a new position. He is already the foremost expert on 'Mentals, and he will now be our olive branch."

Frank raised an eyebrow.

"Rayn, please stand." Suzie remembered him. He'd help them find the village of the 'Mentals by explaining about the strawberry smell.

"Rayn is now Director of Death and 'Mental Relations. If any of you have concerns about 'Mentals, you will direct those concerns to him."

"An olive branch," muttered Frank.

Rayn's mouth widened into a grin. Blonde curly hair hung low over his portly face.

"Classes begin Monday," said Hann. "I expect excellence from each of you."

He sat and the hall applauded.

* * * *

They walked toward Eagle Two, passing through the earthy mounds of the College. In front of them, West Tower shot into the sky: a contorted mountain of rock, twisting and heaped like an enormous stalagmite. Behind them, she knew its twin East Tower also climbed far into the clouds. Between the two mountainous towers stretched a labyrinth of long rocky mounds. The College looked more like a maze of canyons than a complex of classrooms. There were some grassy courtyards, but most of the College was rough, natural-looking stone. To her right, Suzie saw a large cube of perfect black: the Examination Hall. She paused, pushing a strand of hair out of her eyes. The Hall stuck out on campus like it'd been dropped from the sky. She'd had her Final Test there last year, and now would never need to set foot in that cube again.

"Suzie, look at this," said Billy, taking her wrist and turning to one of the rocky mounds. Someone had taped a hand-drawn sign to the wall. It showed a girl with long hair and a dress holding a scythe. There was a big red X over the girl.

"JOIN AGC: the Anti-Girl Club," she read. "First meeting on Saturday at five."

"I'll take this down," said Billy, tearing it off the wall.

"I can't believe the teachers didn't see this," said Frank.

"Maybe they did," said Billy. "Half of them are against Suzie too. Now that there's been attacks, the Deaths will blame anyone who's different."

"Like the 'Mentals," said Frank. "I'm glad Rayn is supposed to help relations, but wonder what he intends to do."

"I'm tired of being a target. Can't people just accept me?"

"We accept you," said Billy. He turned and gave her a kiss on the cheek.

When she opened her eyes, she saw Frank blushing.

"I accept you too," said Frank. The 'Mental reached for her hand and kissed it. Now Billy's face turned red.

The two boys glared at each other and Suzie couldn't help but giggle. Were they fighting over her? It was a bit overwhelming, but flattering too.

"Come on, boys," she said, suppressing more giggles. "I want to get the house cleaned before they bring anyone new."

"I wish they'd reconsider letting me move in," said Frank. "Now that Hann's the Headmaster, maybe I should ask again."

"The Board already turned you down twice," said Billy. "We'll see you all the time, just like last year."

Frank grimaced and looked away. He hadn't entered her mind since the attack on Sindril last school year, but Suzie sometimes sensed something from Frank, as if their emotions were connected. Right now Frank seemed annoyed, but not at the Board. Was it jealously over Billy? She liked Frank a lot, but Billy had her heart.

They turned a corner, and Suzie smiled. "Hello, Eshue," she said, recognizing his long dreadlocks. "Haven't seen you since Mors."

"You," the dreadlocked Death muttered. He spun away and finished taping up a sign, before spitting on the ground. The sign was another poster for the Anti-Girl Club.

"Well, I guess we know who's been putting these up," said Billy..

"Let's go home," said Suzie. She glared at Eshue's back as he strode away. Grabbing a corner, she tore the poster off the wall.

* * * *

She stood in Sindril's office. A large crystal sat on his desk.

A wing moved within the crystal, an eye emerged.

Runes poured around her, burning her arm.

"Help me," she tried to say.

Pain everywhere. The world shattered.

"So weak, so worthless..."

She burst into a billion pieces of light.

* * * *

"They're supposed to bring someone in today," said Billy, pouring her a glass of orange juice. Outside the window, the morning sun dawned over the canyons and mounds of the College.

"I heard you screaming again last night." Sitting at the table, he frowned.

"I keep having the same nightmare." Lifting the glass, her fingers trembled. She placed it back down and took Billy's hand. "Every night I'm back in Sindril's office. Only, when I stare into his crystal, it bursts. There's weird marks and lights, and then it feels like I'm exploding. That's when I wake up."

"I'm not an expert," said Billy, "however, you have more to deal with than anyone here. You went through a huge ordeal when you took down Sindril, and part of your mind probably never got over it. They pressure you just for being a girl, so it's no wonder you feel like you're going to explode."

"That makes sense, but why do I keep having the same dream? Do you think it means something more?"

"I really don't know. In the end, it's just a dream. Eshue and those other jerks are real, but even they aren't strong enough to hurt you.

You've got friends, and you're a great person, Suzie." His fingers tightened around hers.

She smiled.

They looked up when someone knocked on the door. Billy rose and answered it.

"Eagle Two number Six. You must be William Black," said a Death, looking up from a clipboard.

"That's me," said Billy. Suzie stood and joined him at the door.

"You have a new housemate," said the Death. "This is Thomas Huff," he said, shoving a frightened looking boy toward the door. "Give him the free room, make him feel welcome, and have him ready for class Monday. You know how it goes."

The Death lowered his clipboard, spun, and walked away without another word. His long, black ponytail bobbed. Turning the corner, the Deaths headed back to the entrance of Eagle Two.

"Come in," said Billy.

The boy swallowed hard and blinked. He reminded Suzie a little of herself when she'd first come to this world. There were red marks around his eyes from rubbing or crying. His black hair was tousled, and hung over his dark brown face. A bathrobe hung over his thin shoulders, not reaching his bare feet. The Deaths must have pulled him from bed.

"I'm Suzie," she said. "Suzie Sarnio. This is Billy. Welcome."

"Tom," muttered the boy.

Billy held out a hand. Tom shifted from foot to foot, tightened his robe, and finally took Billy's handshake.

"You should come inside," said Billy.

With an awkward nod in Suzie's direction, Tom shuffled into the kitchen. Billy led him toward Jason's old room, and Tom entered, closing the door.

"They left clothes and stuff already," said Billy. "Must have used a scythe to get in while we were sleeping."

"They can just come in here whenever they want?"

Billy laughed. "Yeah, it's pretty creepy when you put it that way, but they've got better things to do."

While Suzie finished her breakfast, Tom emerged from his room. His eyes were even redder than before. He'd changed into a striped t-shirt and blue jeans.

"Do you want some breakfast?"she asked.

He nodded and she rose to get him some cereal.

"Is this real?" asked Tom.

"It'll sink in soon," said Billy. "This is the beginning of my third year here. Suzie's starting her second."

Tom nodded but seemed not to hear. Suzie poured him a bowl of cereal and a glass of OJ. She sat again.

"It's not that bad," she said. "You'll make friends, and you'll find that this place is truly amazing."

"This is really the World of the Dead?" Tom's fingers clenched and released in ceaseless rhythm. His brow furrowed.

"Yep," said Billy, placing his hands behind his head and grinning. "We're Deaths. You are too."

"So we—"

"Reap souls, use scythes, yeah the whole shebang," said Billy. "Don't think about it too hard. While I'm on that subject, don't fret about the Final Test either. You'll get there when you get there."

"Feels like déjà vu," she laughed. "Billy gave me the same speech last year, but he's right. After you finish eating, we'll show you around. You're going to have a good time here, I promise." She reached out and patted his hand.

For the first time since arriving, Tom's expression relaxed. He gave an awkward half-smile, but pulled his hand back.

* * * *

"You sure about this?" asked Billy.

"I have to," she said. "If Eshue's starting a club to pick on me, and the teachers won't stop him, I need to do this to show I'm strong."

"You can show it other ways," said Frank. "You heard what Hann said, they'll make an exception for you. You don't have to be on a team." He tossed a stone into Silver Lake. It skidded over the surface and then sunk into the glassy waters. To their right, the lone grassy hill of Widow's Peak looked down at them. The town of Weston was behind them, and the College was somewhere behind that. Billy and Tom sat near the water's edge. The sky was clear and sunny, with a light smell of strawberries hanging in the air.

"No, I'm sure," she said. "Tryouts are coming up soon, and I'm going to compete. *Just* because I'm a girl."

"It's not that," said Frank. "It's a tough sport. You were attacked with a boskery blade last year, you know better than most. Those things hurt like hell. They're designed to paralyze you, besides, there's never been a girl player before."

"I know." She remembered when Frenchie had struck her at the tryouts last year. Was she crazy? She'd woken from the same recurring nightmare feeling like she had to *do* something. She had to prove that she wasn't different, just because of her sex. She could *fight.* When Billy mentioned tryouts, it seemed to fit, yet now she wasn't sure.

"Look," said Billy. "We all think you're strong. I'm impressed that you'd even think about going for it. However, it's more than the normal trouble with the sport. Boskery takes a ton of talent on the scythe. Let's face it, Suzie, you're not the best at scythe work."

"I admit I'm not," she said, "but you're both stars from the championship team. Billy, you said you're losing a few players who've graduated."

"I'm not throwing the results," said Frank. "If you want to make the team, you've got to earn it. Billy's right, it's not just the danger, it's using the scythe."

"I've got a couple of weeks. Will you guys help me practice?"

"I will," said Billy. Frank scowled.

"I'll help too," said Frank. "Don't want Billy to have all the fun. However, when tryouts arrive, you'd better earn it yourself."

"Sorry, but what's boskery?" asked Tom. Suzie laughed and started to explain.

* * * *

After a day of showing Tom around, Suzie found herself liking the new boy more and more. There was an innocence about him and a feeling of fear mingled with her own hope that he'd adapt. When she looked in his eyes she saw herself a year ago. They sat at the table in Lower Hall enjoying a dinner of gorgers. Hers tasted like spaghetti.

"Suzie," said a voice behind her. She turned.

"Frenchie?" she said, swallowing hard. This couldn't be good. Frenchie and his brother Luc had picked on her more than anyone else last year.

"What do you want?" demanded Billy. He jumped up, facing Frenchie with clenched fists.

The tall, lanky black boy shuffled on his feet, and peered around Billy. "Can I speak to you for a minute outside, Suzie?"

"You'll talk here," said Billy. "Let me guess, you and your Anti-Girl Club want—"

"I'm not in that," interrupted Frenchie. "They asked, but I refused. I think it's awful, and the teachers should be embarrassed to let it exist. I don't think Hann knows yet."

"So why are you here?" asked Frank.

"Please, Suzie. Just a minute?"

"I'll go." She rose and followed Frenchie to the stairwell and out the door.

Frenchie leaned against the earthen wall outside, looking at the dusking sky. His deep-set eyes looked away, watching the sunset. The College's canyon walls deepened into vivid reds and browns. East Tower rose in front of them, casting twisted shadows below. Suzie waited, one hand twirling a strand of hair.

"I've been thinking." Without looking at her, he straightened, one hand on the rocky wall.

"Yes?"

"I treated you very badly last year. Now that Luc's gone back…I realized we shouldn't have acted so—"

"Mean?" she prompted.

"Yeah. I want you to know, I'm different now. I felt so confused. Back when Luc attacked you at the Reaping, things started to change."

"What are you trying to say, Frenchie?"

"Francois," he said softly, turning to her. "When you did that thing with Sindril, we all saw it in our minds. You showed us how he communicated with Dragons and betrayed the Deaths. It was amazing, Suzie. You changed the Headmaster and the entire College. I was so impressed—"

"And?"

"I'm just saying to give me a chance. Let's start again. Please?"

In truth, Luc had been the bigger problem last year, and he was gone now. Even so, she hesitated.

"I know you're reluctant," said Frenchie. "I saw one of those Anti-Girl signs. Kids are gonna start picking on you again. I'm on your side, Suzie. I want the bullying to stop."

"Thank you," she said. "We can start again, but it won't take much to remind me what happened last year. I don't trust you."

"I'll prove you wrong," said Frenchie. He held out his hand and she shook it.

Walking back into the Hall, she couldn't help but wonder if it had been a good idea.

"What did he want?" asked Billy.

"To be friends. He wants to start again."

"Don't trust him," said Frank. "He's hiding something."

You were hiding something last year, Frank, and we're still friends.

"People pick on you because you're the only girl here?" asked Tom.

"Some do, yeah," she said.

"Well I think you're really nice," said Tom.

"Thanks."

"Back home in Tennessee," he continued, "I got a lot of grief for being black. My sister and I were isolated—the only black kids in McAulen's Park. Our neighbors, their neighbors, everyone was either white or had no kids. You should have seen us when we tried to go the pool or the playground. Mom wanted to move, but dad insisted on staying put. I know what you must go through. Now, I'm missing. Mom and dad must be so worried."

He looked down at the table, pushing his food away.

"You're only here for a year," said Suzie. "You'll pass that test, just like Jason did."

"And you?" he asked.

"It's why I have to prove that I'm strong. I'm here for good."

"You are strong, Suzie. You'll show them."

She smiled at him.

* * * *

"On-On-Only one n-n-new st-st-student?" asked Cronk.

Suzie sat next to Tom in Art, which was her first class. At least this year would start off well. Cronk had been her favorite teacher last year, and the only teacher she actually considered a friend.

"T-t-tell us a-a-about yourself."

Tom stood. Last year, a different housemate had stood at the same desk. Tom was nothing like Jason. After only three days, his confidence had grown. He walked to the front of the classroom with a wide smile.

"I'm Tom Huff from Tennessee, and am still a little creeped out by this world. Though for a World of the Dead, it's not anything like I expected. I'm getting used to it, with some new friends." He met Suzie's eyes and she felt herself blush. "I signed up for Art because it sounded fun. I drew a little back home."

"Thank you, T-T-Tom."

Tom sat back down and smiled at Suzie again. Cronk handed them each a blank sheet of paper and pencils. They were instructed to draw one thing they'd done or seen over the summer recess. Tom, as the only First Year in the class, was free to draw anything.

Suzie focused on her sketch, letting the pencil flow. At first, she considered drawing the dream haunting her every night. She saw herself back in Sindril's office, exploding into light and shattered glass. No, Billy was right—the dream was just projected fears. It didn't mean anything.

She drew a long line across the page, and the rest of the image quickly emerged. A ship, on its way to port, covered in flames. A cloud of smoke lingering in the sky. The class drew to a close, and she looked up. To think there had been more than one attack.

"What's that?" Tom asked her.

"At the beginning of the summer, we saw one of the attacks. We were in Mors, the port city. This is what people have been talking about, and no one knows for sure who it is."

"Everyone knows it's the 'Mentals," said a boy behind her. "I saw one of the boats too. Looked awful."

"What did you draw?" Suzie asked Tom.

"It's my family, back home. I miss them." Tom wasn't much of an artist, but she could make out the smiles on the faces of the three figures.

"You didn't draw yourself with them?" she asked. Her eyes drifted to the window, to the mountainous tower looming over home.

"I'm not there."

Cronk collected their papers, and they headed into a corridor. Suzie helped Tom figure out where to go before turning.

She walked down a flight of stairs and outside into a grassy courtyard. Passing the black cube of the Examination Hall, she continued through the labyrinth of canyons. The gnarled stalagmite of West Tower stretched far into the clouds above her. She walked to the base of the enormous rocky mountain and entered one of the doors, then took an elevator to the seventh floor.

"Welcome to Scythology," said a short balding Death, while Suzie hurried in the door. Twenty other Second Years already sat at their seats. She recognized a few, though she didn't have any friends here. The teacher wore a chain necklace with a large charm at the end.

"I am Professor Domen." The chubby Death had rosy cheeks and bright eyes, yet seemed old somehow. "Last year, you all took courses on History and Theory. Scythology continues both of those subjects, while also expanding into the artistry of Deaths. Your appreciation of our unique culture will deepen.

"There is more to Deaths than the...well, the business," he continued, pulling down a screen. He dimmed the lights and turned on a projector. "Given the current mortamant crisis, it is perhaps more essential than ever to understand what makes Deaths special. We have much to learn, so let us begin. Does anyone know what this image shows? Yes, you in the back, what's your name?"

"Jackson, sir. Clarence Jackson."

"Well, Clarence Jackson, what do you think this is?"

Suzie looked at the image of an ancient metal coin. On the coin's face was an etched image of a scythe blade attached to what looked like a donut.

"It's a scythe, you can tell by the blade. It's drawn on some sort of coin."

"Very observant, Clarence, but not what I was looking for." Clicking a button, the image changed. It showed a drawing of a large scythe blade, attached to a wheel. A Death stood under the blade.

"You see, this is no ordinary scythe. Notice the circular shape of the handle, and the immense size. It is believed to be one of the biggest scythes, though of course no one knows for sure."

"Professor Domen?" asked a boy sitting a row ahead of Suzie. "It's a myth, isn't it? The hourglass shaped jewel near the hilt gives it away. A friend of mine told me about that. It's called Grym."

"Very good," said Domen, smiling. "This is an artist's representation of Caladbolg, the First Scythe, or as it is commonly known, Grym. It is a particular passion of mine, and has been since I took Scythology in my second year. This charm around my neck is a different artist's interpretation of Caladbolg. And here, we see yet another." He clicked the button and the image shifted to a painting of a group of Deaths. Six of them held a single massive wheel. An enormous blade snaked up from the wheel, longer than the entire group, edging its way out of the painting. At the base of the blade a green hourglass sparkled.

"Legend states that the First Scythe was forged by the gods themselves. All other scythes were forged in its image. None have ever been so powerful, and yet so compliant to their user. In one story, the

Creator of this world pulled a shard of rock from the ground, and breathed life into it. He attached it to a great ash tree, but the blade was too large to wield. The handle of a scythe is called a snath. We will discuss snaths at length in our next unit. The snath of Caladbolg was an entire tree. No one could lift it, so a circular steel snath was fashioned. The jewel was an emerald, stolen from the Mortal World, and fashioned into the shape of an hourglass. Some say that the First Dragon fought the Creator himself, melting that emerald onto the blade and accidentally tempering the most powerful scythe ever."

Suzie raised her hand.

"You must be Suzie," said Domen. "Something of a legend yourself."

"You talk of legends," said Suzie. "Was the First Scythe real?"

"Many would say no." Domen sighed. "I'm sure there have been exaggerations. Yet, the accounts of a First Scythe, the true Sword of Deaths, are too common. The tales of a blade with the circular snath, and the emerald shaped like an hourglass have been passed for a million years. No, Suzie, I believe it is real, just as you are." He laughed. "Though, if it ever existed, it has been lost. It's no more than an ancient tale now.

"Which brings us to our first assignment," he continued. "Caladbolg has inspired stories and songs in the World of Deaths since history began. We will continue to discuss some of the stories today, but for homework I want each of you to write a poem, song, or short story, inspired by the First Scythe. It is due in one week."

Suzie jotted the assignment down in her notebook. Homework on the first day of the school year? She sighed, and Domen showed the next slide.

After lunch, Suzie had Careers. She saw a few students from Scythology class, but still none of her friends.

"Everyone wants to be a Certified Death, and ferry souls." His low monotone droned on with a dull buzz. "However, there are other careers for Deaths. I chose to pursue Academia."

Unable to stay awake while the insipid teacher described jobs available in the World of Deaths, she doodled in her notebook, thinking.

What would she do after she graduated? Would she become a Certified Death? She had a hard time picturing it.

The class finally ended and she went to Applications. She smiled at Billy, Frank, and Tom. She'd start and end the day in classes she liked. Then she frowned when Eshue walked into the room, tossing his dreadlocks over his shoulders.

"Have a seat," said a stern-looking Death, striding into the room. He spun to write something on the board, and Suzie noticed the long, black ponytail. It was the same Death who'd brought Tom to their door.

"My name was once Jose Ochoa," he said. His expression was dour, and he had a scar beneath one eye. "I bore that name until two years ago, when I joined the honored ranks of the Silver Blades. Tell me, *children*, who knows what the Silver Blades are?"

There was something about the word *children* that Suzie didn't like. Eshue raised his hand and Ochoa nodded.

"Every Certified Death is required to bring a minimum number of souls to the Hereafter," said Eshue. "Every transport is recorded, and if you do extra you get a bonus."

"Very good, continue," said Ochoa.

"Transport more than three thousand in any year, and you're awarded with a Black Star, which can be worn on the robes. It is a high honor."

"It is indeed," interrupted Ochoa. "Notice that I have *eight* of them pinned to my robe. More than any living Death to this day."

He waited a moment. Eshue and one other Death applauded. Suzie looked at Billy, who raised an eyebrow. Hann had a black star on his robe, but she'd always assumed it was just decoration.

"Every Black Star is a tremendous honor," said Ochoa, running his hands down the front of his robe. "It takes massive scythe control, ceaseless discipline, and unwavering determination to earn one. There is but one honor higher, the highest honor possible to a Death, the Silver Blade. Does anyone know how you become a Silver Blade?"

"It's nearly impossible," said Eshue. "You have to be the top-performing Death, bringing in more souls than anyone else, for years."

"*Seven* consecutive years," said Eshue. "Plus a total count of over fifty thousand Reapings. Do both, and you are counted as one of the greatest Deaths of all time. It is an achievement few have ever achieved. I am one of only two living recipients of the Silver Blade. The other is Lord Coran himself."

Billy raised his eyebrow again. Considering how little he'd said when dropping off Tom, this Death certainly liked to talk.

"As a Silver Blade," he continued, "I was given the right to take a new name. You probably know, Deaths take new names when they are certified, relinquishing all ties to the Mortal World. Yet few are given the opportunity to take a *second* new name. I am now called Erebus. I am the most skilled Death alive. You are honored to be here with me, and I look forward to inspiring you. With hard work and immense determination, someday one of you might shed your name and join the ranks of the Silver Blades."

"He's modest too," whispered Frank.

"Now," continued Erebus, "You all know that there is a mortamant shortage. Because of this, I am limiting all teams to four-man mixed-age groups." Suzie smiled. Four Deaths to a team meant she could join Tom, Frank, and Billy on Reapings.

"I have assigned teams based on a number of factors. I want all of you to succeed. The teams are listed on sheets here at the front of the room. Please come take a look, and assemble with your teammates. If you are a First Year, and do not know the other names, I will assist."

Suzie walked to the front of the room and scanned the lists. She saw Frank's name, followed by three she didn't recognize.

"Suzie," called Billy. "Over here."

She walked to a list at the end and read the names: Tom Huff, Billy Black, Suzie Sarnio, and Eshue Boro.

"No," said Suzie. She walked to Erebus. "Excuse me?" she asked. "I was wondering if there's any way we could make a change? One of my old teammates—"

"Absolutely not," said Erebus, spinning around. "Teams are set, and I will not move anyone. You're with two of your housemates, a gift since I felt sorry for you. This is not a place for women."

Her fingers tightened into fists, and her shoulders clenched. She bristled, ready to protest, but he spun away. "Assemble with the rest of your team."

"Bad Luck Suzie," said Eshue. "You'd better not drag us down."

CHAPTER FOUR: BILLY

Flirting with Deaths

"You sure about this?" Billy had asked.

"I'm sure."

Billy scratched his neck with nervous anticipation. Suzie hadn't listened to his warnings, or to Frank's. She walked onto the field in tight blue jeans and a loose black tee-shirt, her determined head held high. The wind tousled her long, black hair.

Ever since she'd failed her Final Test, or perhaps even longer, Billy hadn't been able to stop thinking about her. Those thoughtful eyes, adorable freckles, and soft lips. Was it wrong to feel joy when she failed her final test? Even now, months later, he closed his eyes each night hoping to dream of her.

To his right, a massive circle of grandstands ringed the boskery field. On his left, the two mountainous Towers of the College stretched above the gleaming Ring of Scythes. In front of him, stood the large open practice field, spotted with trees and small wooden towers.

All around Billy, a crowd of Deaths taunted and jeered. His fingers clenched.

"Hey, Suzie," said Frenchie.

"Hi."

He handed her a boskery scythe, and she struggled to keep the blades in the air.

"She can barely even hold it," said Frank.

She gripped the handle with both hands, so that one scythe blade arced above and the other curved up from below.

Frenchie mouthed something.

"What's he saying?" asked Billy.

"He's telling Suzie he hopes this year starts off better," replied Frank.

"How can you tell?" asked Tom.

Frank didn't answer. His 'Mental powers were strange, and at times scared Billy. How powerful was Frank? Could he read Billy's mind? Of course he *could*, but *did* he?

On the field, Frenchie nodded and walked back a few feet. Billy had shown her how to use the blade, she'd be okay. She turned it, moving her hands over each other. The blades circled, starting to spin. She rotated again, but one hand hit the other and her arms collided. She leapt back. The boskery blade fell to the ground, and the stands erupted in laughter.

Billy swallowed hard, turning to Frank, who shook his head.

Suzie bent down and picked up the blade. Not a good beginning to the try outs. She took a deep breath, and started the blades swinging again, moving it like a great propeller.

Like I showed you, let the blade carry its own weight around.

She moved her hands in rhythm, and the boskery blade spun.

"Ready?" called Frenchie.

Frenchie's blade spun in a perfect circle of silver.

She nodded.

Frenchie ran toward her, raising his blade. She held her own higher. The blades touched and a charge of energy rippled through the air, tangible all the way to the stands. The blades clashed again, and the boskery scythe slipped from her hands. She stumbled backward to avoid hitting the blades.

No. "I wish we could—"

"Have faith in her," said Frank.

Frenchie leaped over the blade on the ground, and came toward her. Suzie fell and rolled to the right. For a moment, she vanished from sight, and Billy stood. Frenchie jumped back, kicked by Suzie's foot. She rolled again and lifted her boskery blade. She held it in both hands, but didn't spin it. Frenchie came toward her again, but she blocked his advances. He reached into his pocket.

The yellow flag flashed for an instant, but it was enough.

"Stop!" shouted Billy, running on the field. "The Gray Knights will take her. She's in."

Frenchie smiled. He put his blade on the ground and then took Suzie's. "Good job."He tucked the yellow flag back into his pocket and walked away.

"You didn't have to do that," she said, while Billy escorted her off the field. "You guys are the champion team, how can I join you?" They hurried toward the stands. The next person to try out walked onto the field.

"I think Frenchie would've taken you if I didn't," he replied.

"I dropped the blade twice. I wasn't good enough."

"You were fine. You didn't get nicked once, that's big. You also blocked him without spinning the blade, which takes talent of its own. And that move when you fell. Suzie, you were great."

"Billy, you took me because I'm your... your friend. I wanted to prove myself—"

"You did," said Frank, walking up to her. "Billy and I were watching, and he's right, you're just who we need. You'll need to train hard, but you're a Knight now."

"You really think I was good?"

"I know Frenchie would've taken you." Billy kissed her on the cheek. The warmth of pride and joy tingled in his heart.

"Are you two dating now?" asked Frank, walking behind them. They left the tryouts and passed beneath the Ring of Scythes.

"We're just friends," said Suzie. Billy felt his cheeks blush.

"Because I thought you were great too." Frank leaned in, kissing her on the cheek himself.

"Hey! She's our teammate now. We need to, you know, respect her." Billy took her hand, leading her to one side of the path.

"I respect her," said Frank, taking her other hand.

"Boys." Suzie laughed. "Don't you have to stay for the rest of tryouts?"

"We only had one opening," said Billy. "It's filled, so we're done."

"I can't believe I made it. Are you sure you guys weren't going easy on me?"

"I didn't want you to try out." Frank shook his head. "I still don't know if I really want you to play, but Billy and I both realized Frenchie was going to draft you for the Seekers. When you kicked him, he pulled out a yellow flag. That's how you signal a team. One of them was supposed to come out, but we saw it first. If Billy hadn't come down there, you'd be a Dragon Seeker now."

"It was your help with training that really did it." Suzie grinned. "Both of you. I'm surprised they were planning to take me."

"You showed everyone that you're strong enough to play and make a team," added Billy. I'm proud of you."

"Hey, wait up!" called a voice behind them. Tom ran down the road, waving his arms. "That was amazing! You made the team."

"I did," said Suzie. "I'm a Gray Knight now."

* * * *

"I'm glad you're on my team," said Billy the next day. They sat on a narrow iron bench in a stone courtyard; Suzie held a book and pile of notes. Wisps of browning grass poked up between the gray slate slabs at their feet. Behind him, a canyon-colored wall ran for about thirty feet before folding back toward the rest of the College. West Tower rose above the labyrinth of mounds to his right.

"Me too, I think. I'm kind of nervous. Honestly, I didn't think there was any chance that I'd actually make it. I just wanted to try out, so people would know I'm not scared. With that stupid club and teachers continuing to pick on me, I need to make a stand. This'll show people like Eshue. I still can't believe he's on our team in Applications."

"It's tough, I know," said Billy, "but between you, me and Tom, what can he get away with? If Eshue tries anything, we'll be there looking out for you."

Suzie smiled and he put his arm around her.

"Thanks, Billy." She stood. "It's all overwhelming."

"What is?"

"Last year everyone picked on me, and now you and Frank like me. I'm flattered but also confused. It's so different now. People seek me out this year. I really like you, Billy. But I don't know what I feel for everyone else."

"All right. We can slow down. We're just friends. For now, at least." *I know what I feel, and we belong together*.

"What are you working on?" asked Frank, walking up.

"I'm supposed to write a story about a mythical scythe called Caladbolg. Can't really think of anything."

"Caladbolg?" Frank shrugged. "Doesn't sound familiar."

"It has an hourglass in it, and a circular handle. They say it was made by the gods or something. I started to outline a story about it being found with buried treasure, but it's not very good—"

"Wait, you said it has an hourglass and a circular snath?"

"Yeah."

"That's Grym," said Frank.

"Yeah, they call it that sometimes."

"Well I don't know about the gods, but I do know it's supposed to be the first scythe." He glanced around, lowering his voice, in the secretive way Frank sometimes used. "The 'Mentals have their own legends about Grym. Some used to call it Longclaw or Death's Finger. It's a cursed blade, they say."

"Cursed?" asked Suzie. "Well that's something I can use in a story. Maybe some people go looking for it and they get cursed."

"That sounds like a good story to me." Frank smiled, putting his hand on her arm.

Billy tightened his grip, pulling her back into his embrace. Frank glared.

"Listen," said Frank. "If you need help with this, or if you want to prepare for Boskery, I'd be happy to, you know, give you some private lessons."

She raised an eyebrow.

"She's getting private lessons from me," said Billy.

"I am?"

"I mean, if you want to."

"Thank you both for the offer," she said. "I will write about a curse now." She rose, stepping away from them.

"You're welcome, Suzie," said Frank. He grinned broadly right in Billy's face.

"Well, I'll let you get back to your homework," said Billy."Let me know when you want some more help."

Suzie walked away, and Frank left in the opposite direction. Billy lingered.

Just friends. Now other Deaths were starting to notice her. She was the only girl in their entire world, of course he'd be foolish to think she'd want him.

"Hey, Billy." Tom sprinted forward, his eyebrows knotted in worry.

"Hey, how are you?"

"I was wondering if I could talk to you for a minute."

"Sure, what's bothering you, Tom?"

"It's Erebus. Our teacher in Applications. The guy's really scary."

"He's not so bad."

"He's got all those awards and stuff. He's like a star, and he doesn't seem to like new Deaths. Eshue's not much help either. He's always mean to Suzie."

"Eshue's a bully."

"Well, do you think I'll ever be good at scythes? Could you maybe give me some private lessons?"

Any time helping Tom was time away from Suzie, time Frank would use to steal her away.

"I'm sorry, but I've got too much work."

"I understand, thanks anyway. Hey, what do you think of Suzie? She's really cute."

"Yeah," said Billy. "She sure is."

CHAPTER FIVE: SUZIE

Sparks

Suzie looked around the office. She'd only been here once, yet knew every detail. The plush rug, the massive desk, the oversized windows hundreds of feet above the College.

"Hurry," said Billy. "Hann will be back in an hour."

"I just want to see."

She crept up to the desk. The crystal ball stared back at her. She stepped closer, looking in, and clutched something in her pocket.

Everything blurred except for the crystal ball. Something moved inside.

"You are weak."

The Death laughed, waving his scythe, and the room vanished. Two immense eyes rose behind him, surrounded by leathery skin. She heard the beating of wings.

"You are weak," said the Death. "You're nothing at all, Suzie. Just a girl." He laughed again.

The world burst into light, shattering into shards.

She raised her arm, desperate.

Sunlight streamed through the window and Suzie awoke. She dressed quickly and went to the kitchen.

"Morning." Tom smiled before taking a bite of toast.

"Good morning," Suzie replied. He'd asked her for some private help on the scythe. Unlike Billy and Frank who were helping her, Tom had sought *her* help. The reversal made her smile.

Today was a big day. Three private lessons in addition to the four daily classes. She'd help Tom at lunch, then meet Billy right after Applications, before tutoring with Frank after dinner. She took a gorger from the fridge and concentrated on the taste of eggs.

Suzie hurried out of the door thirty minutes later, still stuffing papers into her bag. She glanced at the story she'd written about Caladbolg. In it, a group of pirates became stranded in the World of the Dead. Convinced their only way home was to use the most powerful scythe ever created, they set off in search of Grym. The pirates met a ghost who told them where the First Scythe was buried, but when they opened the treasure chest, the pirates found their own bodies. They had been ghosts themselves all along.

Okay, not the best story ever. She'd probably been too preoccupied with boskery, but it was still fun to write. It was the most creative thing she'd done outside of Art class.

She walked through an alley between canyon walls. The twisted stonework of West Tower cast a dark shadow over the earthen ridges, which snaked around the campus like a maze. A maze she knew. This was no foreign world anymore, this was home.

"W-w-what's b-b-bothering you?" asked Cronk, halfway through Art. She stared ahead without touching her paper.

"I'm just thinking. I have a lot on my mind."

As the pen touched paper, her fingers trembled. The crystal from her dreams loomed behind every thought. Tightening her grip, a massive scythe blade with a circular snath emerged in ink.

"Cronk?" She rose at the end of class.

He looked at her and smiled.

"Can I bring this to my next class?"

Cronk nodded, a wide grin still plastered across his pockmarked face. She left and hurried through the maze of stone, toward Scythology. Professor Domen greeted her at the door.

"Susan, how are you today?"

"I made this for you, sir. I thought you might like it." She handed him the picture.

"Quite an illustration of Caladbolg. You have a real talent. Thank you, I will hang it up right here on the wall."

He took the picture and went inside the room to get some tape. Suzie started to enter, but noticed something hanging on the opposite side of the hallway.

"Rally tonight: AGC," she read. Anti-Girl Club again. She tore the poster down and threw it in a trash can. Then she walked into the class. She'd drawn Grym: an item that filled people with wonder, while Eshue drew pictures of her with X's through them. Did it even matter that she'd made the Gray Knights?

She soon forgot the incident, listening to the other stories of Grym: the First Scythe. Most of the students had given the assignment less thought than she had, but a few stood out. Her favorite was by a chubby boy named Simon.

"The God of Deaths," read Simon, "made the First Scythe to sever the Mortal World from the World of the Dead. The blade was made from his own tooth. To hold it, the God of Deaths tore a hole in the sky. He spun the ripped sky into a circle, forming the circular handle, and sealed it to the blade with an hourglass. The hole in the sky hardened, and became the moon. Where the great cut separated the worlds, debris still litters the sky today, called stars. If you follow them, you'll eventually find the First Scythe."

"Very inventive," said Domen. "Nicely done, Simon. Mystical and poetic, a nice contrast after Suzie's pirate ghost tale."

She blushed, though Domen smiled at her.

"No homework tonight. Tomorrow we look deeper into the origins of the Caladbolg story, and see if evidence supports a historical Grym."

Suzie closed the book and slipped it into her bag. She passed through the canyon maze of the College, and walked through the Ring of Scythes. With everyone at lunch, the boskery practice fields should be empty. Tom waited there, his lips twitching in a nervous grin.

"I didn't really think you'd come," he said.

"I want to help. I know what it's like to suddenly find yourself in this world, with no friends and no clue how to fit in." She thought about the poster she'd seen. Even with friends, she was still the only girl.

"Well, I'm ready." He took a bite of a gorger. Her stomach growled as she realized she hadn't brought anything for lunch.

"I don't have any practice scythes, but there are some training handles in the shed there. Billy told me how to get in."

Her stomach growled again when they walked to the shed.

"Did you eat?" asked Tom, taking another bite.

"I forgot to grab something."

"Do you want a bite of this?"

"I don't want to take your lunch, Tom."

"Suzie, you're here to help me. The least I can offer is some of the gorger. Here, take the rest. It's ham and cheese." He extended a hand and offered it to her.

She hesitated, but took the gorger. Chewing, she pulled up a mat outside the shed door. The key was there, just as Billy had said. She unlocked the supplies, and pulled out two handles, passing one to Tom.

"The trick with scythes is the blades. The metal's alive somehow, it doesn't always do what you think it will."

"The metal's alive?"

"It's not that simple," she said. "It doesn't talk or anything, but it knows where to take you, and you'll feel the blade's… I'm not sure how to say it."

"What?"

"The best word I can think of is *hunger*. You'll feel it when we go on Reapings. Right now we're just holding the handle. I failed my first test last year because I hadn't learned how to hold the scythe or swing it right."

Tom held the snath in both hands like a baseball bat.

"No, you want to spread your hands like this." She tightened her top hand, moving to the side so he could see. Then she pulled her hands apart from each other, and spread her legs into a wide stance.

Tom adjusted, but still held the snath wrong.

"Make sure the lower hand is tighter, the upper hand will be fighting with the blade if you're holding it too tightly. That was my problem." She dropped her handle and stood behind Tom, helping him with his grip.

"Like this?"

"A little higher and looser with your left hand."

"How's this?"

"It looks good," she replied, letting go of the pole. Tom took a practice swing.

"Keep it loose on top, but tight with the lower while you swing. Try again."

Tom frowned and swung again. Stumbling on a patch of grass, he dropped the handle, and then fell, crashing into Suzie's legs. She collapsed on top of him, and they both laughed.

"Not like that," she said, still giggling. "Let's try that again." She rose, a wide, toothy grin stretching across her face.

"Thanks for your help, Suzie."

"Sure. Thanks for the gorger."

He smiled and she helped him up.

Several tries later, he still struggled with his grip, unable to maintain the balance needed for a smooth swing. Beads of sweat trickled past his knotted brow when he finally threw down the handle.

"I can't get it."

"You can, it just takes practice."

"You'd better get to class soon."

"We'll practice more tomorrow, and you can always work on your grip at home. It's not as simple as it looks."

She blushed. He definitely had a crush on her, though she didn't tell him that she knew. She smiled, and then said goodbye. There are definitely worse things than being liked.

An hour later, Professor Stanton repeated a question to the class.

"What will you do after you graduate?" he asked. "Will you go on to be a certified Death, ferrying souls? Remember, your one-page response is due on Monday."

She put her notebook in her bag and rose, thinking about his question. She was improving with a scythe, but still struggled. Her one Reaping last year had been a disaster, but that had been Luc's fault.

Suzie walked down a flight of stone steps and left West Tower, heading across campus. Applications was in one of the largest rooms in the entire complex, a mound of stone that looked like a mesa, rising from the canyons of the College. She passed the solid black cube of the Examination Hall and rounded a corner.

"Watch it," said Eshue.

"Sorry, I wasn't looking."

Eshue grunted and started to class, with Suzie behind him.

"Why?" she asked, rounding another bend. "Why do you have to run that club? Can't you just leave me alone? I'm sorry I punched you, but get over it."

"You're bad luck," he replied. "Now you're on my team in class. How many Reapings will we botch? I need to graduate. You don't. You're just a freak in this world. My father warned me about you."

"Look, I'm sorry that you don't like me, but we have to work together in class. If your father and you both got brought to this world, you know what it's like to be in an unfair position. Neither of you wanted to be here, and now you both are—"

"He's not my blood father." Eshue rolled his eyes, waving his hand with dismissal. "How stupid are you? He took me in and calls me son. I was brought here when I was only seven, too young to start at the College. They sent me to Mors, where father raised me. It happens from time to time, they said, a young boy brought here too soon. You are different. No girls ever come to the World of the Dead. When we heard about you, father warned that something bad would happen. I didn't believe him. Then you struck me without warning, and I slipped, falling into the Lethe. I touched the cursed water because of you, and a boat caught fire off the coast. That was no coincidence."

"I had nothing to do with that, and you know it. You were there, Eshue. We saw the boat, we didn't start it."

They arrived at the entrance to class. Billy was waiting for her outside the door.

"Father warned me that there is only one thing worse than touching the Lethe. Girls."

"Leave her alone." Billy stood with a tense jaw and clenched fingers. "She's got enough to worry about without you stirring up trouble."

Eshue brushed by him and walked toward the back of the class.

"Welcome all," said Erebus.

"Thanks," Suzie whispered to Billy. They watched Erebus polish one of the black stars on his robe.

"Today will be a bit different. I want to discuss important scythes. I know Second Years are studying mythical blades, so I shall show you true power. Several of the greatest scythes can be seen here at the College, in the Armory. Collect your things and please stand. We are going to take a field trip."

Erebus led them out of the room and into the canyons of the College. It was cooler today, and the overcast sky threatened rain. They walked double-file through the narrow corridors between earthen mounds. Suzie hurried to the front of the procession.

"Are the scythes in the Ring of Scythes actual scythes, or were they just made for that Ring?" She stared as they neared one of the twenty-foot high arches of polished metal.

"A little of both." Erebus strode forward without pause. "The blades were taken from scythes used by the first Deaths, but they were not nearly large enough or numerous enough to form the Ring. Extra mortamant was added, and the blades were re-forged into the massive scythes circling the campus today." They continued around a bend and then walked to the pier where she'd boarded a boat to Mors.

"This is where it started. I still can't believe my father even took her on board." Eshue complained in the background, loud enough for her to hear.

They continued past the pier, toward a series of mounds. Suzie didn't know this part of campus. The road narrowed into a downward-sloping alley. The rocky walls grew higher on either side. They stopped at a massive boulder blocking their path.

"This is the entrance to the Armory." Erebus pulled a large white disc from his cloak and placed it on the stone face. The rock rumbled and started to glow. Then the front of the boulder vanished, and a doorway appeared. Within the gloom, Suzie saw the faint glimmer of flower lights starting to shine. Erebus waved his hand and led them inside.

The path continued to slope downhill, leading into a cave. Stalactites hung from the ceiling like stone icicles, dripping water toward the damp floor below. Stalagmites grew from the cavern floor, rising like miniature versions of West and East Towers. Behind the folds of colored stone, small white flowers clung to molded rock, sprouting in crevices, and glowing with a dull white light. The air smelled of musty stone, and yet had a familiar quality. She turned to Frank. He must have smelled it too. Strawberries. The smell of 'Mentals.

It was cooler here beneath the College. The cave widened into a large hallway. Columns of stone extended from floor to ceiling, pillaring the cave in a grand procession. The walls were folded with reds and yellows, and ribbons of gold and silver wove throughout, catching the light of the flowers. A series of large glass cubes sat in the center of the hall, reminding Suzie of display cases from a museum. Inside she glimpsed the flash of scythes. On the edges of the room, massive wooden chests stood stacked on the floor and in recesses in the rock. The entire room looked like a treasure trove.

"Everyone find a spot where you can see," said Erebus, standing next to one of the large glass cases. Suzie felt something on her cheek. She brushed it off, and saw a flutter. She turned to the glass case, then saw it again. A fly landed on her leg. She tried to hit it, but of course missed. It flew away.

"Inside this case you will notice six scythes. These were used on the front lines against the Dragons in the Great War. They are six of the oldest intact scythes in existence, each being about one million years old."

"Sir?" asked one boy, raising his hand. "How can these scythes be that old? A million years is like dinosaur times."

"No," said Erebus. "Dinosaurs lived far before that, and mortamant is not a material of the Mortal World. These scythes have lost their power, yet they remain preserved forever." The handles were rotting in places, but the blades seemed almost-new.

"Take this scythe," he continued, pointing. "Notice the ten-foot snath and seven-foot serrated blade, one of only two serrated scythes. This is Tuoni, the Blade of Penance; last used by Donn during the Great War. Donn and General Masrun led an attack on what is today East Tower. Storming the Dragon defenses, their assault turned the tide in the war. Donn slew three Dragons with this blade."

The tour lasted the rest of class. She loved looking at the scythes and hearing stories. Moving from case to case, the fly seemed to follow her. She hadn't noticed any insects in the World of the Dead before, but this one wouldn't leave her alone.

* * * *

Frank gave her a smile. She adjusted her grip on the boskery blade and spun it. One blade started to fall, and she let the momentum carry the blade into a spiral.

"Good," he said. "Applications wasn't so bad today. Eshue seemed mellower than usual. I don't remember going on field trips here at the College. Usually we only leave class for Reapings."

"Yeah," she replied, trying not to lose focus.

She pushed her right hand down, until it hung directly below her left. Then she hurried to switch her right hand to the top of the handle. The two enormous blades started to spin. Miscalculating the distance, her fingers pushed the blade out of her grip. Suzie jumped back to avoid getting nicked.

"The blades will pull themselves, but you still have to guide them. Let your top hand move the entire circle." Frank picked up the double-bladed scythe.

She took a deep breath, and then accepted the boskery blade. She moved her hands again, this time focusing more on the spinning metal and less on her hands. The mortamant swung around, pulling the blade in a circle.

"Good, now take a step. This is where you have trouble."

She moved forward, keeping the boskery blade fluid in its motion. In front of her, the two scythe blades spun into a single ring of silver. She took another step, and one of the blades hit the ground. Losing her balance, she dropped the blade, leaping to the side so the metal wouldn't strike her.

Suddenly, the ground trembled. A sound like thunder erupted from nearby West Tower.

"What was that?"

Another tremor shook the ground.

"Come on," said Frank. "It came from over there." Suzie ran after him, barely having time to grab her books. Outside of the practice field, other Deaths sprinted, pointing in all directions. It reminded her of Mors and the burning ship.

"There." Frank waved to a plume of smoke rising outside the Ring of Scythes. Stone and debris catapulted into the sky, while a cannon-like explosion blasted her ears. The ground heaved again.

"Are they bombs?" Suzie's eyes widened in fear. Her heartbeat quickened, thumping against her ribs..

"It's the 'Mentals," screamed a Death behind her. "We're under attack again."

Deaths ran in every direction at once, with no one sure of what was happening. A second explosion roiled the ground, tossing a new cloud of dust into the air. This time, a massive wave of white energy shot up from the Ring of Scythes.

"It's not a 'Mental attack," said Frank. "'Mentals can pass through the Ring. Something just got repelled."

"Use your powers," Suzie whispered to him. "See who it is."

"If I'm discovered—"

"No one will know in this confusion."

The ground heaved again, leaving a buzzing in one of her ears. The buzzing shifted. No, it wasn't from the blast. Could that stupid fly have followed her?

"All right," said Frank.

He planted his feet and froze, staring at the Ring. His eyes glazed, even when another explosion shook the ground. Stones fell out of the College's walls, shattering on the ground. Another wave of energy coursed skyward from the scythes, blasting light into the sky.

"Stay calm!" shouted the booming voice of Hann. He rode toward the Ring of Scythes on a black horse, followed by a group of mounted Deaths wielding scythes. They charged through the Ring of Scythes and waited just outside the Ring. Silence fell like a fire blanket.

"Show yourself!" shouted Hann, apparently yelling at their attackers.

"No," whispered Frank.

"What is it?"

"I swear I saw a man, only it couldn't possibly have been—"

"Who did you see?"

"For a moment, the smallest fraction, I thought... No, he wouldn't have been—" Frank frowned. "No, I was mistaken."

"You weren't wrong," said a voice. "I saw it too."

Suzie spun around. Standing behind her, stood a scrawny child with wide eyes and a malnourished look. Suzie's mouth dropped in astonishment.

It was a girl.

CHAPTER SIX: FRANK

The Fly and the Ointment

Impossible. It couldn't be her.

"Michi?" Frank's eyes widened. "Is it really you?"

"It's been a long time, Plamen."

"Not here." Frank shook his head in disbelief. "We can't talk here." He took Michi by the arm and hurried away. The sallow-faced girl had a dark cloak with a yellow skull on it, identical to the training cloaks Suzie and the Deaths often wore.

This was no Death. He hadn't seen his friend for years, but he'd never forget her.

"Hey wait," said Suzie, jogging to catch up with them. "Someone tell me what's going on."

Frank glanced behind. Two more explosions shook the ground. The air stank of smoke and dust. He staggered, but kept moving. How was she here? Had she been in the College for long?

The confusion around the explosions drew the attention of the other assembled Deaths, so they were able to slip away easily. Suzie followed the pair back toward Frank's house. He entered and started to close the door, but Suzie grabbed it.

"I want to know what's going on," she demanded.

Frank turned. "Those explosions were caused by Sindril."

"Sindril set bombs?" Suzie's eyebrows rose. "That doesn't seem like his style."

"He was riding the air, a whisper on borrowed wings."

"Suzie, this is Michi, an Elemental I grew up with before I came here."

"I am honored to meet you, Suzie." Michi's expression was unreadable.

"Where'd you come from?"

"I was part of the attack on the College last year. I was accidentally trapped in that room with the scythes. I saw you with a group and clung on. I didn't even have the strength to change to this form until I saw Plamen. Seeing him—" She blushed, and Frank blushed in return.

"What do you mean you clung on?" asked Suzie.

"She's an arthromorph," replied Frank. "Every 'Mental has one thing they do well, one ability if you will. I am a seer. Seers control minds. Arthromorphs control, well—"

"Bugs," finished Michi. "I control insects. I myself can take on insect form, like the fly that clung to your shirt earlier. I'd been living like that for months, since it's easier for me to stay alive in insect form when food is scarce."

"Take this," Frank handed her a gorger. "Why didn't you reach out to me? You knew I was here on campus."

"I tried," she said. "You weren't looking. Besides, a seer can make contact, not vice versa. What's more, I used too much of my power. I feel so weak, Plamen. I'm—"

"Eat, and then relax. We'll talk when you've rested."

She used too much power. What did it mean? The wolf in the darkness, lurking behind his thoughts. The power was terrifying. What would happen if he used *too much*? What was the cost?

Michi devoured four gorgers before agreeing to rest. Frank brought her to his room and helped her lay on his bed. For months, the only girl he'd thought about was Suzie. Three years ago, his life had been so different…

* * * *

"Plamen, wait up," shouted Michi.

The young Elementals dashed through the woods. Plamen gasped for air, but couldn't stop smiling. He jumped over a mass of twisted roots and leaped onto a log.

"Is that the fastest you can run?" He sat on the log, watching Michi stumble out of the overgrown forest. She frowned at him and twisted her face into a grimace. His leg started to itch, and Plamen looked down.

"Ew, stop it." Dozens of ants crawled up his legs. "All right, Michi, I'm sorry. Come on."

She smiled, and the ants froze in mid-crawl. He brushed them off his legs.

"It's amazing how much power you have already. I have dreams but that's it. I can't even do anything when I'm awake."

"I'm a girl, we develop faster."

"Do your parents know?" He wiped the last ant away. Michi sat beside him on the log.

"No," she replied. "I don't want them to know. My mom said something about the cost of our power. If I tell them I already use it they'll just fuss and tell me not to."

"If it means sticking a bunch of ants on me, *I'll* tell you not to."

She laughed and punched him in the arm. "You're funny."

For a moment they said nothing, looking up at the sun streaming through the trees. A gentle breeze blew across Plamen's face. He turned to see Michi watching him.

"Is it true?" she asked.

"What?"

"You know what. Are they really going to send you away?"

"My dad wants me to work with one of his friends. In the In-Between." Plamen sighed. "I've met Athanasius, he's pretty nice."

"How long do you think you'll be gone?"

"I don't know."

She picked an ant off the log and watched it scurry across her finger.

"I'm going to miss you," she said.

"Yeah."

Without warning, Michi looked up and kissed him on the lips. She pulled back, smiled, then jumped up and ran back into the woods.

Plamen sat in stunned silence. He watched her disappear into the trees, then continued to gaze in that direction.

* * * *

Frank brought himself back to the present. Michi lay in front of him on the bed. He opened a drawer and pulled out a small glass jar. Athanasius had manipulated strength, a rare ability, even for 'Mentals. Frank unscrewed the top, reaching into the silvery liquid.

"This is a strength ointment," he murmured, dabbing some onto his finger and smearing it on Michi's arms. She opened her eyes but said nothing.

"Frank," said Suzie gently, "what in the world is going on?"

"We were kids together. Michi is a good friend."

"I got that. You must be surprised to see her here."

"That's an understatement." He chuckled.

"Frank, what about Sindril? What did you see? Has he returned?"

"It's hard to explain, I didn't see him there, but I *felt* him." He turned, meeting Suzie's gaze. "There was something else, too. Something massive. It might've been a Dragon, I've never actually seen one."

"I saw him." Michi propped herself up on her elbows. "Suzie, you showed Sindril's face to all of us last year. I saw that same face riding the wind, attacking the College."

"So he's returned. Do you think he's come back for me?"

"I don't know," replied Frank.

"We'll protect you," said Michi. She started to cough, and Frank reached into the ointment again.

"Take it slow," he said. "You're still weak. You need to build your strength more." He held out a hand and Michi clasped it in her own. Frank avoided Suzie's eyes but sensed her staring at them.

"It's so good to see you, Plamen," she said.

"You too."

"How were you trapped in the Armory?"

"I followed a group of Deaths down a series of corridors. There was fire everywhere and smoke filled the air. I became a beetle to dodge an attack within the Armory. I got knocked onto my back and when I scrambled to my legs the door had shut. I spent a week searching for any hole small enough for me to crawl out in insect form, but there were no exits."

"What will you do now?" asked Suzie. "Will you return to the forest, and the other 'Mentals?"

"You can stay here with me," said Frank.

"Tensions with the 'Mentals are higher than ever," said Suzie. "Frank's disguised as a Death, but you're a girl."

There were other 'Mentals here, but none who knew him like Michi did. His friends were all Deaths, it would be nice, no it would be *wonderful*, if she stayed. Was she in danger? No, he'd protect her.

"You should stay," said Frank.

"We do need friends and support," said Suzie, "but your parents must miss you."

She stopped and looked away. Frank knew Suzie still missed her other home. The one she'd never see again.

"I don't know if I can stay." Michi frowned, sitting up on the bed. "Thanks for the ointment, I feel better."

"Michi, you're better than anyone at staying out of sight. Who's going to notice a fly in the window, or a spider under a desk?"

"You want me to stay here and remain in insect-form?"

"Just for a while. You can visit Karis whenever you want to."

"Karis?"asked Suzie.

"Our village," said Frank. "Where you met my parents last year."

"Well, I'm sure mother misses me, but a few days won't make a difference. I am going home after that. Though maybe I could come back and visit."

"You'd always be welcome." Frank smiled, and Michi smiled back. "One thing, though. My name's not Plamen anymore. It's Frank."

CHAPTER SEVEN: SUZIE

Standing Up

The world exploded in shards of light.

Suzie awoke covered in sweat. The same dream again. What did it mean?

Rolling to her side, she looked past the curtain at the College of Deaths. Another girl. Though she'd met female 'Mentals last year, this was different. Frank knew this girl, Michi, and Suzie sensed she'd be around a lot. She'd have another ally against the foolish war many of the Deaths, including Eshue, seemed to want. It was good, right? After all, she liked Billy. She didn't need another boy paying attention to her. Frank flirted, but after last year's secrets, she'd never return his affections.

Besides, she had bigger issues. Sindril was back. There'd been no official word on the explosion, but she believed Frank and Michi. He'd returned and was teaming with the Dragons to attack the College itself.

She'd been so glad to be rid of him, but never stopped fearing his possible return. She took a deep breath, her fingers clenching and releasing. *He said I'd come to him; that I'd be drawn to the Dragons. What's changed?*

She got up and walked to the kitchen.

"Morning," said Tom.

"Good morning."

Billy stepped into the kitchen, rubbing his eyes. "Where were you yesterday? We all ran down to see the attack and you scampered off somewhere. Frank too. I kept looking for you."

"I went to Frank's house."

"You were there a long time." Billy frowned. "You must have come back after dark. What were you doing there?"

"We were just talking." In the end, Michi and Frank had asked her to keep the strange girl's presence a secret for now. They insisted they'd share with her group of friends, but only after Michi had a chance to go home and talk to her mother. Her father had apparently died shortly after Frank left for the In-Between. Suzie disliked the idea of keeping secrets from Billy. She might tell him later, when Tom wasn't around.

"Yeah, I get it." Billy avoided her eyes. His embarrassment stung like lemon on a wound. She'd let him down by lying, but at the same time a part of her was flattered at his jealousy. She'd definitely have to tell him about Michi.

"You should eat or you're going to be late," said Tom.

Suzie nodded.

* * * *

"I know many of us are concerned about the attack on the College yesterday," said Professor Domen, surveying his class with a raised eyebrow. "I, along with each of your teachers, have been asked to inform you that all precautions have been taken, and the College is completely safe. No one came within the Ring of Scythes, and an investigation has been launched."

"It was another 'Mental attack, wasn't it?" shouted someone in the back. "Like the boats over the summer."

"I do not know. There is no word yet. I share your suspicions, but we must not jump to conclusions."

He agrees with them, thought Suzie. *He blames the 'Mentals too.*

"At any rate, we are going to move on. Erebus took many of you to the Armory. Tell me, during your excursion, did anyone notice anything unusual? I hope someone saw."

I saw a fly who turned out to be both a 'Mental and Frank's old friend.

"There was a drawing on each of the scythes in the Armory," said a boy Suzie didn't know. "They all had an inscription about Grym, except two that resembled pictures of the First Scythe."

"Excellent, and correct on both counts. Most of the great scythes used in the war bear an inscription of Caladbolg. Two were carved in similar fashion to Grym. Why is that significant?"

Suzie yawned; the teacher was obsessed with this First Scythe. Last year, she'd been obsessed herself with the idea of a Dragon Key, an object which would let her return to the Mortal World. She still didn't buy Kasumir's explanation that it was just a story. Once the year settled down, she'd go to the library and start looking through books again. She smiled. Her library. She'd been away too long, she needed to go back.

"Suzie, are you listening?"

"Yes, professor, I—"

"Do you agree?" Domen raised an eyebrow. *Agree with what?*

"Absolutely," she replied.

"So you believe the first Deaths were fools?"

"No, I just—"

"Whatever you are daydreaming, Suzie, I'm sure can wait until later."

"I'm sorry." She frowned, looking down at her book. A drawing of Caladbolg looked back at her.

An hour later, Suzie walked toward Frank. He held out a boskery scythe, handing it to her with a smile. She finished her gorger, and took the double bladed scythe in her hands.

"Thanks again for helping me."

"Sure thing," he replied. "You put your left hand here, in league with the right. Remember the weight of the blade will carry it around."

She held the boskery blade, feeling the power of the scythe in the weight of the blades, and heard a slight buzzing in one ear. She looked to the side and saw the flicker of a fly. She raised an eyebrow at Frank.

"She was curious," he said. Suzie nodded and continued the motions he'd shown her. With practices rapidly approaching she needed all the extra help she could get, yet she found her eyes darting from corner to corner wondering where the fly was hovering.

She spun the blade, but heard a buzz. Losing her focus, she faltered.

"Concentrate."

She shouldn't be here. She's judging me.

"Suzie, you're not even looking at the blade. Are you taking this seriously?"

"I'm sorry. Let me try again."

By the end of her session Suzie's arms dripped with sweat. She handed the blade back to him and leaned against one of the stony walls, suppressing a frown.

"You did well today." Frank smiled weakly.

No I didn't.

"You're a good teacher."

She strode toward Applications that afternoon, after half-sleeping through Careers. Erebus stood in front of the class holding a scythe. His ponytail hung to one side of his face, which was locked in a scowl.

"Sit down quickly," he said. "I'm afraid I have bad news. The mortamant shortage continues, and with the recent attacks, student Reapings have been placed on hold. Your first Reaping is therefore delayed."

"Delayed?" asked Eshue. "For how long?"

"That hasn't been decided yet."

Strange, thought Suzie. For all her time in the World of Deaths, she'd only been on two Reapings. She knew there'd be many more ahead. *Splitting souls from bodies and escorting them onward. Our job*. She glanced at Tom, who appeared relieved at the news.

"Of course, from what I've seen, none of you are ready to Reap. Still, I am disappointed. Your first Reaping will be in three weeks, and that will be your only chance before Styxia. In the meantime, grab your practice scythes. You will have a test on Friday."

"Professor?" said Eshue.

"Yes?"

"We've been getting a lot of bad luck this year."

"That's true," said Erebus.

"I was wondering if you'd like to join a rally my group is having tonight?" He looked at Suzie and grinned.

"Your group?" asked Erebus.

Suzie was appalled. To ask the teacher to join his stupid club was bad enough, but in front of the entire class?

"That's right. We're called the AGC. We plan to take a burning effigy to Silver Lake and toss it in."

"That's outrageous," said Suzie, jumping to her feet.

"There's nothing wrong with protest," said Erebus. "We're short on mortamant, so he's re-creating the attacks of the summer."

"It's a stupid sexist attack. AGC stands for Anti-Girl Club. He's not upset about the mortamant, he's upset that I punched him. Which, I'll add, he deserved."

From the corner of her eye she saw Tom staring. Billy smiled, then got up and stood beside her.

"She's right," said Billy. "I don't know if anyone else here is in the AGC, but you should all be ashamed."

Eshue glanced from left to right. Erebus touched one of the stars on his robe, but said nothing. Eshue sat down in silence, and for an awkward minute no one spoke. Then Frenchie started to clap.

Soon the whole class was applauding. Eshue ran out of the classroom.

"You have courage, Suzie." Erebus waved the class quiet again. "I apologize, I did not know what group he was a part of. I'll speak to the other staff and make sure the AGC is disbanded. However, no assaulting other students off the boskery field."

"I won't hit anyone. You'll really disband the club?"

Suzie's pride swelled. Beside her, Billy took her hand and squeezed.

"Yes," said Erebus. "Let's get back to work now."

Suzie ran to the front of the room and took a beginner's blade, which she brought to Tom.

"The class liked it when you stood up to that bully," he said.

"It felt good," she replied. She gripped the handle and let the scythe fall; a trail of green light followed. "See that light, Tom? Billy and I will help you make your own trail."

"You've come full circle," said Billy.

"Only with your help."

CHAPTER EIGHT: WILL

The New Recruit

"Call me Will," he said when Suzie walked into breakfast.

"What?" she asked

"I don't want to go by Billy anymore," he replied. "I went to bed thinking about it. Standing beside you yesterday when you stood up to Eshue, and now preparing to go to your first boskery practice, I don't feel like a *Billy* anymore. That's a kid's name, and everything's changing. I'll tell them at practice too. I'm Will now."

"All right, Will, if that's what you want," she said.

"Feeling older?" asked Tom with a laugh.

"I am. My third year at the College, and my life's spun 180. At first, I wanted to go back, but now I can't imagine a different home. Suzie's here, and I have friends, and now I'm teaching others in boskery. People look up to us, Suzie."

"Well if everything you've said made you want to change your name, maybe I should change mine too. Suzie spent a year being attacked. Now that I'm standing up for myself, how does Susan sound?"

"Sounds beautiful to me," said Will.

Suzie, no *Susan*, smiled. They were growing up together. It was silly of course, using different nicknames and expecting things to be different, but Will *felt* different. He might be a Death, but he'd never felt so alive before. Finishing his eggs, he gave Susan a squeeze on her shoulder.

"Today will be great," he said. "I know you've been working hard with Frank and me. Now we get to put it to use."

Susan left to finish getting ready, while he stayed in the kitchen with Tom.

"Will, I'm really not afraid," said Tom, "but I do want to go home. Suzie told me you didn't even take your Final Test, your chance to go back to the Mortal World. Is that true?"

Will nodded. "My mom and I fought a lot, and things got even worse whenever my dad was around. No one misses me in that world. Things were strange here, but I didn't feel isolated. There's nothing for me there."

"I know it's months away, but I hope I pass. I want to go home."

"Our roommate last year passed, so it is possible. If you go, you'll forget you were ever here. Yet, if you stay, the life you used to know drifts farther and farther away. My old life is like a dream or a story. It's no more real to me now than Suzie's questions about Grym."

"Susan, you mean."

"Yeah," said Will. "That'll take a little getting used to."

Tom lowered his voice, glancing toward Susan's room. "You like her, don't you?"

"Yes." Will grinned. "A lot."

"I had a girlfriend last year, named Emily." Tom sighed. "I dreamed about her last night. I wonder what she's doing now. Does she worry about me? What happens to her if I don't come back?"

"She'll find someone else and live her life," said Will. "I'm not trying to sound harsh, but I'm sure it's happened to everyone here. Even our teachers were once regular kids back in the Mortal World." Over the summer, he, Frank, and Susan had played a game where they tried to guess their teachers' original names and places of origin. Cronk proved the hardest. He'd had so many jobs in the World of Deaths no one could even guess what he'd been like in the Mortal World. Will smiled. Susan had joked that Cronk probably stuttered so badly when choosing a new name after certification, they'd just called him Cronk. It was mean, but might even be true.

"I'm ready," said Susan, emerging from her room. She wore tight jeans and a loose gray shirt. She'd tied her long black hair into a ponytail. Her gray eyes sparkled above her playful grin. She was beautiful.

"We'll see you later, Tom," said Will.

"Have fun at practice."

Will led Susan out of Eagle Two. They met Frank in a courtyard, and then headed through the College.

"You guys ready?" asked Frank.

"This'll be fun. Susan's been working hard."

"*Susan*? Are we on formal terms now?" Frank laughed.

"It's not a joke. I told her I'd like to go by Will now. Susan's decided to go with a change too."

Frank studied them. "You're serious. All right. Changing names is fine, but don't alter your boskery style."

Will laughed, and they continued through the Ring of Scythes. Passing under the immense blades, the three stepped onto the boskery field. "Hey guys, hope you had a good summer," he said to the rest of the team.

"It was nice, but we're ready to work," said Mel. "Frank, since Dave's graduated, we want you to be captain. You won the championship for us in the end, after all."

"All right," said Frank. "I just found out myself, we won't be playing this year with Billy or Suzie."

"What?" Mel turned to Will in surprise. "We talked about this, and we were fine with your decision. If you're still concerned about having her—"

"Don't worry," said Frank. "These two are playing."

"You just said—"

"We're going to call them Will and Susan," said Frank.

Will nodded and glanced at Susan. She stood her ground, grinning.

"Well then, Will and Susan," said Olu, "let's get to work."

Frank led the team toward the sheds with boskery scythes. They took a few practice scythes, but most of the training would use actual blades.

"You know what they feel like if you get nicked," said Will, speaking softly to Susan. "Be careful."

"I had a good teacher," she replied. "I'll be fine."

"All right, Gray Knights," yelled Frank, "pair off. I know some of you haven't practiced for a couple of months, so we'll start with basic moves."

Susan stood facing Will, gripping the handle. The two blades glinted in the sun, like a shining *S*.

"Just like we practiced," he said. *She'll do fine.* Susan moved one hand around the other, spinning the blade. Will spun his own, while hers moved faster.

"Attack," said Frank.

Susan ran forward, and he deflected the blades with his own. He felt the force of her spins, and shifted his weight to counterbalance. She came toward him again, handling the scythe even better than he remembered at their training sessions.

"Hold," said Frank. The team paused. "Everyone in this line, move down one. Let's get used to different partners."

Will knew it'd happen, but he couldn't stop the lump from rising in his throat. He smiled at Susan, watching her take a new stance across from Gordon. The slim boy's thick, curly red hair caught the sunlight.

"Scythes ready," said Frank, "and begin."

Olu stood in front of Will, spinning the blades into a silver circle. They whirled at him. Will watched, spinning his own scythe defensively, but he kept glancing to the left. How was Susan doing? He saw Gordon shift legs and move forward. Susan parried and—

"Ah!" shouted Will. Olu's blade sliced into his leg. Paralysis coursed into his entire lower body, and he sank to the ground.

"Hey, we're still in light training," said Frank, coming over.

"I was going easy on him," Will heard Olu say. The world blurred, but he kept focusing on the ground and his own pain.

"Are you all right, Will?" asked Susan, bending down.

"I'm fine," he grunted. *Should've watched my opponent instead of watching you.* Olu helped him off the field.

Grimacing, he clutched his leg. Susan moved to a new partner. She dodged two of his parries, then pressed forward. The woman swinging a blade had grown so much since the day she'd first appeared at Eagle Two.

A fly flew across his vision, landing on a blade of grass. He waved a hand, and it flew away. After the pain subsided, Will stood and joined the others. Frank waved the team into a huddle.

"We're moving into plays and drills," said Frank. "Susan, I want you and Will to flank the quadrant. I'll be Protector at the tower. Feng, Mel, back them up. Let's see if the four of you can get the ball past me. Then we'll move on to other groups."

Will nodded and caught the ball Frank tossed toward him. Frank headed to the nearest tower. Four similar towers stood on far sides of the two-acre circular boskery field. When all four teams played, the field became a war zone of endurance. Will walked toward the tower.

"Come at him from the right," Will said to Susan. "I'll come from the left. He'll come to me since I have the ball. I'll toss it to Mel, who will throw it to you. If he rushes you, toss the ball back to Feng. If we cross mid-way, one of us should be able to get the ball past him. He can't take on four at once."

"We still have to get it up the tower," said Mel.

"If three of us distract him, whoever's free will scale the tower." The other three nodded.

"Let's see what you've got," called Frank.

Grasping the ball firmly in the crook of his arm, and holding the boskery scythe with a single hand, Will jogged to the left.

"Go," said Will. Susan sprinted toward Frank from the right, with Feng trailing. He and Mel ran toward the tower from the left.

Frank grasped his boskery scythe, but held his ground.

Will ran until he was only a few feet from Frank. Frank moved one hand over the other, spinning his blade into a circle. He kept his back facing the ladder. Will got close, then dropped his blade and tossed the ball backward. Feng caught it, then launched it high into the air. Frank's blade stopped. He watched the ball. Not pausing to see if Susan caught it, Will grabbed his blade, and let the momentum pull the scythes toward Frank. Frank raised his scythe, blocking Will's attack.

Looking up, he saw Susan toss the ball. Frank sprinted forward, striking the handle of Susan's boskery blade and knocking her double-scythe to the ground. The ball missed Mel and landed in the dirt, where Frank scooped it up.

"It's not our fault she throws like a girl," said Mel, struggling to catch his breath.

"I'm sorry," said Susan. "Juggling both the ball and scythe is tough."

"It was a nice attempt," said Frank. "The diversion was good. Try again, same play, but let Susan start with the ball. In fact, let her try it without a scythe. There are still three blades to one. If you three can't protect her with those odds, you won't help the rest of the team."

Susan put her scythe down, and took the ball from Frank. Since when had Frank taken charge like this? Will had been so focused on Susan, he hadn't noticed the changes in Frank. Maybe it was his 'Mental side showing, but Frank's confidence had also grown. Will and Mel jogged back to the left of the tower.

"Go!" shouted Frank.

Will and Mel ran toward Frank, spinning their boskery blades. Susan sprinted forward, clutching the ball in both hands. Frank's blades sparked when Will struck the mortamant. Metal screeched against metal. Frank pulled his scythe back and swung toward Mel. Feng approached, staying close to Susan.

"Should I throw it?" she called out.

"No need," said Frank. "I'm busy with these three. Get to the ladder."

Will attacked with a new invigoration, trying to pull Frank away from the tower. He slashed downward, aiming for Frank's thigh, but Frank jumped up, and slashed out with his own scythe. Will focused on Frank. Feng and Mel helped push Frank to the center of the field.

Amazing, thought Will, watching the circle of metal Frank spun, blocking three attackers at once.

"I did it," shouted Susan. "I'm here." Her voice came from above, she must've scaled the tower.

"Hold," said Frank. The four boys stopped their scythes, breathing hard. "Well done, Susan."

The rest of the team joined them, clapping.

"Let's get another group," said Frank. "Olu, take over as Protector."

Frank walked to Susan and patted her on the back, then whispered something into her ear. Susan smiled and joined him on the sides.

Will watched, trying to ignore his rising jealousy.

Frank saw his stare and smiled. He turned back to Susan, raising his voice. "You did great." He tossed her a canteen of water.

"Thanks, all that extra training really paid off." She took a long drink.

"I'm glad."

Will sat down, motioning Susan to sit beside him.

"Thanks but I want to talk to Frank a bit more. He had some other great ideas."

"Yeah, okay," said Will, fighting the urge to frown. Susan and Frank walked away.

My plan would've worked if we tried it again. Frank just got lucky. She likes him better, doesn't she?

Will admitted, he didn't know how Susan felt.

He needed a new strategy. The only girl on campus was worth fighting for.

CHAPTER NINE: SUSAN

Shadows in the Library

Susan ran her finger along the edge of the ancient book. *Lovethar's diary*. Real or not, the mere suggestion of an ancient book connected to the only other female Death intrigued her. The 'Mentals had magic, so perhaps this truly was her diary.

Frank's birthday gift had sat on her dresser for weeks. This was the first time she'd opened the book.

Lovethar's diary, she thought again. What had the other female Death dreamed of? What had her world been like? If Lovethar really lived a million years ago, did she even speak? Was she a proto-human, some sort of Neanderthal, or one of the mysterious Donkari, the ancestors of Deaths, she'd heard of last year?

She smiled. Maybe Lovethar had admirers too.

Susan opened the leather cover carefully, turning to one of the pages in the center. The smell of old paper wafted up with a cloud of dust. The pages were covered in runes of some sort, yet while she stared at them the markings dissolved into English.

It must be the same magic that lets us all communicate here. I wonder if it's another 'Mental trick, or if just some property of this world.

Even while words formed in front of her, Susan had a flash. She remembered runes pouring over her skin, slicing into her arms, and a room exploding in light. Could these be the same runes from her dream?

Blurry figures coalesced, and the words became legible.

Grym is unbearable. It fights with me day and night, yet I feel stronger now.

Susan looked up suddenly. *Grym?* The thing she'd studied in school? She read on.

The others fear me. When the war is done, I will bury Grym. Even Orryn doesn't like it. We need it though, if we want any hope of defeating Ryuuda's army. They've taken over the stone citadel and the two towers. We hide in the forest, waiting. It won't be long now.

"Hey, what are you doing?" asked Will, poking his head through the open door.

She closed the book.

"I was looking at the diary Frank gave me," she replied. "Lovethar mentioned Grym."

"You think that book's real? Paper doesn't last a million years, Susan."

"We've seen what 'Mentals can do, so yes I think it is."

"Well I just wanted to say how amazing you were yesterday. Really glad you're on our team."

"Thanks, Will."

"You didn't have to stop reading, I wasn't trying to interrupt."

"I didn't think I'd be able to read it," she said. "It's written in runes, yet when I look at them the words turned to English."

"Can I see?"

Nodding, Susan opened the book. Again the strange writing blurred and coalesced into recognizable words.

"Definitely magic," said Will. "I'm sure you're going to enjoy reading this. Even if it's not Lovethar's, you love books."

"The 'Mentals made this readable, I'm sure they could make it last if they wanted. It *is* her diary. The part I just read mentioned Orryn, who Kasumir told us about. They were lovers."

"The Elemental and the Death, yes I remember. Distant ancestors of yours."

"Very distant," laughed Susan. "Still, you are right, I like books. Would you like to go to the library? We haven't been this year."

"Okay. It's probably still a mess. We never put the shelves back after Sindril attacked you."

"All the more reason to go. Lovethar talked about burying Grym. If she hid her blade somewhere, maybe we could find it. The First Scythe was the most powerful scythe in the World of Deaths. With Caladbolg, we could do anything, even return to the Mortal World."

"Giving up on a Dragon Key?"

"No. However, we have two chances now. If we use the diary, and cross-reference it with books we find in the library, we have an opportunity that no Death had before."

Will smiled. Susan's determination coursed through her veins, sending shivers of excitement down her arms. She took Lovethar's diary and led Will out the door. They walked through canyons and mounds, weaving their way through the web-like maze of the College. Passing beyond the Ring of Scythes, they walked along the road toward the Southern Forest. Susan wondered how far the forest reached. Last year, she looked over the world from the top of West Tower. One forest stretched to the horizon south of the college, while a separate forest mirrored it to the north.

They left the path, trudging through newly fallen pine cones and over brambles. Ivy covered the fading and cracking paint on the walls of the hidden house, half buried in the hillside. Susan paused at the door, glancing at the boy beside her. She'd been hard on Will the past few days; he cared deeply for her, and she didn't want to push him away. She touched him lightly on the arm, grinning.

The door creaked as they entered the cramped front room. Susan walked to the curtain and drew it aside, remembering Sindril's machinations. He wanted her dead, and now dared to attack the College directly. However, he'd never return to the library. Frank had promised her the albino would guard it.

"You okay?" asked Will.

"Just thinking about last year," said Susan. "I'm going to have to face Sindril again eventually. Whatever the Dragons want me for, and whatever they've promised him, I'm still a target."

"You're never alone. You'll always have our support. Come on." He touched her arm lightly, pointing to the red book, and the hidden entrance. They pulled the thick book's spine down. With a slight tremble, the bookcase turned, revealing a hidden wall and the words *Librvm Exelcior*. Passing through the illusory wall, Susan and Will walked down a narrow staircase. White flower lights glowed beneath a layer of dust, each blossom brightening with their approach. Entering the library, Susan gasped.

"Where's the mess?" asked Will.

Expecting heaps of books and knocked over bookcases from her encounter with Sindril, Susan was surprised to see neat and orderly rows. She'd never seen the library this clean. Even the stone slabs predating the books were arranged in rows along the walls.

"Who do you think did this?" she asked.

"Look," said Will. He pointed to a small sheet of paper taped to one of the bookcases.

I cleaned to make up for attacking you. I know what it means to be a target.

"It must be from the fearmonger," she said.

"The albino?"

"I don't even know his real name."

"There's something on the back," said Will, pointing to the paper.

She turned the paper over. The writing on the other side was smeared and hurried, like an afterthought.

behind third stone on south wall

"What do you think that means?" asked Will.

"Sounds like he's leading us to something. Let's see what's there."

"I think that's south." He pointed. "It's also where most of the stones are. Do you think he meant third from the right corner or the left?"

"You look from the left, I'll look from the right." She hurried to the corner, going to the third stone. Like most of the others, the tablet was covered in runes and images. Flames encircled an elaborate key at the top of the rocky slab. Heaving with her full strength, she pulled the stone to one side.

"I don't see anything behind this one," she heard Will shout.

"It's here," she replied.

Will hurried over while she stared at the wall. The library's walls were rock, stretching far underground beneath the tiny house above. Most of the limestone walls looked cave-like, similar to the canyon mounds of the College. Streaks of color ribboned both the library and the campus, between sections of beige, red, and tan. Behind the stone, however, a white area larger than Susan stretched up from the floor. Deep black scorch marks lay across the white surface.

"What do you think that is?" asked Will.

"Almost looks like a door, but these burn marks are what's really odd. They're concentrated all along its edges."

She ran her hands along the white but couldn't find any crack or separation. It wasn't a door, or didn't seem to be. Door or not, the area clearly suffered a serious attack.

"Do you think the albino did this? The burns I mean?" asked Will.

"I don't see why he would. Besides, Frank said 'Mentals only control one thing. The fearmonger manipulates fear, so how would he burn this?"

"If he didn't do it, why write it on the paper?"

"Well, it's different at least. Maybe he was curious, or thought we'd be curious about it. We're in here from curiosity, right?"

She heard someone coming down the steps.

"I'm curious why you didn't invite the rest of your friends," said Frank, walking into the library. Tom followed behind, his eyes wide.

"This place is amazing," said the younger boy. Susan forgot she'd never shown Tom the library. A third pair of footsteps surprised her; Michi stepped off the stairs.

"Who is that?" exclaimed Will. Another thing she'd forgotten.

"Susan didn't tell you? This is my friend Michi," said Frank. "We're visiting my mother's village tomorrow, but wanted to spend today with everyone."

"A girl?" asked Will. "You knew about her, Susan?"

"Yes. She's a 'Mental, trapped here last year after the attack. I met her in the Armory."

"Nice to meet you," said Will.

Susan watched his face, noting the shimmer in his eye when he shook the Elemental's hand. Is this what he felt when she talked to Frank? She'd never known jealousy before, and disliked the taste it left in her mouth.

"What are you doing?" asked Michi.

Susan gestured to the marks on the wall. "The fearmonger cleaned the library, but mentioned something he'd found. We're trying to figure what it is."

Michi walked to the wall and ran her fingers along the edges of the white mark. She rubbed one along a burn, and sniffed.

"This was done long before I was born," she said. "There's 'Mental magic here."

"It looks sort of like a door," said Tom.

"That's what I thought," said Susan, "but we can't find any way in. There aren't even spaces on the side."

"Let me try something," said Michi. She closed her eyes and held out her hands, trembling. The tips of her fingers darkened and turned black, then crumbled off and started to fly. Ten tiny insects flew at the scorch marks, while Michi grimaced.

"Your hands," said Will. "Are you all right?"

The 'Mental girl didn't respond, but watched the insects crawl over the wall. Michi rocked back and forth. Frank reached an arm around her waist, holding her.

"Easy now," said Frank.

Tears welled in Michi's eyes. Ashamed at her earlier pang of jealousy, Susan stared at the stubs of the other girl's fingers. The insects flew back toward the Elemental's hands and Michi was whole again.

"There are words," said Michi, gasping for air. She lowered to one knee, clearly in agony. "On the outside. Words carved on the wall."

"Just relax," said Frank. "Sit down." He helped prop her against one of the stone slabs. Tom reached into his sack, and pulled out a bottle of water which he handed to her. Michi sipped, then massaged her fingers.

"I'm sorry, it's been a long time since I've done anything like that. I forgot how much it takes from me."

"You said there are words on the wall?" asked Susan.

"Yes, too tiny for us to see with our eyes. It's a message for other 'Mentals. It says:

Dragon's bane,

Death's pain,

Never to wake again.

Shadow of fear,

Let no man near

The Creator's blood."

"What does it mean?" asked Tom.

"It's a curse," replied Frank. "Probably intended to keep people out. If this is 'Mental magic, there could be an entire complex behind this wall. Yet, we'll never get in unless we know how."

"An entire part of the library we've never seen?" Susan's body trembled with new excitement. "I came because I was looking at Lovethar's diary. Now, we found something amazing."

"The albino found it," said Will. "Besides, if it's a cursed entrance, how are we supposed to get in?"

"Michi and I can ask Kasumir tomorrow," said Frank.

"What are all these other books?" asked Tom. "Why is this place separate from the College?"

"We found it last year," said Susan. "You have to promise not to tell anyone, and you too Michi. You can tell the 'Mentals, but otherwise this is our secret place."

"I understand," said Tom.

Susan walked to where she'd left Lovethar's diary, and picked up the ancient book. "We'll worry about that cursed area some other time, after Frank asks his mom about it. Now, let's see if we can find any mention of Grym."

"The First Scythe?" asked Frank.

"Lovethar mentioned it; I think Grym belonged to her during the war. I'll look in the diary, but I want to see if there's any other mention of Grym or Caladbolg."

Tom walked to the stones. Frank helped Michi up and the two walked toward a bookcase, with Will trailing.

"The way your fingers turned into bugs was amazing," said Will.

Frank reached down and took Michi's hand. Were they more than friends? Susan sat at a table, looking down. She tried to focus on Lovethar's words but questions started circling her mind.

I'm curious, but it doesn't matter. I'm not some kid anymore, I'm a Reaper. It's time to act like an adult.

She opened Lovethar's diary, and dove in, allowing the runes to become words.

CHAPTER TEN: FRANK

A Sliver of Soul

Rayn's office was crowded with trinkets and books. Frank watched the Death place an emerald hourglass on a shelf, between an assortment of other baubles. It seemed Rayn used his new office as Elemental liaison to hoard knickknacks from across the World of Deaths. What a freak.

Frank stifled a laugh. The irony was ridiculous. Susan worried his absence would be noticed, so here he was suggesting a meeting with the 'Mentals.

"Explain this to me again," said Rayn, opening a porcelain jar and taking a long sniff before putting the top on and frowning.

"The College is low on mortamant," replied Frank. "They've already limited the number of Reapings this year. We're trying to foster better relations with the Elementals. If I can find where the 'Mentals live, perhaps I can ask them to help us make more."

"What about your friends Suzie and Billy? The ones who went last year, why aren't they going?"

"Susan and Will are behind in their class work. I'm ahead in mine. If you make me an official representative, the 'Mentals will listen. They might not agree, but what if they do? We'd be prepared, both for Reapings and in case there's another attack."

Again, Frank fought the urge to laugh out loud. Of course he'd go, with permission or not. Still, Will's suggestion to ask about mortamant was a good one. Their first Reaping was coming up, and despite being a 'Mental, Frank found himself looking forward to it. Maybe he'd spent too much time pretending to be a Death.

"I'll not lie." Rayn prodded a small clock on his desk. Did he ever stay still? "The Council is nervous. I never liked Sindril, myself, but for him to attack the College directly? Frightening. You and I both know the 'Mentals had nothing to do with those boats. They were on fire, attacked from the sky, and yet the idiots here still don't know who to blame."

"You think Sindril caused the attacks?" asked Frank. He'd yet to hear a Death admit Sindril's culpability. "The boats and the College?"

"No," said Rayn, sharply. "I think Dragons caused both. Yet we all know Sindril's gone to live with the Dragons, so the difference is negligible." He paused, raising an eyebrow. "This speculation remains between the two of us, of course."

"Absolutely," said Frank.

"Very well, I hereby appoint you an official representative of the Deaths. Follow the trail that Susan took last year, and I'm sure you will find the 'Mentals. If you can convince them to help us replenish our mortamant supply, I will make this position a permanent one, and will even offer a stipend."

They'd pay him? The last time he'd worked was in the In-Between. He'd abandoned Athanasius. It seemed the right thing to do when Susan first appeared. A pang of guilt welled in his throat. Sindril would pay dearly for murdering his friend.

"Thank you, sir."

"I'd come with you myself, but since the attack, I dare not leave. I don't think you should go alone. If your friends are busy, select another Death to accompany you."

"I have a friend who'd like to come along," said Frank. *More than a friend*. "I'm not going alone."

"Take this," said Rayn, lifting something from one shelf. He held an ornate ivory sheath, and withdrew a silver dagger. "This is a mortamant knife. Like the training daggers, it allows transport back to the College if you nick yourself. However, this blade also allows attack. If you cut a foe and draw blood, they will flee, no matter how minor the injury."

"Will I face enemies?"

"Beyond the Ring of Scythes, especially in the forest, there are many you should avoid. This knife is a loan, not a gift, but be careful."

Frank nodded.

"Report to me when you return." Rayn returned to his shelves, studying the knickknacks he'd collected.

* * * *

Frank paused at Silver Pond, glancing back toward the two distant towers of the College. The rising sun hung low in the sky behind the campus, silhouetting the writhing mountains against a salmon pink backdrop.

"We're clear," said Frank, "you can take off your hood."

Michi pulled her hood down, shaking out her long auburn hair. Her face remained thin, and a tan ring surrounded each eye. She might never fully recover from her months trapped in the Armory. Every time he looked a her, Frank's heart pulled in opposing directions. She was beautiful, and the first girl he'd ever liked. Yet, she was a voice from the past, a reminder of Plamen, and the life he'd given up.

"I can't believe they think we're a couple of Deaths going to ask 'Mentals for help," she said. Her voice lilted with a playfulness he'd missed.

"They have no reason to doubt us, and they need the mortamant."

"Deaths are stupid," she quipped. "Why do you want to be one?"

"I don't. I live with Deaths to help our people. I work with Susan, and others, to help bring change to the world."

Michi cocked an eyebrow. "You've gotten a lot more idealistic from the boy I knew," she said. "You're not just hanging around them because Susan's pretty? I'd be jealous."

"No, that's not it at all." Frank's cheeks burned and he turned away. "I admit, I like her—"

"Oh, I know. You can't keep your feelings from me, Plamen."

"Frank," he murmured.

"Oh, lighten up. I'm not trying to *bug* you."

He groaned at the pun and continued toward the Northern Forest. His parents lived in the village of Karis. Vyr lay farther to the north, with rumors of smaller scattered villages even farther away.

They crossed an open plain of grass and dandelions, and entered the dense forest. No paths wove between the trees, yet each of them knew the way well.

"Susan said she followed a scent to find Karis last year," said Frank.

"How many times have I told you, you stink?"

She hasn't changed at all. Frank smiled, then dropped to ground.

"Michi, get down!"

A deafening scream split the canopy above them. A shadow swept over the trees. Pine cones scraped his knuckles and grass brushed against his face. Glancing up, he saw Michi cowering. The screech rang through the forest again.

"It's circling back," she said.

The shadow neared, and the screech deafened Frank. He clutched his hands to his ears, turning up to see a long shadow with wings. He had to know.

Reaching deep into his inner self, he tugged at the power. He only needed a little to raise his vision above the tree line. The world blurred, and for a moment his body slipped away. He drifted up to look.

He'd seen pictures, but nothing prepared him for the spectacle in the sky.

A creature like a massive snake, a hundred feet long, soared above. It had two great wings, talons of steel, and a monstrous head capped by horns. The Dragon's blood-red scales pulsed and quivered with every flap of its leathery wings. Traces of black and gold glinted on the creature's underbelly. It glided over them, before veering westward, toward the distant mountains.

Frank released his power, and floated back into his body, breathless. He lay still, waiting for sign of the Dragon's return.

"What was that?" asked Michi, coming over.

"A Dragon," he replied. "I've never seen one in person."

"Why was it here?"

"Let's not stick around to find out. Come on, let's get to Karis."

They rose. Michi's hair hung wildly around her face, and she'd torn her shirt while diving to the ground.

"Maybe I should use insects to keep watch," she suggested. "I can post them on the tops of trees."

Frank nodded, his mind still going over the details of the Dragon's body, both terrifying and beautiful.

Michi shut her eyes and lifted her hands. The air buzzed as flies flew past them, darting into the sky. Michi swayed, then stumbled.

"What's wrong?" asked Frank, catching her.

She murmured something, but stared lifelessly.

"Michi? Are you all right?"

"Too many." She swayed, putting trembling fingers on her forehead. Frank helped her lean against a tree, then reached into his bag for water, raising it to her quivering lips.

"Slow. Just relax. Did something happen with the Dragon?"

"Not the Dragon," she said. "I've been reckless. I've spent too much of myself since Susan found me in the Armory."

"What are you talking about?"

"My power." She fell silent and stared ahead again. This was no good, she couldn't move, but there was a Dragon who might return.

"Come on," he said. "I'll help you walk; you can lean on me. Let's get moving."

With Michi leaning heavily on his shoulder, Frank stumbled forward through the forest. Tripping over a tangle of roots, he lost his grip and she slipped.

"I need rest," she whispered.

"The village is still hours away. I want to get there before the Dragon returns."

She shook her head. "There's nothing we can do. We can't outrun him."

Damn. They couldn't continue like this, but why was Michi so weak?

"You used to outrun me every day," he said. "What happened?"

"Our power has a terrible cost. Haven't you noticed yet?"

He shook his head. Behind his conscious mind, the wolf lurked, its hungry eyes wanting to leap forth and consume him. *What would you take from me, if I used too much?*

Everything and more.

He didn't know where the response emanated from, but the answer was true. He knew it.

"Give me another minute or so," she said between gasping breaths.

Frank crossed his legs and gazed up at the dense canopy. Shafts of golden-green light slipped between leaves, warming the dark forest below. The air was damp, unlike the scratchy dry pine needles beneath him. A faint hint of moss and mud lingered on the breeze.

"Are you all right?" he asked, watching her.

"I will be, yes."

"I'll bring you to a healer in Karis. They'll be able—"

Her eyes widened. "You really don't know, do you? There's nothing they can do."

"If you're sick, Michi—"

She laughed, shaking her head. Brushing a strand of hair out of her face, she smiled. "I'm not sick, Frank. No more than you are. Come on, let's get going."

She struggled to her feet and took a deep breath. Holding her hands palm upwards, she opened her mouth. A strange rumbling growl rolled from her lips. A fly buzzed, whizzing by Frank's ear, then another and another. A swarm of insects sped to Michi, until black clouds of tiny squirming bugs encased each hand. She closed her mouth, clenched her jaw, and her eyes widened. Her pupils pulsed with a burst of white light, so bright that Frank shielded his gaze. *What has she done?* He looked up.

Michi smiled. At her feet lay two piles of dead insects. *She's found a way to draw power from other beings?*

"Come on," she repeated. She ran through the forest, and Frank struggled to keep pace. They continued for an hour, crossing tiny streams, and ducking between branches. Frank wanted to ask, but didn't.

She loves insects. She'd never kill a bug; not Michi.

He squeezed through a thicket of birches. A large boulder sat amid the undergrowth.

"Let's pause a moment," he said.

"You said we needed to hurry," she quipped.

"Michi, those insects you called—"

"I needed the strength. You'll understand one day."

Frank started to speak when a deafening shriek pierced the woods. They exchanged a silent acknowledgement, and crept to the side of the boulder.

"We might be able to hide beneath the stone," Frank told Michi. He used his mind, grazing the power without diving into its depths.

The shriek screamed through the forest. The Elementals huddled on the rock's edge, grasping for a crevice. Frank reached into his pocket and clutched the hilt of Rayn's dagger. Tingles of warm energy coursed through his skin, rippling in waves from the mortamant blade.

A third scream blasted leaves to the ground. The forest floor trembled and trees quivered in the face of the Dragon's fury.

"Something's changed," said Michi. "He knows we're here."

"Don't be ridiculous," said Frank. For a moment the forest quieted.

Crash!

The canopy overhead tumbled down, trees snapping in half. A smell of sulfur choked Frank. A blast of heat swept through the forest. White-hot flames engulfed the woods, disintegrating trunks and leaves in a conflagration. Fire rushed around them like a tidal wave against a beach. The boulder protected their backs, yet even the stone grew hot. Smoke stung his eyes like acid.

Frank pulled out the dagger. The Dragon's scales covered its entire body. He'd never get close enough to draw blood. Yet, one nick of his own blood and he'd be home.

The Dragon's blast ceased. *So much destruction in a single blast. How did the Deaths ever defeat creatures like this?* Acrid smoke billowed around the ashen ruins of trees.

"Hold my hand." His breath quickened as he clutched the dagger. The boulder radiated heat behind them like coal in a furnace. "I'm going to bring us back to the College."

"Wait. I've used my power. It's two against one, we should fight."

"Fight a Dragon? Are you insane?"

"We're Elementals." An edge he'd never heard her use before crept into the words. "We're the most powerful creatures in this world."

"I can't get close enough to use the knife. If we could draw blood, he'd flee."

The Dragon screamed and leaped into the sky, circling the decimated woodland. Its ruby scales glinted with gold in the sun. Through a haze of smoke and ash, Frank saw its eyes glowing blood-red. It opened its mouth, baring massive white fangs.

"Good plan," said Michi.

There was nowhere to run or hide. Frank froze, like a Reaped soul staring at the scythe. He edged the blade to his thigh. A single nick. He grasped for Michi's hand.

"Frank!" shouted Michi. "Snap out of it. Use you power, and take control. Take his mind."

Behind the paralysis of his fear, the wolf of his power growled. It gnawed at him, begging to be set free.

Help me, Frank implored.

Soaring into the sky, Frank's energy shot like a fountain. The wolf opened his mouth, breaking through.

A wall of armor. A body of flame.

Fury and fire.

Fire.

Beneath him, the tiny bodies of two Elementals clutched to a rock. His breath was flame, and his fury could obliterate them.

Heat.

The Dragon's ancient mind extended infinitely around him. Anger and flames meant nothing, the Dragon held wisdom and a deep sense of duty. This was unlike any mind Frank had entered. Clutching desperately in the dark, the wolf snarled.

In a second, my body will die. I hold him here, or I fail.

A pool of red, lined with white flame pulsed and trembled before him. The wolf jumped. Digging the claws of his power into the pool, Frank held the Dragon.

Through the eyes of the beast, he saw a cloud hovering with something silver. The ancient eyes focused. A swarm of insects held the mortamant knife. The Dragon struggled, but Frank's grip held. The knife flew straight to his right eye and pierced it.

Pain tore through Frank's soul, roaring into a scream that shattered the heavens. He fell out of the Dragon's mind, landing in his own body. The mortamant knife tumbled to the sooty crater, while the beast roiled in agony. With a deafening cry, the creature extended its wings and sped away.

Frank's head spun. Before passing out, an overwhelming sense of regret filled his heart. The magnificence of the ancient mind lingered in his thoughts. His eye ached, as if his had been the one gouged.

"You did well," said Michi. She held him in her arms; the world and its smoky ruins fading to a blur.

* * * *

Frank drifted in and out of visions. He paced an endless library, where a thousand years of knowledge lay stacked in spotless shelves. At the center of the ancient vault, a wolf clawed the ground.

The Dragon screamed.

Frank opened his eyes.

A vase of flower-lights glowed to his left, lighting the dim room. Sitting up, Frank recognized the bed. It'd been a long time since he lay here.

"Welcome," said mother, walking in. Her face seemed even more skeletal than when he'd seen her last spring. Kasumir's eye sockets were solid pools of darkness. The rings of white and gray he remembered had vanished; a solid mass of black formed the space within each eyelid. Her skin was lean and paler than the whitest alabaster. She wore a dress of silky blue.

"Mother. How did we—?"

"Michi sent some of her insects to tell us what transpired. We rushed into the forest, and carried you both here to Karis." She paused, turning away. "I entered your mind. Forgive me for the intrusion. You were unconscious, and I needed to learn the Dragon's fate."

"Did I hurt it?"

Mother faced him, her mouth twisted. "Yes, and I see that troubles you. How long were you inside the creature?"

"Only a few seconds. Michi was swift."

"It might have been too long," said mother. "You've been unconscious for four hours."

"What?" Frank pushed the sheet away and stood. "Why didn't you wake me?"

"We tried. Sit down, son. I've spoken with Michi already. You're not children anymore. Now that your powers are nearing maturity, you must realize the price."

Frank rubbed his head, thinking of the wolf clawing the ground. "You mean I'll black out if I use my power?"

She shook her head, and Frank was amazed to see a tear fall from one of her black eyes. In all his life, he'd never once seen her cry.

"It's not that simple," she replied. "The cost of our power is soul. Each time you draw on your hidden abilities, a sliver of your soul vanishes. Use too much, and you go mad or die."

"And you didn't tell me before? Why would you let me use my abilities at all? Why do you use yours?"

"Some things are worth the cost. I've watched Dragons attack ships. I saw a female Death enter our world, and knew she was a descendant of Lovethar. Yet for those gains, I have lost my normal sight. I no longer sleep, and soon I shall perish."

"Why are you telling me this now?" asked Frank.

"This is a dangerous time for you," she said. "Your powers will increase, and you shall be increasingly tempted to use them. Plamen, you must resist if you can. Use your gifts from time to time, but be aware of what you pay. The less you use your power, the longer and happier your life will be." She turned away.

"Mother—"

"Rest. When you're ready, there is much to discuss."

CHAPTER ELEVEN: SUSAN

An Ill-Equipped Reaping

Susan glanced at Tom and Will. Frank still hadn't returned after a week. Erebus hadn't asked anything, which meant Rayn had spoken to him.

"I can't believe he's not back yet," she whispered.

"I'm sure he's fine," said Will.

Erebus strode into the classroom, his face twisted into a scowl. He slammed a letter onto his desk before looking up at the class.

"It's come to this," he said. "Unbelievable."

No one spoke, but Suzie guessed it had something to do with the mortamant shortage.

"For the first time since the War, we're falling behind. By preventing student Reapings to conserve mortamant, the Council caused a glut of undelivered souls. Now it's up to the classes to bail them out." He laughed. "If I wasn't babysitting you, I'd personally retrieve every soul out there. A Silver Blade like myself, a *master* of the craft, has no need to ever fall behind. Yet, even I must follow orders." The smile left his face. "Disgusting," he said, looking at the class.

"So we'll be Reaping?" asked Billy.

"Not in the normal fashion," Erebus replied. "When a soul lingers in the Mortal World, its ties to flesh weaken. You'll be in your teams, with impure scythes. You'll be transporting some of those souls. Older students will wield the scythes, First Years will observe. Perhaps this is good for some of you, an early challenge."

"What do you mean impure scythes?" asked Susan.

"The scythes won't be fully mortamant. They'll work, though."

The number of the older boys murmured. Susan remembered her first Reaping and glanced at Tom with sympathy. She'd be fine, but there was no *normal fashion* about a first Reaping.

"I don't think you are ready," said Erebus. "I know this was sudden, but we're going today. Those fools can't allow any more souls to wait. The Council ordered this Reaping, so grab your teams and tethers, and I'll get the scythes. For those who have Reaped before, prepare to transport three souls instead of one. The scythe will guide you."

"This is insane," muttered Will. "Can't believe they're having us fix their mess."

Eshue crossed to their group. For a moment, Susan had almost forgotten he was on her team.

"Your friend's going to miss all the fun," he said. "Where's he been? Decided to drop out of school?"

"Frank's busy on Council business," snapped Will, "Which is more important than quibbling with you."

"Yes, I've heard the rumors. He some kind of 'Mental lover now, gone to beg for their help."

Not far off, thought Susan. "Come on, grab your tether and let's get ready," she said. "We've a job to do, and will need your help."

Eshue nodded, seeming mollified. He clicked a chain to his belt and pulled the cord taut, then fastened his tether to her, Will, and Tom. Erebus walked over with a scythe. Its blade glistened with a copper sheen, different from the normal silver. He handed it to Eshue.

"Three souls, and return. Don't mess up."

Susan turned to Tom, starting to ask if he was ready, but Eshue swung the scythe and the world split.

The room swirled into a torrent of blurring colors. They tore through the In-Between, with its double sun, and the scythe started to screech, like a nail on a chalkboard. Sparks flew toward her, while smells and time melted into a river of glowing light.

They hit the ground, and Susan fell, colliding into Tom. The tether pulled taut, yanking Will and Eshue down with them.

"Watch it," said Eshue, struggling to his feet.

"I've never heard a scythe screech like that," said Will. "These really are impure."

Susan's elbow stung where it'd scraped. A row of narrow cypress trees lined a gravel road, heading down a hill. The sun hung low in the orange and gold sky behind them. In the valley below, streetlights clustered in a small village, which climbed the adjoining hillside. Old buildings with yellowed walls and terracotta roofs clustered around a stone bell tower. The air was mild, filled with gentle cypress aroma.

"Let's get this over with," said Eshue. He lifted the scythe, walking away from the road.

"We're in the Mortal World?" asked Tom.

"Only to do our job," said Susan. "We can't go home."

"Our job," said Tom. "Right."

Beyond the trees, the grass bent beneath their shoes. Small stones and tiny wildflowers littered the hillside. Eshue adjusted his scythe, then pointed. A faint glow shone from the grass. He raised the snath and let the blade fall. A streak of sparks flicked off the scythe, and then it stopped mid-air.

The glow sat up. Part man and part cloud, the blur of light frowned at them.

Eshue pulled the scythe back and swung a second time, forcing it downward. A shriek pierced the air and Susan clamped her hands over her ears. In an instant, the soul came into sharper focus. A cloud of gold light enveloped the man and then burst outward, knocking Eshue into the air. Their tethers caught and the other three Deaths staggered.

Eshue landed hard.

"Are you all right?" asked Susan, hurrying to his side. His arm bled into the grass. Without pausing to think, she ripped the bottom of her shirt and tied it onto the gash, pressing close. "Will, help us, Eshue's hurt."

"What happened?" he asked.

"Keep pressure on his arm." She turned to the still-glowing soul. "We're here to take you onward. Don't be afraid."

The man crossed himself and clasped his hands in a sign of prayer. "I am ready," he replied. "Take me to Saint Peter."

"Do you have those daggers Hann gave us last year?" asked Susan. "The ones that let you go back? He needs a doctor."

Eshue moaned, sitting up. "I'm okay, he said.

Will shook his head. "Erebus didn't bother giving them out. We can't go back until we retrieve all three souls."

"I can't use the scythe," said Eshue.

"I'll take it," said Will.

"The soul was *stuck*," warned Eshue. "It wouldn't budge."

"The scythe is weaker," said Susan. "It doesn't have the power to do this easily. Will, I think you and I should use the scythe together. We've both handled scythes before. Tom and Eshue can help hold the souls."

Will smiled. "All right, let's do it. Tom, hold onto him tight. It's going to be a bumpy ride."

"I am ready," repeated the soul. "I am ready."

Tom took the man's hand.

"Wait," said Susan. "What's your name?"

The man smiled. She'd been criticized last year for asking, but as a Reaper, this was her way.

"Giacomo DeRosa," he replied.

"Come on," said Will. "Two to go, and Eshue's hurt."

Eshue clutched his arm. The shirt reddened where he held it above the elbow.

Susan and Will each grabbed the handle of the scythe, arranging their hands on the snath. Susan felt the tingle of hunger creep over her, the strange sensation that showed mortamant, yet this was different. The scythe seemed crazed and weakened, like a desperate cornered animal. This wouldn't be easy.

"On three," said Will. "One, two…three."

They swung. Instead of easily slicing through time and space, the blade sawed through the air in a rough gash. Every atom pushed back at the metal, sending sparks into the sky. The world ripped open, and they dove into the tear.

Colors bled into a whirlpool of sound, which faded into the taste of steel. Through every sensation, Susan struggled against the impure scythe. Will's hand slid down, touching hers; both dripped with sweat.

The universe turned and shattered, exploding into starlight.

The moon shone overhead. Voices spoke in a language she didn't recognize. Susan staggered, her feet stepping in wet grass. A pond in front of them reflected a pagoda rimmed in white electric lights.

"Let's find it quickly," said Will. The scythe tingled when she passed it to him.

Susan glanced at the others. Tom held Giacomo's hand. Eshue grimaced, clutching his elbow.

"There," said Will, unhooking his tether. They walked to the pond. The water shimmered with hundreds of reflections, but one corner of the waves shone differently. An elderly woman with gray hair and a long dress floated face down underwater, her soul glowing.

"Stand on the edge and swing," said Will. "If we dislodge it, she'll come the rest of the way."

Will and Susan each grasped the snath of the impure scythe, allowing the blade to drop. It screeched like nails on a chalkboard, pulling them down. Susan fell into the pond with a splash. The icy water choked her nose and she spat, sputtering to the surface. The scythe floated beside her. The soul spun in the water, her dead eyes staring blankly ahead.

"Will, you'd better come in," said Susan. "Maybe we can get her from here."

"Hurry," said Eshue. "People are coming."

Susan heard worried voices. From the corner of one eye she saw someone point. Will jumped in the water, and she pulled the scythe toward him. They grasped it and swung, forcing the blade into the floating soul.

"Pull," said Will, when the scythe caught.

They yanked backward. Will and Susan splashed back into the water, and the soul tore free. It hovered above the surface, staring. Susan and Will climbed out to find Eshue and Tom with their hands raised.

A uniformed Asian man pointed to them, shouting. When he saw Susan and Will emerge from the pond, dripping, he yelled louder. Then his eyes widened and he fell to his knees.

Susan felt the woman's soul behind her. She took her hand.

"Re-latch," said Will.

Everyone snapped the tether back on and Will and Susan grabbed the scythe, letting it fall. The uniform man stood again, pulling out a gun. He yelled, gesturing to get down.

"Please," said Will to the soldier. "We just want to help."

She watched the trembling soldier point the gun at Will.

Bang.

The sound pelted her ear. Would the bullet reach them?

The scythe fell, blurring the air. She slipped away from the scene, spinning into a whirlwind of colors.

Smash.

Something slammed into the scythe. They bounced in the vortex; Susan clung to the snath, while it pulled away. The scythe dragged through the tear in dimensions; sparks collided with the Deaths. They tumbled into the gash of sound and light.

Crack.

The sound echoed through the void, knocking Susan to her face.

She opened her eyes, struggling to her knees. A fierce wind whipped past her, and she crouched again.

"The scythe," she heard Will say. "They shot it."

Turning her head, she saw the blade lying on stone. The handle had split in half; half of the snath lay a few feet away.

"Help," called a voice to her right. She rose carefully, fighting the wind. "Help me!" it repeated.

Susan turned. They'd landed on a peninsula of stone, overlooking an ocean. The outcropping was only about thirty feet wide, with sheer rock cliffs dropping fifty feet to the choppy water below. The wind howled, freezing her soaking wet clothes, and stinging her face. The sunset lit up the land behind them, a coast of green grass and more jagged rock. She walked to the cliff face.

"Help," said Eshue, clinging to the cliff face. Susan reached down a hand.

"Take my hand," she said.

He grabbed it and she pulled, falling backward onto the rocks at the top of the peninsula. The shift in weight helped Eshue climb over the rim. He turned away from her.

"What is happening?" said the soul of the Asian woman.

"Just stay calm," said Susan. "We're trying to help you."

"It'll be all right," said Giacomo.

Susan sat up, peering toward the next outcropping of rock down the coast. The ruins of a medieval castle clung to the sides and top of the next peninsula.

"Where's the soul?" asked Tom.

"There," said Susan, gesturing. "In the window of that ruin. See the glow?"

"The scythe broke," said Will. "The handle snapped in half. We're done. Trapped here until we die."

Susan stood, unlatching the tether. She fought the wind, shivering in the bitter cold. The taste of saltwater lingered in the air, and the ocean below pounded against the rock face. She walked to the blade and lifted it. It tingled.

"We're not done," she said. "With no handle, it'll only take one person. I'll go. It's on that next outcropping. I'll bring the soul back and then we'll all go home."

"Will it work?" asked Tom.

"I'm going to try."

She started toward the mainland. A path of sorts ran across parts of the rock.

"Susan," called Will, but she didn't turn.

"Stay there," she said. "Watch the others."

She made her way carefully back along the stones. The wind lessened near the mainland. She stuffed the blade through the loop in her belt, where the tether attached, and got to her knees. Easing herself over the edge, she climbed down the cliff. She stopped every few minutes, whenever the wind picked up.

She reached a narrow strip of shore and jumped down, walking to the next outcropping, which she now saw was an island adjacent to the shore. Caves riddled the bottom of the enormous stone island. The ocean pounded, surging back and forth against the rocks. A wooden bridge extended toward the castle ruins, and a path led to the bridge. It was roped off, but she climbed over the rope easily, and crossed to the ruins.

The glowing soul sat up at her approach. A middle aged man with a beard. Next to the glowing soul she saw a smashed camera. To her right, she saw the finger-like projection of rock where the other Deaths and two glowing souls waited.

"I'm here to help," she said.

Pulling the blade out of her belt, she paused. She couldn't swing. She pushed the blade over the soul, but nothing happened. She tried sawing the top of the glow, but the blade quivered in her hand. On instinct, she then grabbed the broken blade and stabbed the top of the soul. Sparks flew; it clawed into the caught soul. She wrestled the blade free and the man stood.

"What the hell is all this about?" asked the soul, speaking with a British accent.

"No time to explain," said Susan. "I'm a Reaper, just follow me." She put the blade back in her belt and started toward the bridge again. The man hesitated, then followed. She stopped, turning.

"I'm sorry, I forgot to ask your name."

"Clive," said the man. "Am I...am I—?"

"You're dead," replied Susan. "We'll take you on."

"Is Sally here?" asked the man. "My wife?"

"Not here," said Susan, "Perhaps you'll find her wherever you're going. Come on, we've tarried too long."

The sky overhead darkened, and the crash of water on stone intensified. They crossed back over the bridge and walked to the next outcropping. She climbed up the rocks, and Will extended a hand to help her up. Clive half-walked and half-floated behind her.

"You did it," said Will. "Even with a broken scythe."

"Let's go," said Susan. "You three hold the souls, and I'll use the blade."

"Will it work without the handle?" asked Will. "Before, we needed two people—"

"I cut Clive's soul by myself. It'll work, it just takes effort."

Will nodded.

"What's your name?" Susan said, turning to the Asian woman.

"Nuo Bai," said the woman with a nod. "You speak Mandarin?"

"No," said Susan. "You've died. I wish we had more time, but I'm glad to have met you."

Nuo nodded again, looking at her own glowing hand.

"Tether up," said Susan, clasping hers back on. "Each of you needs to hold a soul."

"We're ready," said Will.

Susan pulled out the blade. If it cut Clive's soul free, it should bring them home.

She stood, shivering, and sneezed. Her soaking clothes clung to her while the freezing wind bit into her face and skin. Her hand trembled, lifting the blade.

"Please," she whispered.

She stabbed the air and the blade caught. The pressure jerked her hand, but she dug her feet in, thrusting the scythe farther into the air. Filaments of white light rippled from the blade, while the air splintered into shards of color. Tension mounted and then the scythe yanked forward, drawing Susan and the others through the tear.

Her body burned with fire. Colors and sounds screamed past her ears. The whirlwind cascaded into a torrent. The sun appeared, divided into two, then exploded into starlight.

Color.

Sound.

A whirl of worlds colliding.

Thunder echoed all around.

Susan sat up on the narrow beach net to the Door. A sheer cliff behind her rose at a 90 degree angle, straight up for miles, blocking most of the sky. A hundred feet into the ocean, a second cliff shot toward the sky, made from upward flowing water.

"What is this place?" asked Tom.

"The Door to the Hereafter," said Will.

The wall of water thundered toward the heavens above, vanishing into the horizon. Above them, a narrow strip of cloudless sky ran the length of the beach, which stretched beyond sight in front of and behind them.

"There," said Susan. A stone bridge emerged in the water, leading to an enormous metal door, a hundred feet high.

She walked forward, and the three souls paused on the edge of the bridge.

"You need to cross," she said. "Whatever answers you seek, lie on the other side."

Clive, Nuo, and Giacomo thanked her, walking toward the door, where they vanished into white light.

"Hardest Reaping ever," said Will. "I wonder if the others had crummy scythes too."

"We still have one final trip," said Susan."Everyone hold tight."

The blade barely tingled when she lifted it.

"We'll help," said Will. He put his hand on hers. Tom joined, putting his hand on top.

Eshue paused.

"She saved your life," said Will. "She could've let you fall after the way you've acted."

Eshue mumbled something, then added his hand to the others'. They pushed the blade downward. Sparks flew and the scythe screeched. Susan pushed down, crying out as the broken blade sliced into her skin. Will, Tom, and Eshue pushed harder, easing the blade farther. The world shattered into light.

The final trip seared her skin. Every color that passed tore into her bleeding hand.

Susan opened her eyes to see the smiling face of Erebus.

"We're back." She gasped, dropping the broken scythe to the ground.

CHAPTER TWELVE: WILL

Dragon's Bane

Will watched the scythe fall, stepping up to Susan to help her.

"The scythe broke?" asked Erebus.

"Yes," replied Susan, "but we completed the job. All three souls are in the Hereafter."

Erebus nodded slowly. "I'm impressed. Three groups returned early, having failed. You are the first to have succeeded with all of the souls. I'll make a note commending you in each of your records, and you're free to take the rest of the day off."

"Sir," said Will. "I want to mention that *Susan* deserves most of the credit. She retrieved the last soul herself, insisting that we finish, even after the scythe broke."

"Noted," said Erebus. "Eshue and Susan, you're hurt. A few others had injuries as well. I want all four of you to see Medic Kuriel, he's right over there."

Kuriel bandaged Suzie's hand and gave her a pill.

"Were you injured?" asked the medic.

Will shook his head.

Ten minutes later, they left the class.

"Thanks," muttered Eshue, frowning.

"Stop the AGC," said Will. "A *girl* saved you today. Don't forget it."

Eshue frowned, then nodded. "I'll stop the club."

"I'll hold you to that," said Susan.

Eshue limped away and Will stared at the world's only female Death. Her raven hair streamed from her sweat-streaked face. Her clothes, still damp, clung to her skin, showing every curve in her young body. She was stunning.

"Let's get out of these clothes," said Will, starting toward Eagle Two.

"Are Reapings always that tense?" asked Tom.

Will laughed. "No," he said, "but if this mortamant shortage continues, they'll only get harder."

"They sent us to Reap with a defective scythe," said Susan. "I'm not surprised the others failed. I wonder how they got back. Maybe the scythes got confused. I just wish we hadn't been seen, and could've helped those souls more."

"Susan, you were amazing," said Will. "Don't worry about being seen. You took charge of our group. I would've given up, but you kept going."

"I just did what I had to," she replied.

"No, you did more," said Will. They walked to Eagle Two and entered. In the kitchen, Frank sat waiting for them, his eyes wild.

"Frank? Are you all right?" asked Susan.

"I have a lot to tell you. It looks like you have a lot to tell me as well."

"Let us get changed," said Will, shivering.

In his room, Will tore off the soaking robe and stepped into the shower. The hot water stung on his cold skin. He changed, thinking about Susan. There was no doubt any more. He loved her. He couldn't think about her face without butterflies swarming his stomach.

Stepping into the kitchen, he saw her hugging Frank.

"Will, listen to what Frank's been through," said Susan. "He fought a Dragon."

Will grabbed an apple while Frank recounted his trip to Karis.

"If I kept using my power, I could take on a Dragon again, but mother says every time my abilities are used, part of my soul is lost."

"A part of your soul?" asked Susan. "What do you mean?"

"Elemental power feeds off of our souls. Each time I use it, I die a little, or go crazy. I guess the more I use power, the less of *me* there is inside."

"That's terrible." Susan's voice dropped to a whisper. "All those times you contacted me last year. All those visions. It cost you part of your soul?"

"Yes," replied Frank. "I didn't know then. I've used my power rarely since, but have to be careful. The Dragon was strong. It took a massive effort to fight it at all."

"You shouldn't use your power again." Susan frowned, shaking her head.

Will sat. "I can't believe you fought a Dragon."

"And nearly won." Frank's lips parted in a wide grin.

"What was it doing there?" Will bit into the tart fruit.

"They're attacking the boats. Dragons are behind the mortamant shortage."

"Why?" Susan's finger twirled around a lock of hair. "Why would they do that?"

"The 'Mentals think they want to provoke the Deaths into a second war. Though why they'd want to fight now, after all this time, is a mystery."

"What do we do?" asked Susan.

"Well, I'm supposed to report to Rayn. The 'Mentals will help us, but if war's coming, we're all in trouble."

"I'm amazed you took on a Dragon." Susan stood, grasping Frank's shoulder. "You're so brave."

Will bristled. Susan had rescued a soul with a broken scythe, while Frank battled Dragons with magic. What had he done?

Will swallowed. "Susan is brave as well. You should've seen her take charge of the craziest Reaping I've ever seen."

"Tell me," said Frank.

Will, Susan, and Tom told their story. Will watched Susan's eyes linger on the 'Mental.

"I can't believe they sent you out with those scythes," said Frank. "Did you tell Erebus you were seen?"

"He was glad we returned, and got the souls." Will shrugged. "We don't need to tell him."

"We'll tell him tomorrow." Susan sat again, leaning on the table. "We won't keep that a secret. I'm sure he won't mind our initial omission."

"Of course," said Will. "It's better to tell him. You're right."

Frank raised an eyebrow, glancing at Will.

Susan leaned back, smiling. "Let's go to the library. My hand hurts a little, but with the rest of the day off, I want to compare that spot we found to Lovethar's diary."

"You're the only person I know who'd choose to spend all her free time reading books." Tom shook his head. "I just want to relax. The Reaping exhausted me."

"You can stay here. I'll go alone if no one wants to come."

Will wanted to stay and relax. His body ached from the three Reapings. How did she still have energy?

"I want to read up on the War." Frank nodded. "I'll come."

"I'm coming too." Will glanced at Frank. *You're not going without me*. "It'll be fun."

Tom yawned, turning. "Aren't you tired, Susan?"

"A little tired, sure, but invigorated. Eshue might stop teasing me, and Frank's proven that the Dragons are behind the mortamant shortage. This is no time to relax."

Tom shrugged, leaning back in his chair. "Suit yourself."

Susan brushed a few stray strands of hair off her face and rose. She went to her room. Will glanced at Frank. "Michi stayed with the 'Mentals?"

"She did," said Frank. "Will... About Susan, I—"

"Yeah?"

Susan returned with Lovethar's diary. Frank shook his head.

What were you saying about Susan?

"Come on," she said. Will followed her and Frank toward the Ring of Scythes. Susan put her hand on Frank's arm, whispering something in his ear.

"Hey, no secrets." Will sprinted, catching up.

Susan smiled but said nothing. *Was the smile for him or Frank?*

They came to the Ring, and Susan pointed up. "There's plenty of mortamant there. Do you think the Deaths would consider melting the Ring of Scythes down?"

"It'd leave the College defenseless." Frank gestured. "My mother told me a spell extends around the campus through these scythes. That's why Sindril attacked it from the outside before. Dragons can't fly directly to the Towers."

They continued into the forest, then to the library. Susan walked straight to the wall.

"Do you remember the message Michi found?" she asked.

Frank nodded and recited it:

"*Dragon's bane,*

Death's pain,

Never to wake again.

Shadow of fear,

Let no man near

The Creator's blood."

Will frowned. Did Frank possess magic memory too?

Susan sat on the floor, by the gap in the wall, and opened Lovethar's diary. Frank walked to one of the shelves and pulled out a dust-covered book.

"This entry talks about mortamant," said Susan. Will sat on the floor beside her, watching her dark eyes scan the page. Her hair fell over her freckled face, and she brushed it aside. "The Deaths opened a new mine last week," she read, "a direct source of new metal across the sea. The stronghold at Mors continues to fortify. However, the Dragon army launched an attack on two boats. All-out war seems imminent."

"Doesn't sound that different from what we're experiencing now," said Will.

"Orryn showed me a forge today," she read. "Elementals line a tub of molten mortamant, bending their powers together, and folding it into the forming scythes. The process amazed me. General Masrun demanded larger, more powerful scythes, to help launch a counterattack. The Towers seem lost. Dragons again hold the entire area."

"Masrun?" asked Frank.

"Maybe he led the Deaths?" suggested Will.

"I saw something about him on a different page," said Susan, flipping forward in the diary. "Here it is. I met General Masrun today. A tall brute, with a bracelet shaped like an hourglass. He accused me of treason in front of the Council. I pled for two hours, and in the end was sent away with a warning. They need the Elementals, but fear them. If the Deaths win the war, I fear for Orryn and my friends."

"She was right on that count," said Frank. "A million years of distrust and subjugation, and you still fear us."

"I don't," said Susan.

"You know what I mean," said Frank.

"Did you find anything about Dragons there?" she asked, closing the diary. "Ow."

"What happened?" asked Will.

"I got a paper cut. I guess these old pages are still sharp."

"'Mentals preserved it too well." Frank smiled.

Susan put her finger in her mouth for a moment, then put the book down. Will hurried to his feet, reaching a hand to help her up. Ignoring him, she leaned back, and reached out to the wall, propping her hand against its surface to stand. She grimaced when the cut brushed against rock.

The wall rumbled.

"What's happening?" asked Will.

The library floor shook. Susan stumbled and fell into his arms. Behind them, the wall glowed.

"Your cut," said Frank. "You touched the wall with blood, and triggered something."

The glowing wall divided, and a door emerged, sliding open with a thunderous roar. A cloud of dust caught in Will's throat; he struggled not to cough. Susan turned. Behind the door, he saw a single closet-sized compartment. Susan walked forward, approaching a table sitting in the chamber's center.

"What's this?" she asked, picking something off the table. "It's a bracelet." She held a wide gold band with inlays of silver, running toward a massive emerald-colored hourglass.

"With an hourglass," added Will. "Didn't you just read about that?"

"You think this is Masrun's bracelet?" asked Frank. "Why here? Wouldn't that be in the Armory?"

"Maybe it's got some sort of power," said Susan. "Or perhaps they lost it, and someone else put it here." She unclasped the band and put it on her wrist.

"Do you think that's wise?" asked Frank. "If it has 'Mental power, and was hidden, the bracelet might be dangerous."

"Feels fine to me," said Susan, "though it tingles a little, like a mortamant blade."

"You should take it off," said Frank. "The cost for my power is part of my soul. Who knows what cost that bracelet has."

"You don't even know if it's magic," rebuked Susan.

"It was locked up and hidden." Frank's eyes widened. "Your *blood* opened the door. They weren't hiding a plate of gorgers. That thing was there for a reason."

"Fine." Susan unclasped the band. "I'm still keeping it."

"She's made up her mind. We'll see her wearing the bracelet soon." Will smiled. "Besides, there's no danger she can't face."

"Thanks, Will." She took his hand, squeezing. Frank frowned, and Will couldn't stop grinning.

"Do you really think this is Masrun's bracelet?" Will raised his eyebrows.

"She mentioned a bracelet with an hourglass. Now that I look harder, an hourglass jewel near a circle...if this had a blade, it looks like Grym, the scythe we studied in class."

"Maybe Masrun modeled it on the Caladbolg legend," suggested Will. "What did the poem say? Dragon's bane? Well the First Scythe would be the biggest weapon against the Dragons."

"Maybe you should show the bracelet to your teachers," said Frank. "Or at least bring it to my mother."

"No." Susan drew her hand back. "It was hidden and protected. I'm not showing this to anyone else until we learn more. Start going through the books, and not a word about this to anyone when we return."

Will nodded, taking a nearby book from a shelf.

"If you say so," muttered Frank, "but I think it's a mistake."

Susan placed the bracelet beside her and opened Lovethar's diary again. Frank scowled at Will, but opened a book. Will pretended to read, but turned his attention wholly to Susan. The beautiful young woman before him dove into the diary with the same zeal she tackled every problem. She was absolutely amazing. Will smiled, trying to focus.

CHAPTER THIRTEEN: SUSAN

Teammates

"You are weak," said Sindril. "You're nothing at all, Suzie. Just a girl." He laughed.

"Leave me alone," shouted Susan. She walked forward but stopped. A sharp, shooting pain coursed through her.

"So weak, so worthless."

"Go away! Leave me alone!"

The world shattered, splitting into fragments of glass. The glass flew forward, burying shards in her skin. So much pain. She looked down. The glass was gone, but she saw markings on her hands. They crawled upwards, toward the hourglass on Susan's bracelet.

"I will help," said a voice.

Susan gasped for air, struggling to breathe. Something clawed at her neck, pulling her down, ripping her apart. Her arm burned from the inside.

She exploded into a burst of light.

* * * *

Susan placed the bracelet in a drawer on top of Lovethar's diary, thinking about the dream. She opened her closet and pulled out a pair of worn jeans and the gray jersey with an emblem of a knight on the back.

She drew a tight gray armband onto each arm, then put on a pair of black gloves.

Game time. After only a month of practice, the Gray Knights' first game of the season had arrived. As the reigning champions, the Knights were favored. *Now we find out if I really deserve to be on the team.* She smiled into the mirror, then strode into the kitchen.

"I'm ready," she announced.

Will wore an identical uniform, with a red C on the front, for Captain. Frank had made him co-captain after their third practice.

He grinned awkwardly. "You'll do great, Susan. Just remember the basics: turn, rotate, pivot, attack. The Soul Rippers sucked last year, we beat them every game. I'm sure this will be no different."

"Anyone want to explain this game to me?" asked Tom. "Last time I asked you guys started talking about Dragons and 'Mentals again."

"I guess we have been a bit distracted," said Susan. "With the mortamant shortage, Frank's return, and that insane Reaping two weeks ago, it almost seems silly to play boskery. We could be at war any day."

"That's the best reason to keep the season going," said Will. "If everyone sits around waiting for something to happen, we'll be at each others' throats. Besides, what better way to keep our senses sharp than boskery?"

"Still didn't answer my question," said Tom.

"In a normal game, four teams compete," answered Susan. "I didn't go until the final game last year, but I loved it. The team with the most points wins, and you get points by getting the ball up a tower past their Protector. Teams can help or hurt each other by forming alliances."

"First match of the season is a show," said Will. "It's a chance to see the new teams before the real games begin. Each team plays one game against a single rival, and the results don't count toward the season. The stadium's booked all week with these two-team games. The true boskery season starts next week. That's when things get interesting. For this game, we'll only be on half the field. Dragon Slayers are playing the Skull Smashers on the other side at the same time we play. Basically if any of the Rippers get the ball past Frank and up our tower they score. Same for us going the other way."

"If no team wins by the end of time, the two Protectors battle. The last one standing wins," added Susan, remembering Frank's fight to secure the championship for the Gray Knights during Styxia last year.

"Do the blades really paralyze?" asked Tom.

Susan laughed. "Oh yeah, and they hurt like hell."

"Well, be careful," he admonished.

"Susan's one of the best on the team," said Will.

"You don't have to lie." She pulled a stray hair out of her eyes, grinning.

"You're a lot more flexible than the others, and you climb a lot better too."

"Those were only practices."

"We saw you during the Reaping as well." Will smiled.

"You were amazing then." Tom nodded. "Besides, Will's one of the captains, I'm sure he knows who's best on his team."

"And he's completely unbiased." Susan rolled her eyes, and poured a small cup of juice. Gulping it down, she tossed the empty cup into the sink.

"Hope to see you in the stands, Tom," said Will. "Enjoy the game."

"I will, and good luck to you both."

Will and Susan left Eagle Two, proceeding south through the College's canyon labyrinth of earthen mounds. Susan glanced at the black cube of the Examination Room.

"Tom's test should be a lot easier than mine was," she said. "When he gets to the end of the year."

"Every test is different." Will shook his head. "Only two passed last time."

They continued through the Ring of Scythes. Approaching the boskery field, they joined a throng. Most of the school was either watching or playing. A makeshift barrier bisected the circular two-acre field. Frank stood at the base of the nearby tower with the rest of the team. Will waved the seven teammates into a huddle.

"This is where our hard work pays off." He put his hands around Frank's and Susan's shoulders. "We set the bar high last year, but don't worry about expectations. Remember our training. Play to each other's strengths. With only two teams on the field, it's more about skill than strategy." They broke the huddle with a shout.

Frank carried over a bag with seven boskery blades. Careful not to touch the metal, Susan grasped the handle of the double-bladed scythe. The snath quivered in anticipation, sending tingles down her arms. She looked up at Gordon, Olu, Mel, and Feng. They were all counting on her.

The crowd in the stands cheered when the Gray Knights strode toward the middle of the field. Across the no-man's land she saw boys in bright purple jerseys. She recognized a few from class, but most looked older.

"If you get in a jam," whispered Will, "just yell for help."

She'd taken charge during the Reaping, but he still tried to protect her. *He means well, but I'm going to do this without any extra help*.

She held the blade ready, one hand over the other. The referee, on horseback, dropped a ball into the field, then rode off.

The Soul Rippers sprang toward the ball with incredible speed. A mohawked boy grabbed it. Two players sped toward the Knights' quadrant, flanking the player with the ball. A fourth trailed behind, spinning his boskery blade. Just like in a regulation game, only four opposing players could enter an enemy's quadrant.

Will and Mel countered, swinging their blades into the two flanking players. One was nicked and fell, but Mel lost his blade in the process. The mohawked boy ran toward Susan. She moved her hands, starting to spin the blades into a circle, then sprinted forward.

The mohawked boy threw the ball backward to a teammate, then dove straight at Susan. His blades whirled with fury; she tried to counter. She ducked, barely missing one, then jumped. She reached out with her scythe but when metal collided with metal, her blade spun into her own leg.

Susan crashed to the ground in agony. Her leg burned from within, searing and throbbing. The mohawked boy continued into Knights territory. For five minutes the world passed in a blur; she could only stare at the sky.

"That's what you get for taking a girl," she heard someone yell.

"Get her off the field already," said another voice.

"Don't worry about it," whispered Will, kneeling by her head. He sprang back up and ran.

The pain subsided and Susan stood. She turned to Gordon.

"Still nil, nil," said the redhead with an encouraging smile. "Will's pushing." She turned toward Ripper territory and saw Will approaching the tower. She counted three Gray Knights, each in a fierce struggle. Susan sprang into their territory, dodging two players and twirling her blade into a circle of spinning metal. She then threw her scythe at an enemy player.

"Will! Eagle to the nest," she shouted.

Will backed up, shielding blows from their Protector, and rolled the ball toward her. She scooped it up and leaped onto one of the ladders scaling the twelve-foot tower. She climbed to the top in a flash, and tossed the ball into the bucket.

The referee's whistle blared and the crowds cheered.

"Great job, Susan," said Will, helping her down. "You came out of nowhere."

Susan's heart pounded so hard she could barely respond, but she gave a thumb's up.

Play resumed, but the momentum never changed. Gray Knights scored twice more before the game ended. At one point, Susan blocked two attackers at once, knocking one of the Rippers' boskery blades into his partner's arm, and paralyzing both players.

"Gray Knights win!" shouted the ref, collecting the ball an hour later. Will and Frank hoisted Susan onto their shoulders.

Susan grinned, allowing the ecstasy of the win to sweep over her. She listened to the cheers of the crowd and waved.

"They booed me at first, but now they love me," she said.

"Don't know if I'd go that far," said Frank, "but they do recognize you've got talent with a blade. You're also one hell of a climber. That first score was great."

"Thanks." She smiled. They helped her down at the edge of the field, and they all headed through the stands. At the Ring of Scythes, Mel and Olu paused. "We need to celebrate. It's only our first win, but it's our first win with the new team."

"The first coed team in boskery history," added Frank. "No small feat."

They followed the road away from the College and headed to the town of Weston, a ten minute walk from campus. Will entered a bakery and returned with a bag of cookies. They sat at the fountain in the center of town, surrounded by small white brick houses and stores.

"You took me here on my first day in this world," Susan said to Will, taking a cookie. "Before going to the lake."

"I remember," he said. "Your eyes wide with terror, but wonder. The girl I knew last year wasn't as brave as you are."

"No. It took me some time to find my courage, but you helped."

Will smiled.

Susan remembered her first kiss, when Will's lips met hers following the Gray Knights championship victory. His smile held warmth and comfort. She slid her hand into his.

CHAPTER FOURTEEN: FRANK

The Most Wanted Death

Frank awoke to a buzzing in his ear. He forced his eyes open, squinting at sunlight streaming through an open curtain. Michi stood at the window, gazing at him.

"Michi?"He pulled the bed sheet up to cover his bare chest. "What are you doing in here?"

"I'm sorry to wake you," she said. "You scream in your sleep."

"No I don't," he replied, sitting up. He gathered the sheets closer to hide his state of undress.

"You do." She cocked her head. "You yelled about a wolf hunting, something about lurking in the back of an enemy's mind."

If my power lurks behind my waking thoughts, perhaps it struggles to emerge when I sleep. Is the Dragon I fought the "enemy," or am I?

"What are you doing in my bedroom? I didn't know you'd even come to the College."

"I only arrived this morning." She gave him a penetrating look. "You said something else in your sleep. Something about *Susan*."

"Oh?"

"Do you have feelings for her?" Michi stepped closer, touching his cheek.

"I don't know, what does it matter?"

"Plamen, I care about you."

"Thank you again for saving me in the forest. I should've stayed longer in Karis, but I wanted to tell my friends what'd happened."

"Have you told Rayn?"

"I told him the 'Mentals would help the College. I didn't tell him about the Dragon attack. He wants to meet me again tomorrow afternoon."

"I'm coming with you."

"Why? Michi, what's going on?"

"After you left, Kasumir had a vision of a Death working with the Dragons. She thinks its Sindril."

"That's nothing new," said Frank.

"In her vision, he mentioned the Mines of Donkar. Don't you see? If Sindril reveals the locations of the mortamant mines, Dragons could attack the source of the Deaths' power. We have to stop them before that happens."

"Does he know where the mines are?"

"That's what I intend to ask," she said. "Your mother also wanted me to check up on you. She sensed your power growing. I feel it from here."

"That's not possible."

"Perhaps my insects have a sense others lack, or maybe I just know you well enough. There's a *hunger* lurking behind your smile. Something dangerous yearning to break free. Kasumir thinks you should return to the village."

"I don't need to go back, I'm fine."

She raised an eyebrow. "Is it your girlfriend?"

"She's *not* my girlfriend," he replied. "Wait outside, I'm going to get dressed."

Michi laughed, tossing her hair back. "You wish she was your girlfriend?"

"She's just a friend, and she likes Will."

Michi leaned forward and gave him a peck on the cheek. "Don't forget your own kind." She rose and walked out of the room, winking before she shut the door.

"Geesh." Frank exhaled slowly, and then rose. He pulled on a shirt and reached for a pair of pants. *Michi sensed his power? Mother's just worrying, being over-protective.* He put one leg into the jeans, and felt something brush by his ear. He saw a fly flit toward the window.

"Michi, that better not be you." The fly didn't respond, but landed on the windowsill. He turned his back to the insect.

She hasn't changed a bit. He grinned, and finished dressing.

"Your shirt's on backward," she said, when he emerged from his room. "Bit distracted?"

"Well I wasn't expecting company," he quipped, pulling the shirt around.

"You missed me. If you're not returning to Karis, and I expect you won't, I'm staying here."

"To keep an eye on me?"

"Exactly. I can't let Susan have all the fun."

"We're just friends." Frank reached for an apple.

"Good."

Frank finished a hurried breakfast, then the two of them left his room in Lion Three. Outside, a cool breeze blew through the stone canyon. A painting of a lion outside his door graced the rock face. He led Michi down a ramp, through a maze of earthen mounds. West Tower loomed in front of them, its sinuous stone sides disappearing into clouds above. He turned at a mound with an image of an eagle clutching two scythes.

Frenchie stood outside her door, holding a small bouquet of daisies. The young Death stepped up to the door, but then backed away and paced, staring at the blossoms.

"You waiting for an invitation?" asked Frank.

Frenchie jumped back, startled, and bobbled the flowers. They fell to the ground.

"Looks like you've got competition." Michi tossed her hair back playfully.

"Sorry about the flowers," said Frank, helping Frenchie gather the dropped daisies.

"It's fine." Frenchie reassembled the bouquet. "I was just bringing these, for um, Susan."

"Flowers for Susan?" Michi's lips widened into a broad grin.

"Who's your friend?" asked Frenchie.

Frank's mind raced. *Why was she walking around in human form?* There was no time to think of a proper excuse.

"This is Michi, an Elemental who's visiting."

"A female 'Mental?" asked Frenchie. "Does she work here?"

"I'm considering employment at the College. I hear you treat my kind better now, since Sindril left."

The door opened and Tom stepped out, almost hitting Frenchie.

"Sorry, didn't see you," said Tom. Frenchie quickly hid the flowers behind his back.

"Tom," said Frenchie. The younger Death nodded and walked past them.

"Hey, Frank, great job at the game." Tom patted him on the back. "I'm looking forward to seeing more."

"Thanks."

"I'm Tom." He turned to Michi and extended his hand.

"Michi," she replied. "Don't want to bug anyone, I was just hanging with Pl— with Frank."

"What's going on out here?" Will poked his head out the door. "What are you all doing?"

"I was just leaving." Tom nodded to Michi. "Pleasure to meet you."

"Could I speak to Susan?" Frenchie shifted from foot to foot.

"About what?" asked Will."What are you hiding?"

"Nothing. I just wanted to ask her something."

"You'd better show me what's behind your back." Will placed his hands on his hips.

Frank tried to suppress a smile. It was clear Will still didn't trust the boy who'd bullied Susan last year. Frenchie frowned, but revealed the daisies.

"I don't think they're poison," added Michi. "You should call Susan. She seems to be the most wanted Death around."

"Susan." Will turned. "You've got visitors."

"Just a second," called Susan from somewhere inside.

Will, Frenchie, and Frank each avoided the others' eyes. A breeze swept through the canyon. Frank stared at his shoes. Silence.

"I heard you won your match," said Frenchie

"Yeah, same for you," said Will, after another awkward pause.

"Good job," said Frenchie.

"You too," said Frank.

"Oh for crying out loud," said Michi. "You boys are pathetic." She walked past the three Deaths and entered Eagle Two. "Susan, you'd better save these fools from embarrassment."

"Hey, Michi." Susan gave the 'Mental an embrace in the doorway. "Didn't know you'd returned."

"Just got here today. How've you been?"

"I'm okay."

"Susan," interrupted Frenchie, who'd placed the flowers behind his back again. "Could I speak to you in private?"

"I don't keep secrets from my friends," she replied.

"It's just that I wanted to ask you something, you know, alone."

Frank watched the expression on Frenchie's face. Will shuffled his feet.

"Frenchie, whatever you want, just say it. I'm tired," she said.

Frenchie held out the flowers. "Would you care to have dinner with me on Saturday?"

Susan's eyes widened. "You're asking me out?"

"If you're not busy," added Frenchie.

"You've got a lot of nerve," said Will. "After the crap you put her through last year."

"I'll think about it," said Susan. "I'll tell you tomorrow in class."

Frenchie nodded, turned and hurried away.

"You're not going to accept, are you?" asked Frank.

"Come inside," said Susan. "You too, Will."

They walked to the couch and sat, with Susan between Frank and Will. Michi grabbed one of the kitchen chairs and faced them.

"You've gotten awfully popular." Michi tossed her hair again.

"I can't believe his nerve," said Will. "Asking you to dinner like that."

"You're upset because you didn't ask her first?" Michi's eyebrows raised.

"What? No," said Will. "I meant he bullied her last year."

"Look." Susan placed the flowers on the table. "What can it hurt? He apologized to me last year and he's been nice so far this year. It's just dinner."

"I don't think you should either," said Frank. Michi glared at him, and he turned away. *If I tell Susan I have feelings for her, I'll lose Michi. Yet Susan belongs with someone like Will, not that jerk Frenchie.*

"Susan," said Michi. "I think you and I should give the guys a chance to catch up. I have news from Kasumir."

"Let's talk in my room." The two girls strode into Susan's bedroom and closed the door.

Frank and Will sat in silence for a moment.

"You hungry?" asked Will.

"Yeah."

"I've got some sandwiches. Want one?"

"Thanks," said Frank. Will handed him a soggy peanut butter and jelly sandwich. Frank took a bite.

"You think she'll go out with him?" asked Will.

"I guess it's not our business. It's up to her."

"Michi was right."

"Oh?" asked Frank.

"I should've asked her. I keep thinking she knows how I feel, but she's got so much else going on."

"It's not too late. Ask her to go with you instead of Frenchie."

"You know, Tom asked her out this morning," said Will.

Frank choked on a bite of peanut butter. He forced it down and put the rest of the sandwich on the table. "What?"

"Yeah, that's why he was sad when he left. She said the same thing. Told him she'd think about it. He told me this morning."

I thought if anyone was going to be with her, it'd be you," said Frank.

"Or you," said Will, looking down at the carpet. "You've got all those amazing powers. You took on a Dragon. You're the one she likes."

"Will, you're a good friend. I didn't mean to get between you and Susan."

"You haven't." An edge crept into Will's voice.

Frank wondered what the girls were discussing. He felt the power stirring. The wolf growled in his subconscious. If he reached into Susan's mind, he'd discover who she liked.

The wolf snickered. *Use the power, and* force *Susan's heart.*

The thought tickled the back of his mind, but Frank pushed against it, disgusted.

"I think Susan should be with you." Frank's fingertips drummed against his knees. "I'm not going to stand in your way."

"I thought you—"

"Don't ask," said Frank. *I'm too dangerous.* "I think it's best if I stay her friend. *Only* her friend."

"Doesn't matter anyway." Will's head shook in disbelief. "Two guys asked her out in a single day. I've blown my chance."

"You're fine. You just need to do something special. Let me help."

"How?"

Frank reached toward the power. It'd cost him, but if it helped Susan choose Will, it'd be worth it. She had to be with someone right. She deserved better than Frenchie or Tom. His own feelings didn't matter, he couldn't put her in harm's way.

The wolf smiled at him, flowing into his mind. Frank pushed the power outward. The room darkened and gentle music began to play, streaming into each mind. For a final touch, he put a suit on Will, which only Susan's eyes would see.

"Wait." Will raised a finger. "Let's do this right. Can you give us some space?"

Frank nodded and left, slipping into the hallway. He closed the front door, but then pried it open a crack.

Susan opened the door. "Frank, is this you?" She stopped, staring at Will. Michi stood beside her.

"Michi, I need to talk to Susan alone," said Will.

Michi nodded and passed them, joining Frank outside. They closed the door, then Frank pried it a crack again.

"We shouldn't eavesdrop," said Michi.

"You're curious too," said Frank. He wondered if she's left a bug in the room.

"Susan," said Will, inside. "I know Frenchie and Tom both asked you out. I know you're the only female Death, so everyone at the College will eventually pursue you. I don't deserve any special attention. However, you have feelings for me. I know you care about me, like I care about you. I'm not asking you to dinner or on a date. Susan, will you be my girlfriend?"

Frank stopped the music and allowed the vision to fade. Michi gave him a coy smile, apparently pleased that he'd helped Will.

"It's about time you asked," said Susan.

CHAPTER FIFTEEN: SUSAN

Shadows of Life

Susan placed the bracelet on a table.

"It's been a month," said Frank. "Maybe you should just ask a teacher. Domen's obsessed with anything resembling Grym. He'd be one to ask."

"I doubt he knows anything about Masrun," said Susan. "Let's look today, and if we still find nothing, I'll ask Domen. Besides, it's our first time down here with Michi, since she found the poem in the wall."

Michi smiled at her. The young 'Mental jumped onto a table, crossed her legs beneath herself, and then smoothed her skirt over her knees. "Back in Susan's secret library, looking for clues about the mysterious bracelet."

"You're acting like a child," said Frank.

"At least I don't go everywhere with a permanent pout," said Michi, grinning even wider.

Susan hopped onto the table beside her, letting her legs dangle off the side. Her boyfriend stepped up and handed her a glowing flower.

"For me?" Susan grinned.

"To help you read."

Their relationship, though official, hadn't changed much since he'd asked her out. Dating wasn't practiced in this world. Boys who dated each other kept it to themselves. The biggest difference so far was a peck on the cheek before she went to her room each night. In public, Will avoided drawing attention.

"Thanks." She placed the flower behind her, and then opened Lovethar's diary.

Tom walked to a shelf of books and pulled something down.

"I wish there was a way to look through everything here," said Susan. "We only ever scratch the surface."

"What do you want to find?" asked Michi. "I'll ask my friends for some help."

"Don't use your power," said Frank.

"Talking to insects takes no power at all, it's a part of who I am." She beamed at Frank. "Sweetie, are you worried about me?"

Oh, and that. Susan and Will weren't behaving differently, but since she'd accepted Will's offer, Michi's advances toward Frank had grown bold, and very playful.

"She wasn't sure it's Sindril. Kasumir said to tell you and no one else, not even Plamen."

Michi's warning lingered in her memory. *A new Death working with the Dragons.* If Frank found out and lost control of his powers, they'd all suffer.

"His power nears the critical point. Whatever I might do, remember my duty is to protect Plamen. Susan, what you feel for Will, I feel for him."

Susan smiled at Michi. The wild-haired 'Mental pointed around them.

"Just ask," said Michi. "I'll help look for information."

"Anything about Masrun or this bracelet. It was hidden behind the wall, it must be important."

Michi raised her arms and two spiders crawled up. Susan stood, startled.

"You heard her," said Michi. "Tell everyone you find." The spiders scurried off the table.

"How do you talk to spiders?" asked Tom. "I've seen crazy stuff in this world, but you've got magic unlike anyone else."

"That's a story I can answer," said Michi. "While we wait for my friends to search, let me tell you about the first Elementals. I'm guessing even Plamen, I mean Frank, doesn't know."

"I skipped classes a lot, back in Karis," added Frank. "Half the time, Michi came after me with an army of bugs."

"Who were the first Elementals?" asked Tom. "Were they brought here like Deaths?"

"No," said Michi. "Over a million years ago, this was a very different place. The Mortal World grew over time. A powerful force emerged billions of years ago, when life first developed there. *Life* gained complexity and purpose, and that power grew.

"However, the Mortal World had a shadow, like an echo. When living souls died, they fell into shadow. Anything that lived found its way to this echo world when it died. The stars themselves cast echoes into the shadowy realm. While Earth was young, its echo, what we call the World of Deaths, took shape.

"Dragons emerged before all other life on Earth. They raised the mountains, dug the oceans, and cut rivers through the land. Their fire sparked all other life as we know it now. They sung, causing seeds to bloom, fish to swim, and birds to fly. Watching over all life, those wise guardians protected and cherished the world. For a time, they maintained a perfect balance.

"However, the Dragons had shadows too—dark, twisted, brilliant shadows. Even as Dragons of Earth nurtured life, Dragons of this world feared it. Every soul that perished from the Mortal World fell into the shadow world of death. The World of Deaths soon became littered with shadow souls. The shadow Dragons gathered those souls, penning them. Like their counterparts, the shadow Dragons shaped the world to suit their needs. They used a wall of water and an iron door to cage souls."

"Wait," interrupted Susan. "You're talking about the Door to the Hereafter? Everything we've been taught indicates that souls move on, the gateway is just one stage of their journey."

"I don't know," said Michi. "It's possible things changed following the War. Today, most Elementals believe there is nothing after death, yet the Deaths firmly avow an afterlife. Either way, the story of our creation is still passed down this way."

"Go on," said Susan.

"Life flourished in the Mortal World, while death flourished here. The shadow Dragons harnessed energy from trapped souls and used it to break through. They attacked the Dragons of Earth. The two sides decimated each other. The last Earth Dragons used their remaining power to seal the barrier between worlds.

"Their final act was to breathe life into this world. They created the first Elementals, the ultimate act of love for the Mortal World. They hoped the Elementals would watch the shadow Dragons and ensure that they never again threatened the living world."

"So the Dragons today are actually the shadow Dragons?" asked Tom.

"Yes," said Michi. "The Dragons lived on in this world, ferrying souls to the Hereafter, until the Deaths came and usurped that job."

"I still don't understand why you have powers," said Tom.

"I know that story," said Frank. "The first Elementals, all twelve of them, had a full range of powers."

"The powers of the Earth Dragons," added Michi.

"Generations passed, and the powers started to dilute. 'Mentals now have one ability, and it varies by lineage. My family are seers, and my powers relate to the mind. Once my powers mature, I'll be a seer as well."

"If the first Elementals were strong, why didn't they fight the Dragons? For that matter, why didn't they stop the Deaths?" asked Susan.

"Things weren't always so bad between us," said Michi. "The first Elementals had powers, but limited understanding. Wily Dragons manipulated them. The College you call home was built by Dragons as a prison for those Elementals. The guard towers, both East and West, watch over the entire complex."

"The College is a prison?" asked Susan.

"It was," replied Michi. "By the time Deaths arrived, Elementals had grown weak from subjugation. For many, the transition from Dragons to Deaths was just a change in jailor."

"Wow," said Will. "I never knew any of that."

"Most Deaths don't," said Frank. "Look what happened when the last headmaster learned about Dragons. Sindril's with them now."

Kasumir suspects another Death's involved too.

Susan tried to wrap her mind around light and dark Dragons wrestling for control of life and death. Her enemies weren't just beasts living in mountains—they were the very gods of this world. A bug scampered across the floor, brushing against Susan's leg.

"They've found something," said Michi. She jumped down, following the spider. They walked to the other side of the library, stopping at a tall bookcase. Michi pulled a worn looking tome from the bottom shelf.

"What is it?"

"I don't know," said the 'Mental.

Susan held the book Michi gave her sideways to see the spine.

"An account of the final days of the Great War," she read, "Recorded by Orryn, Chief Liaison Officer to General Masrun." Her voice dropped off.

"Orryn?" asked Will. "Isn't that the 'Mental Lovethar married?"

"He must have worked with Masrun," she said.

"I'm going to take this home," she said, glancing through the pages. "If this has nothing about Masrun's bracelet, or why they sealed it, then I promise I'll ask Domen."

"I think it's a weapon," said Michi. "Don't you, honey?" She took Frank's wrist, her playfulness returning.

"A bracelet sealed behind a wall, only to open with blood," said Frank. "It's definitely dangerous. You haven't tried to wear it again?"

"No," lied Susan. She'd clasped the bracelet to her wrist a dozen times. It was harmless, but she saw no point in worrying the others.

"Last year we searched for information about a Dragon Key, this year about a bracelet," said Will. "This is going to end up like our last search, nowhere."

"Kasumir claimed the Dragon Key was a myth," said Susan. "I don't believe that. It's all over the oldest stones. Maybe the Dragon Key is related to the story Michi shared. Maybe it's leftover from the first Elementals. That'd explain the writing on the slabs."

"Maybe the bracelet *is* a Dragon Key," said Will, rolling his eyes. "Look, we learned a lot, and Susan's checking a book out. Let's call it a day."

"Checking a book out?" asked Susan.

"You're the one who keeps calling it a library. Though in this case, you'd probably be the librarian."

She laughed and gave him a light peck on the cheek.

"You guys go on ahead. Frank, I want to ask you something."

Michi gave her a quizzical look, but shrugged and headed toward the staircase with Will and Tom.

"What is it?" asked Frank.

"I should've told you sooner," she started. "I didn't want to worry you, but it's getting worse."

"What?"

"A dream. Every night I have the same dream. I look in a mirror and see Sindril staring back. He calls me weak, and then these marks... strange glowing marks appear."

"Marks?"

"Like writing. Almost like the words in Lovethar's diary before my eyes adjust, and the language turns to English."

"Runes," he murmured.

"The marks wrap themselves on my arms, but they burn. There's immense pain."

"You can't feel pain in a dream," said Frank.

"It always burns, even after I wake, I feel where they cut me."

"What else happens?"

"That's it. The mirror shatters and I wake up. I've had it too often to be coincidence. The last time I suffered visions like this, you were causing them."

"I don't know anything about these visions. However, there's a chance—"

"What?"

"My power's maturing and growing. Michi claimed I screamed in my sleep."

"Michi sleeps with—"

"No," he said firmly. "She snuck in to wake me up. She said she *sensed* my power while I slept. If my power's activating in my sleep, it could be reaching out to your mind again. I got used to reaching for your thoughts last year."

"So it *is* you?"

"It might be," he said. "If I'm causing the visions, I'm sorry. It's not intentional, and I don't know what they mean."

"What should I do?"

"I can ask Michi to monitor me. She'd wake me if the power started slipping out of control. Maybe that would help stop these visions."

"Your family's power," she said. "Could these be glimpses of the future?"

"Perhaps, but don't start changing things. We don't even know if I caused your dreams."

The world shattering in light, and the terrible laugh.

"One more thing," she added. "After I found the bracelet, it started appearing in the dream."

"Appearing?"

"When the runes attack, the bracelet's on my wrist. What do you think that means?"

"I don't know."

She walked to the bracelet and diary and put them in her bag, alongside the new volume by Orryn. Lovethar and Orryn, together again.

My ancestors.

CHAPTER SIXTEEN: WILL

A Styxia Surprise

Girlfriend. The word still sounded strange.

Will stared at the pistachio-green ceiling of his bedroom. Rolling to one side, he pulled back the sheets.

It has to be special. Styxia's the only holiday in this world.

He walked to the window, drawing the green curtain aside. Fingers of pink and amber light crept above the College's earthen mounds, reaching into the dawning sky. West Tower loomed high above, its tortuous, gnarled sides wrapped in darkness. Knowing it'd once been a prison tower, the immense stone pillar seemed more imposing.

Opening a drawer, he pulled out a wad of bills. *Enough money for something nice, but what should I get?*

Two years ago, he'd celebrated his first Styxia. Placing the money back, he looked in the mirror remembering the boy he'd used to be. Two years ago, Billy stared back from the same mirror, a terrified, lonely new Death. He'd watched one Reaping, appalled at the morbid job. Struggling in all his classes, watching boskery was the only thing he'd enjoyed.

Will stared deeper into his sapphire eyes. Three years ago, he sat at home arguing with his mother about how'd they spend the holidays. She was torn between one of her new boyfriends. He could still hear her shrill voice.

"I'll do Christmas eve with Jack, but then drive up to Philly and spend New Year's with Juan."

Billy sat in his room, staring at the worn photo. A thin man with dark, straight hair kissed a younger version of his mother. Creases and tiny tears edged the picture. He folded it in half and shoved it back inside his pocket.

"I'm telling you, Marcy, things are picking up," continued Mom's voice, which slipped through the crack in the open door. "Gary? I haven't thought about that slime ball for ages. Don't make me think about him now."

Had Dad given up trying to see him over Christmas? Last year he'd spent an uncomfortable holiday afternoon making small talk. The few words they'd shared then were more than Mom and Billy spoke to each other during most days. However, he hadn't seen Dad in months.

Where are you dumping me this year?

"Who? Oh, *Billy*. No one calls him Will. Yeah, my sister's taking him."

Aunt Nancy. Great. She'd leave him with her laptop and a box of cookies. Maybe this Christmas wouldn't be so bad.

He reached into his backpack and pulled a stack of graded assignments. Flipping through the pages, he saw F's and D's. He shoved them to the bottom of his trash can, burying the work, then laughed at his own foolishness. Like Mom really cares.

Back in his room, at the College of Deaths, a tear fell down Will's cheek.

He'd screamed at Mom the day he left. They'd parted on poor terms, and now she'd never see him again. It wasn't his mother he missed, he'd chosen to stay in this world. Still, it was a life he *might* have known if things were different.

Now, things are *different. I have a girlfriend. I'm the only Death who can say that. I'm captain of the reigning champion boskery team. My life as a Death is better than it ever was back there.*

He took a shower, and a plan developed in his mind. After dressing, he walked into the kitchen.

"Is Susan still asleep?"

"Yeah," said Tom, sipping a cup of coffee.

"Just a couple weeks until Styxia," said Will. "This'll be your first one."

"They've been talking about it in class nonstop," said Tom.

"The parade will certainly be different. In the past, they've used it to showcase 'Mental slavery. I'm surprised they're having one at all this year."

"My teacher said the same thing," replied Tom.

"Hey," said Will, lowering his voice."Take a walk with me, before she wakes."

Tom finished his coffee and the two stepped outside. They went to a small courtyard near West Tower, sitting on a bench.

"How's your year been going?" asked Will.

"Overall, okay I guess. The shock's worn off, but whenever I think I'm used to this world, something new surprises me." He glanced toward the examination room. "Your roommate last year passed his test. Maybe I'll pass too, and this will all be a dream."

"It could happen. Whether you stay or not, the College isn't so bad, and you've got guts. You asked Susan out before I did."

"Lot of good that did," laughed Tom. "Is that why you asked me here?"

"Styxia's the one holiday here. I want to do something special."

"You're asking me for advice?" Tom laughed. "You know her better than me. Why not Frank? He can do something with his magic."

"Not Frank." *He's helped enough, besides, I don't want him to regret helping me ask her out.* "I have an idea, but I'll need your help for it to work."

"Oh?"

Will spelled out the details of the surprise, and then handed him some money.

"This should cover it. If there's any leftover, keep it for yourself."

"Won't I be missed at the parade?" asked Tom.

"I'll distract Susan if she notices. However, all the Deaths in the World will be there. The crowds are huge, so it's hard to see individuals. You won't be missed too much. If your friends don't see you, they'll guess you're lost in the throng. I'd do it myself, but we have to march in the parade. Even if we lose this week, we're still one of the top four teams. Both Susan and I have to be there with the Knights."

"So my one chance to see the Styxia parade will be spent setting a surprise for a girl who rejected me?"

"You can say no," said Will.

"I'm just teasing," said Tom with a smile. "I won't tell her, and everything will be set."

"Thanks, Tom. I owe you one."

"If I fail my test, remember this during boskery tryouts next year." Tom winked. "Kidding again. Sheesh, you Deaths are so serious."

Will shook his head, smiling. They walked back to Eagle Two.

"Good morning," said Will, giving Susan a quick peck on the cheek.

"You've got that weird grin," she said. "What are you planning?"

"Just a new move to show the team. You'll see."

* * * *

Two weeks later, Will walked hand in hand with Susan. They wore their boskery uniforms and red ribbons. Thousands of robed Deaths thronged the canyon passages of the College. The sun hung high in the sky. West Tower, draped in bright red banners, cast a shadow across the sea of men and boys. Susan still drew attention wherever she walked. *My girlfriend*.

They joined the rest of the team. *Tom's by the fountain right now, setting up. This'll be perfect*.

"Shame about last week," said Olu, shaking Will's hand.

"Doesn't matter," said Mel. "We still have the third-best record overall. If we win tomorrow, we'll be champions two years straight."

"This way please," said a Death with long blond hair, waving the team toward a growing line of parade marchers. A cart rolled past, pulled by a horse. Atop the cart, a pile of logs formed a pyre, with a dummy in a dress propped from the center.

"They've taken the 'Mentals out of the parade, but still have a float for Lovethar's burning?" asked Susan. "That's ridiculous, we know she wasn't killed."

"How do you know that?" asked Mel.

"What happens when a Death is killed?" she asked, sharply.

"All memory of them vanishes," said Will. "Every trace that they ever existed disappears, as if they'd never been born. Susan's right, Lovethar couldn't have been killed, or we'd never remember her."

"Maybe it's different with girls?" suggested Mel. "The story can't be made up."

"Can't it?" said Susan.

The cart rolled to a different part of the procession, disappearing behind a group of Deaths.

"You've changed so much of our world already," said Will, lowering his voice. "You'll change their perceptions of Lovethar eventually, but not today."

"I want to jump on the float and scream about how wrong everyone is," she said.

"Just enjoy the parade. There isn't a single 'Mental marching. That's a huge accomplishment. One step at a time." He squeezed her hand.

"I don't get why we're the only ones who realized the contradiction. They teach us over and over, when a Death dies every trace of them is erased. They *cease*. We remember Lovethar; heck the Deaths obsess about her execution during the War. Yet, she was a Death. The story's a lie. She faded, passing to the Hereafter naturally. If she was killed, we'd never remember anything about her. Her presence would be erased."

"Her descendents would be too," added Will. Only Frank, Susan, and Will knew the truth. Susan was a distant relative of the first female Death. If Lovethar ceased, Susan would've never existed either.

"I spoke to some of the 'Mentals," said Frank. "They'll be watching from the stands. First time in history 'Mentals will be allowed to watch the parade."

"Is everyone ready?" asked the long-haired Death.

Susan stood at the center of their team, flanked by Will and Frank. Olu and Mel stood slightly behind, followed by Gordon and Feng. They trailed the Dragon Slayers. Frenchie's team would face them in the finals yet again. They'd play against the Tiger Fangs and the Blue Beasts. It'd be a tough match. Slayers were the top-ranked team this year, followed by the Beasts.

A whistle blasted, followed by a trumpet's blare. Will watched the crowd of Deaths cheer. Stands ringed the College, just inside the Ring of Scythes. The parade circled the entire campus, a two-mile walk. This was the part of Styxia he hated. The first time he'd watched, he'd enjoyed the floats showing dead Dragons, and enjoyed watching the fake Lovethar catch fire. Of course, that had been a 'Mental, followed by other 'Mentals in chains. He turned to Susan and smiled, full of pride.

The teachers marched, followed by the boskery teams. When they reached the Ring of Scythes, red confetti flew from the stands, flying over the parade. Glancing into the crowd, he saw a blend of excitement and boredom. Some Deaths loved Styxia, but the obligatory parade meant a long time waiting around.

Susan waved to the onlookers. Will took her hand again while they marched. They passed a section with some of their friends.

"I don't see Tom," she said.

"I'm sure he's there, lost in the crowd somewhere."

They continued around the Campus. East Tower, also draped in red, came into view and then passed, and West Tower re-emerged on the horizon. At the Lethe Canal, they crossed over the bridge, continuing around the Ring.

"This is where our year began," said Susan, "on our way to Mors."

"Been a crazy year so far," said Will. "Maybe things will settle down now."

"Mortamant's lower than ever," said Frank. "I heard they're planning to melt down the boskery blades following the game tomorrow."

"What'll happen to next year's season?" asked Will.

"At this rate, we won't have a season next year. Tomorrow's game could be the last one for a while."

"I'm glad I got to play this year," said Susan.

"Me too," said Will.

They continued to where'd they'd started. The early marchers were already disbanding, heading back to the College.

"I'm going to go home and relax," said Susan.

"I need to show you something first," said Will. "It's a surprise, just for you."

Frank raised an eyebrow. "I guess I'll see you two tomorrow then."

Will led Susan away from the crowd, toward Weston. Some Deaths walked back toward the town with them, but Will turned from the path, leading Susan toward the banks of Silver Lake. *Everything should be set up now.*

They rounded a bend and saw a plume of black. *I asked for candles, but that seems like a lot of smoke*.

"Did you plan a surprise?" asked Susan.

"Yes," said Will, letting go of her hand, and jogging toward the shore. *Something's wrong.*

A large white blanket lay by the lake, with plates and overturned cups. Food littered the ground in piles. Near the spread, something burned.

"Oh my God." Susan ran forward. "It's Tom!"

They rushed to the boy's side. Will grabbed a bowl from the picnic, and sprang to the lake, then threw the water at the flames. Tom's face stared back, but his eyes were closed.

"He's unconscious, help me get him into the lake," said Will.

"The fire's so heavy."

"He's still alive," said Will. "We have to try."

Will reached into the flames and pulled on Tom's arm. The fire licked Will's skin, scorching and burning him. He held his breath and pulled the burning body toward the water. Susan grimaced, then grabbed Tom's other arm. The three plunged into the lake. Will's arm and face stung, but he ignored the pain, swimming to the surface. He pulled Tom up, then started back to the shore.

Susan sputtered as she emerged from the water.

"The fire's out, but he's not breathing," said Will, between gasps.

What have I done? This was supposed to be a beautiful surprise.

He pushed on Tom's lungs, then opened his mouth.

"I don't know CPR," said Will.

Susan walked over, and without hesitation, leaned down, pressing her lips to Tom's. She breathed out, then moved to Tom's chest and pumped three times.

"I've only seen it on TV, and that was a lifetime ago," she said, gasping for air. She returned to Tom's mouth.

"Try holding his nose," said Will. She pinched his nose and blew.

Tom groaned, turned to the side and threw up a blend of water, vomit, and blood. His face and clothes were covered in scorch marks.

"Tom, what happened?" asked Susan. "Are you all right?"

Tom moaned, his eyes tearing.

"I'm so sorry," said Will. "I should've done this myself. I'm so sorry, Tom."

He turned his charred head again, spitting up blood and starting to cough.

"We have to get a doctor," said Susan. "We need to get help."

Tom shook, and she reached her arms around him, holding him. Tom's blood covered her shirt.

"Help!" she shouted. "Somebody, help!"

Tom murmured, moving his lips.

"I think he's trying to say something," said Will.

Susan and Will lowered their heads, close to his mouth.

"Dragons," whispered Tom. "They're already here."

"What do you mean?" asked Susan. "Tom? We'll get help for you, just hold on."

Tom leaned back, and his body vanished, turning to black smoke. Susan's arms passed through him.

"What's happening?" asked Susan.

"He's vanishing," said Will. "We need to write down—" *No, we mustn't forget.*

"Write what?" asked Susan. She stood, looking perplexed.

"What happened?" asked Will.

"I don't know," said Susan.

He had the horrible sense he'd forgotten something. Something important. Like smoke dissipating in a breeze, the thought blew away.

"Your shirt," he said, pointing."It's filthy."

"We must've hit our heads and fallen in the water." She laughed. "You're soaked."

"Something messed up the picnic," said Will. "An animal. Food got everywhere. I'm sorry."

"This was such a sweet idea." She helped him pick up the spilled food, putting it on the plates.

"At least it fell on the blanket, so it should be clean."

"I'm amazed you set this up yourself before the parade," she said. "It's a wonder the food isn't all gone. Honestly, you should've just bought the food after."

"Well I wanted to surprise you."*What am I forgetting? There was something else.*

"It's weird," she said, sitting down. "I don't remember falling in the lake."

Something in his mind shifted, as if memories and moments were changing. No, it must only be his imagination.

"I remember," he said. "You made a joke about Frank moving in as a second boyfriend. I pulled you in."

"Well it's weird that the yellow room in Eagle Two's been vacant all year. You'd think they'd let him move in."

"If he wants to, let's just have him move his stuff after the match tomorrow. He practically lives at our house already." Will pulled off his soaking shirt.

"Just because you pulled me in the lake, doesn't mean I'm going to pull off my clothes," said Susan.

"You don't want to catch cold," he replied.

"I think it's time we headed back," she said, with a coy smile. "Thank you for the surprise."

"What do you think that is?" He pointed to a spot a few yards away. A burn mark covered the grass.

"Looks like a lightning blast," said Susan. "Right over there is Widow's Peak, where Deaths still insist they burned Lovethar. Someday I'll learn the truth of what happened to her."

"I'm sure you will."

Will picked up his shirt and they started to pack the picnic. He glanced at the burn mark on the ground. Strange to think lightning could hit the ground so near to where he'd set up the picnic. Susan's hair was damp and her clothes dripped, clinging to her skin.

"You are beautiful," he said.

CHAPTER SEVENTEEN: SUSAN

Eagle and Nest

The Death stared at her from the ground, his body covered in burns.

"Get up," shouted Susan.

The body trembled and the boy's eyes snapped open.

"Remember me," he said.

"Who are you?" She clutched him in her arms.

"You are weak," he said. "You're nothing at all. You couldn't even save me." He laughed, and his body vanished into a cloud of smoke.

"No," she whispered. "Come back."

"You should've let me help," said a voice.

She reached into the smoke, and lifted the bracelet, snapping it onto her wrist.

Suddenly, the world shattered, splitting into fragments of glass. The glass flew toward her, burying itself below her skin. So much pain.

Glowing runes clawed up her hands, moving toward the emerald hourglass.

Suzie gasped for air, struggling to breathe. Something tugged at her neck, pulling her down, ripping her apart.

She exploded into a burst of light.

* * * *

Susan awoke covered in sweat. The dream lingered in her mind.

There's something important I'm forgetting.

She rose, yawning. Walking to the window, she watched the sunrise.

I miss snow. It's one thing we don't have at all here.

Amber light crept into the sky behind the distant East Tower. Today was the big day, the day the Gray Knights fought to remain boskery champions. If they did melt the boskery blades, this might be the last boskery match ever.

Thinking back on the fading dream, she opened her drawer.

"I've seen this in the dream," she said, lifting the bracelet. "Will thinks your dangerous, but you're just a piece of old jewelry." She snapped the bracelet on, admiring the emerald hourglass. It fit perfectly. Wearing the artifact gave her a strange confidence, like the cake Athanasius gave her last year.

She slipped out of her nightgown and pulled on her uniform, careful to hide the bracelet beneath her gray armband. She placed a hand on Lovethar's diary.

"Wish me luck today," she whispered to the diary.

She finished dressing, and looked in the mirror.

"I'm strong, and the Gray Knights will win."

"You talking to yourself in there?" asked Will through the door.

"I'm coming," she said, smiling.

She opened the door and they sat down to breakfast.

"You remember what you said yesterday?" asked Susan.

"Hmm?"

"About Frank moving in. I think it's a good idea. We know some of the boys date each other in secret, but you and I are the only open couple in the College. We live together, with no other roommates. People talk."

"Let them talk. They're just jealous," said Will, grinning. "Besides, we have separate rooms. We're not, you know—"

"How about a wager? If the Knights win, Frank moves in."

"No way," said Will. "I'm not going to bet against our team. However, since you're worried about people talking, we'll tell Frank to get his stuff after Styxia. He can take the yellow room."

"Don't worry, things won't change between you and me."

"Is that a promise?" asked Will.

"Yeah."

They finished eating, and walked together to the boskery field, cutting through the narrow canyons and mounds of the College. They heard the crowd before they reached the Ring of Scythes.

"Everyone's going to be there today," said Will. "They're going to melt the blades after the match; everyone's saying so. The last boskery match ever."

"We'll give them something to remember," she replied. Her confident tone masked the butterflies in her belly. Will desperately wanted to win again, and she didn't want to disappoint him or the rest of the team.

With extra bleachers, stands now ringed the entire two acre field. Scattered trees and a small creek cut through the four quadrants. Susan and Will walked through a tunnel onto the field.

"They've painted it," said Will. "That's new."

Light gray paint covered the quarter of the field near them. The opposite quadrant was orange, with red and blue areas on either side. A ten-yard wide beige no man's land sat in the center of the circle, like a bull's eye.

"Colored quadrants?" asked Frank, approaching them from the Knights' tower. Usually, chalk alone demarcated the half-acre quarters.

"It might be the last boskery match," said Will. "They're making it special."

Peering out over the colored field, Susan mentally mapped the positions of the three opposing towers.

"Gather in," said Will, waving the others into a huddle. The ten Gray Knights stood shoulder to shoulder, leaning in. "I don't want to win by points, and I don't want Frank facing off at the end either. We bested Beasts and Tigers during the season. Frenchie's Slayers are the team to beat. We'll team with the Tigers, score on Beasts and Slayers, then strike the Tigers and win. Three and out, that's our goal. Knights!"

"Knights!" they shouted in response.

"Susan," he added. "I want you to make the deal with the Tigers."

"Me?"

"Tell them we'll exchange defenders, to ensure the truce. One of them can stay with Frank; you stick near their Protector. After we score on Slayers, we'll let them score. Stay there until we've scored against the Beasts. I'll get the ball to you. Eagle and Nest play. You'll be up the tower before they realize we're double-crossing them."

"All right," she said. His plan meant she'd miss a lot of the early action, but would ultimately be the key to their victory. She rubbed her armband, feeling the bracelet underneath.

"Good luck," said Frank, jogging to the tower.

Susan strode toward the no-man's land. *How can I convince them I want a truce?*

Noise from the crowd picked up as Erebus trotted to the center of no man's land, riding a white stallion. The Death's long, black pony tail hung over a white and black referee uniform. He lifted the game ball to the crowd, then dropped it.

Susan sprinted forward, her blade in hand. She skirted around three boys, running toward the orange. Holding the boskery blade horizontally, in a sign of truce, she waved her left hand palm upward.

"Talk to Hank," grunted a stocky boy running past her.

She continued into Tiger's territory, holding the blade and her palm still, hoping no one struck her from behind. Someone screamed far behind her, and she caught a commotion in the Beast territory. She strode on until a boy in orange and stripes ran up.

"Awful early for a truce," he said, "and I never thought Will would send his girlfriend over."

A few boys nearby laughed, but Susan kept her composure.

"We will exchange defenders," she said. "Send one of your players to our tower, and I'll stay near yours. We'll each score against the Beasts and Slayers. Then the truce ends."

Hank eyed her. It was a risky gambit. Even if the Knights weren't planning to double cross, if the Tigers scored once in each opposing goal before the Knights did, then the Tigers walked with the championship.

"Would you rather fight one team or three in the end?" she asked. "You had the worst record coming in of the four teams. You need our help, and we don't want to waste time with the others."

"You need help against the Slayers," he mused. "All right, we have a truce. If I see even a hint of betrayal, I'm taking you out of the game, and it won't be for a mere five minutes. Understand?"

"Of course," she said.

"I want your blade," he added.

"That wasn't part of the deal."

"Take it or leave it. Hostages go unarmed. We'll do the same."

"Fine," she said, dropping her boskery blade to the ground.

"Cole," shouted Hank. "Leave your blade here, and go to the Knights' tower. Sam, protect him. Cole's a hostage. Truce with Knights, spread the word."

A blond-haired boy handed his blade to Hank and ran toward the Knights' quarter, led by a boy with an ugly gash on his cheek. Hank held three blades. Even if the hostage exchange was even, they'd maneuvered Susan out of her blade.

"Go on. Tower's over there by our protector, Gavin."

They walked together toward the tower.

"Understood," said the protector, when Hank whispered something in his ear.

Gavin grabbed Susan's left wrist, pulling hard, after Hank walked away. "Try anything, and Will won't have a girlfriend anymore," he said.

"Let go of me," said Susan.

Gavin smelled of body odor and sweat. His hair was black and greasy, and the hint of a beard struggling to grow framed his face. She'd seen him around campus, and remembered him from their last game on the boskery field.

"Frank's doing all right?" muttered Gavin. In the distance, the effects of the truce spread. Knights and Tigers stormed the Slayers quarter together. Will ran toward Frenchie, slashing his leg with a spinning blade.

"He's fine," said Susan. "Hoping for a rematch?"

"If it comes to that."

Frank defeated Gavin at the end of their last encounter. If the tie was scored at the end of regulation, the Protectors all squared off for the win. In the last match, Gavin and Frank had been the final two standing. Few matches were won with a three and out, when one team scored against all three enemies, ending the match instantly.

The crowd erupted in cheers as Mel and two Tigers scaled the Slayer tower. Mel tossed the ball into the goal.

"First point goes to the Knights," said Susan, pumping her fist in the air.

"Don't get excited. It was a joint effort, and the truce's only just begun."

The momentum continued. The two teams ran back across no man's land. Circles of whirling metal clashed, tossing sparks into the air as blades collided. Several players collapsed in paralysis, but she couldn't see who. One of the Tigers held the ball, running into Beast territory. The Knights helped him weave a path through the Beast's quadrant.

Two Beasts converged on the Tiger's player, but he threw it to Olu before going down. Olu tossed it to another Tiger, already scaling the ladder, but the boy missed. Will dove for the ball, scooping it into his armpit and scaling the tower himself. He reached the top and scored.

"That was supposed to be our goal," said Gavin.

"They tried to let you take it. Your players are incompetent."

Susan's body tensed. This was her moment.

Erebus trotted to the center of the field, surround by eager Deaths. Gavin stared at the action. Susan moved slowly to the left.

Erebus dropped the ball and Will grabbed it, running toward Slayer territory. Olu and Mel along with two Tigers flanked him. The play mirrored the first play of the truce, until Olu and Mel stopped, swung their blades and paralyzed the Tigers.

"Betrayers!" shouted Gavin. He grabbed for Susan, but she'd started climbing.

"You bitch," he yelled. He swung his boskery blade, and she jumped to the side. The metal lodged in the ladder, missing her. From the corner of her eye she saw Will, Olu, and Mel sprinting into Tiger territory.

"Eagle to nest!" shouted Will. He launched the ball into the air, throwing it past the tower. She jumped off the ladder, just in time to avoid another swing of Gavin's blade. She scooped the ball off the ground, then scrambled under the tower, using the ladder and sides to shield herself from Gavin's blows.

"Stay in there and you'll never score," he said. "Come out."

She waited until her teammates approached, but heard Hank and others running toward her as well. She crawled out of the back of the tower. Will and Gavin swung their blades wildly, shooting sparks. She started to the ladder again, climbing one hand after the other. Hank grabbed the ladder beneath her, shaking it.

"Will, I need help," she shouted. The ladder shook and she lost her balance, tumbling to the ground hard. The ball rolled out of her grasp, only to be scooped up by one of the Tigers.

Hank held two boskery blades, both spinning in circles of solid metal. She lifted her arm to defend herself from getting struck in the face.

Clang.

She felt the blade strike her arm, but it didn't hurt at all. Shards of Hank's boskery blade flew through the air.

"What the hell?" he said. "She's a cheat."

Blades stopped, and Erebus blared on his whistle. Susan's arm throbbed, not with pain, but with power. She saw the torn armband, and the glowing emerald hourglass.

"Susan," said Will. "What have you done?"

An eerie blue light, so bright it hurt her eyes, encased Susan's right arm, extending from either end of the bracelet. It looked like a blade, formed from light.

"I didn't know," said Susan.

"What is it?" asked Erebus. "A 'Mental charm?"

"I don't—"

"It broke my blade," said Hank. "She was unarmed. That's cheating."

"Knights are disqualified," shouted Erebus. "You have five minutes to clear the field before play resumes."

Will threw his boskery blade down and stormed off the field. The other players followed, staring at Susan.

"You'd better go now," said Erebus.

Silence filled the stands and the field. All eyes stared at her as Susan stood, her legs trembling. The blue light faded.

I wore the bracelet for good luck, and cost us the game.

She trudged toward the tunnel, her head bowed. No one booed or cheered, but she felt every staring eye boring into the back of her head.

The team stood inside the tunnel.

"Guys, I'm sorry."

Will didn't respond, but turned and walked away.

"Will," she said.

Frank put a hand on her arm. "He'll be okay, but give him some space."

She turned and saw play resuming on the field. No one else spoke to her.

She ran through the Ring of Scythes, stumbling through the College, and collapsed on her bed.

CHAPTER EIGHTEEN: FRANK

Melting Pot

"It wasn't your fault," said Frank. "None of us knew the bracelet's abilities."

"You tried to warn me," said Susan. "It was hidden for a reason."

Frank looked across the table.

"Beating yourself up isn't going to help," said Will.

Susan sat between them, her head in her hands. She sighed.

"We lost the match, but learned something amazing," said Frank. "The band came to life, and broke a boskery blade. Not even the strongest scythe could snap a blade apart like that."

"I'm not going to put it on again," said Susan.

"That's smart," agreed Will.

"Let me take it to my mother," said Frank. "I want to know what the bracelet is, and what power it holds."

"I'll come with you," she replied. "I'm responsible for the bracelet. The library wall opened to my blood. We don't know if someone else's would've produced the same effect. During the match, it protected me. My arm became something else, something *stronger*. I don't think it's dangerous."

"It's not alive," said Will.

The three Deaths stared at the golden bangle and its emerald hourglass. Susan picked it up, and stood.

"I'm sorry again about the game. I know how much it meant to you both."

"It's just a game," said Frank.

"I'm tempted to skip the banquet," said Will, while Susan went to her room. "Everyone thinks we cheated on purpose."

"Who cares what anyone says?" said Frank. "Last year, everyone made fun of Susan for being the only girl. At the start of the match, Susan was cheered as a hero. People are fickle, they'll forget soon enough."

"That won't make today any easier."

"Listen, Susan's been strong for us all year. Let's repay the favor."

* * * *

Frank sat beside Susan at the long banquet table under the tent. The disqualified Knights weren't even allowed in the main hall. Last year, the Gray Knights had sat beside the Council, as champions. They'd been the first to be fed, the first toasted, and the first to be praised in every sentence. *The champions.*

Now, they were outcasts. There hadn't been an incident of cheating at boskery in decades. Will held Susan's left hand, and Frank held her right, sensing her tension. No one spoke. They sat at a long table under a tent twenty feet from the hall. During Styxia, one wall of Lower Hall opened, adjoined by tents to accommodate the larger crowds. The makeshift seating was normally reserved for those last to arrive. *Those who were least important.*

Behind his conscious mind, the power paced, longing to spring forward, jumping to Susan's mind. *You cannot protect her*, snarled the wolf. *Release me, and I will comfort her.*

Frank took a deep breath, shoving the power back.

It's only a matter of time before you unleash me again...

"The Dragon Slayers claimed victory in one of the most memorable boskery finals ever," said Erebus, speaking over the loudspeakers. "However, this day of celebration also bears a bitter aftertaste."

Several of the Deaths turned and looked at Susan.

"It was an accident," she said.

"Many of you know, the mortamant shortage continues unabated. The Council therefore decreed that this year's final would be the last boskery match until new supplies of mortamant are discovered. Starting tomorrow, all boskery blades shall be melted and re-forged into proper scythes."

The crowd murmured its discontent.

"We suspected this'd happen," said Will.

"It's still difficult to hear," added Frank.

"Do not let this news sour our celebration today," continued Erebus. "Even now, professor Rayn heads to the 'Mental village to discuss terms of an alliance."

"He left without me?" whispered Frank. "I was going to see him tomorrow."

"They're desperate for help," replied Susan.

Hann stepped to the microphone. Frank watched through the open wall of the tent, which connected to the side of the Hall. The extension occurred every year, for Styxia.

"This College of Deaths," said Hann, "is more than rocks and classrooms and learning. Children from all over the world find themselves here against their wills, struggling to fit in. Yet, in our hearts we are all Deaths. We are the backbone of life, and our job is more important than any other. Long ago, Deaths fought for this right, the privilege of escorting souls. Soon, we might be called to fight again.

"The paths you started led you here. This is home. The College of Deaths stands as a testament to our way of life. I look around and see many faces united in a common goal. The College is a melting pot. With each of your strengths, together we shall forge the mightiest scythe imaginable!"

Deaths cheered as Hann finished.

"Bit much for a Styxia speech," said Will.

"He's prepared for war," replied Frank.

"Do you think it'll come to that?" asked Susan.

"I think until we talk to my mother, you should wear the bracelet," he said.

"What?" Will leaned into the table, his eyes blazing. "We don't know what it does, it's dangerous."

"It protected Susan. If war's coming, don't you want your girlfriend safe?"

Butlers brought food and drink to the table. Someone pinched his arm from behind, and Frank turned around.

"Miss me?" Michi winked, bringing another platter of food.

"What are you doing here?"

"I got a job. Last year they forced 'Mentals to do this; this year we're paid. It's a nice change."

"I'm strong." Susan's fingers tightened around her glass. "That's what you told me all last year in my visions."

Frank glanced around, hoping no one else was listening. He refused to announce his race to the world just yet. The rest of the table ate hungrily.

"You are strong," he replied. "Look at what you did last year."

"I'm going to wear the bracelet, but not for protection. I'm going to wear it because I'm strong enough to deal with whatever magic it contains. My blood freed the bracelet, and it's mine now. I wish I'd waited till after the game, but I'm not afraid of it."

"You're wearing it now, aren't you?"

She patted a bump under her sleeve and smiled.

A power yearning for release, begging to be freed. You two are alike.

Frank shoved his power back to the recess of his mind, suddenly fearful of the object beneath Susan's sleeve.

CHAPTER NINETEEN: SUSAN

Grym Reaper

A crowd of Deaths stared at her, their bodies covered in burns.

"Remember us," they said in unison.

"Who are you?" She clutched her throbbing arm.

"You are weak," said the bracelet. "You're nothing at all." It laughed.

She exploded into a burst of light.

* * * *

Erebus scowled, drawing his ponytail tight. He turned to the class, holding a scythe.

"The new scythes arrived this morning, and the Council's eager to have you resume your duties," he said.

Susan's wrist itched beneath the golden bracelet. She wore the strange band most days. On the rare occasions she didn't, she found herself missing it.

"These scythes," continued their teacher, "are more pure than the crap they stuck us with earlier this year. However, they are *untested*. Bear that in mind on your Reapings. The oldest member of each pair will carry the scythe."

Susan smiled. *He's still letting us go in pairs, which means a Reaping alone with Will.*

Erebus walked to each pair, handing out the new scythes. Eshue stood beside a first-year student named Tim. Frank grinned at her from across the room, and gave a slight nod toward his shoulder. Something scurried on his shirt, vanishing into his pocket.

"Michi's tagging along with Frank," whispered Susan.

"Hope she has fun," replied Will. He waited to get the scythe. "This is lighter than the normal ones," he said.

"It's almost pure," said Erebus, "but boskery blades aren't the same, and apparently the conversion process limited the amount of available mortamant per scythe. I Reaped one soul with every blade in the room; I assure you they function."

"I thought the scythes arrived today."

"I am a Silver Blade." Erebus walked away.

Will snapped his tether to Susan. "You ready?" he asked.

"Let's go."

Will adjusted his hands, letting the blade fall. The room split open; colors and sounds bled into the gash through space. Susan followed Will into a whirlwind of sensation. The strawberry-scented World of Deaths sank into a rancid blur, while thunder pounded all around. Light and dark danced into a stream, flowing through worlds.

"*Susan.*"

She heard the strange voice clearly, despite the confusion. Stars whipped by. The sun split into two, while the In-Between rocketed out of sight. Her arm pulsed with excitement.

They landed, staggering.

"You've got to be kidding me," said Will.

Around them, dozens of others in robes also held scythes.

"Where did those two come from?" shouted a voice to their left. Had they appeared in a different part of the World of Deaths?

"Move, already," the man yelled, "and go back to make-up, they did a terrible job."

A man in jeans tapped Susan on the arm. "That's you, hon, did they miss your face entirely?" He pulled Will and Susan into a corridor. She glanced behind at the other figures. One man reached up and pulled the blade off his scythe, then reattached it.

"It's some sort of film," said Susan.

"Really?" asked the man with a huge eye roll. "What gave that away? For Christ's sake, what were you smoking with lunch?"

He shoved the two of them into a room filled with chairs. "Patty, these two clowns skipped make-up. Get them done fast, we're an hour behind." Susan unclasped her tether and they sat.

"Sure thing," replied a chubby woman with garish neon purple hair. She pushed a cigarette into an ashtray and faced them.

"Look, there's been a mistake," started Will, while a younger woman with curly black hair wrapped a towel around his neck.

"They won't believe you," said Susan.

Patty dabbed Susan's face with foundation.

"We don't have time for this," said Will, standing.

"You'd better sit your ass down now, mister," said the curly-haired woman.

"*Susan.*" The deep, powerful voice echoed in her mind.

"*Yes?*"

"There's a body within the crowd. They think it's part of some game."

A movie.

"Susan, are you all right?" asked Will. "You're staring off into space."

"Staring into space is what you do during makeup," said Patty.

"*Use me. Use my power, and no one will ever stop you.*"

"Who, and what *are you?"*

"I have many names. I've waited for freedom for a long time."

"Are you the bracelet?"

Patty pulled out a black pencil and darkened her eye sockets, then began adding white to her cheeks. In the mirror, Susan noticed a skeletal pattern emerging.

"Susan?" whispered Will. "What are you doing?" He squirmed in the seat next to her.

"*I am no bracelet.*"

"*Did you belong to Masrun?*"

"I belong to no one. Masrun belonged to me for a time."

"Your emerald hourglass, is it modeled after Grym, the First Scythe?"

The voice laughed.

Patty finished, adding some powder, then spun Susan around and pulled off the towel.

"Get back on set. Fran, you finished?"

"If he'd stop squirming."

Will stood, knocking the towel away.

"*I am the First Scythe*."

A bright blue glow enveloped Susan's arm.

"What'd you do to her arm?" asked Fran.

"I ain't do nothing," said Patty.

"Are you all right?" Will asked, walking behind Susan.

"*Enough of these Mortals.*"

Susan's arm jerked upright, and a flash of light exploded outward, shooting across the room. A sound like metal sliding across stone accompanied the wave of light. It slammed into both women, knocking them to the other side of the room. Where the light struck their bodies, an enormous gash opened on both Fran and Patty.

"Oh my God," screamed Susan. Blood poured out of their wounds. Fran had been struck in the abdomen, and her body crumpled against a chair, convulsing as gore tumbled to the floor. The corpse sagged.

"What did you do?" asked Will.

Susan clawed at the bracelet, at Grym, trying to pull it off. The clasp held; the metal sank further into her skin.

"We've got to get help," said Susan.

While she spoke, two glowing souls appeared behind the women's bodies. It was too late, they'd died.

"You killed us," said Patty's soul, staring at Susan.

"It was an accident," she replied. "Will, we've got to Reap them. There's another body in the crowd as well."

Will stared at her, dumbstruck. He'd placed the scythe against the wall. Slowly he turned toward it.

"Why?" asked Fran. She stared down at her bleeding body. "Why?"

Susan trembled from head to toe. She clasped her left hand over Grym, willing it to stop.

Will raised his scythe, and walked to the women.

"We weren't part of your movie," he said. "This was all a misunderstanding."

"You're using one of those props on us?" demanded Fran.

"We're dead," said Patty. "We're dead."

Will's blade fell, severing Fran from her body.

I'm not a murderer.

He turned to Patty, freeing her soul as well.

"I'm not a murderer," she said aloud. "Will, this bracelet *is* Grym. This is Caladbolg, the First Scythe."

Will's eyes widened.

"It spoke to me," she continued. "I heard it in the vortex, then again just now."

"Take it off," he said.

"It acted on its own." Tears poured from her eyes. She'd killed two innocent people. She'd murdered in cold blood. "I didn't mean to—"

"Take the bracelet off."

"I tried, but it—"

Will grabbed her arm. She felt Grym's power start to grow again. The blue glow appeared.

"*I am power. You need me.*"

She fell to her knees, pushing against Grym with all of her mental might.

For a terrible moment, her soul wrestled with that ancient, awesome power.

Will knelt, unclasping the bracelet.

Caladbolg, the First Scythe, left her wrist. The world brightened until she looked behind her at the blood and organ-covered remains of the two women.

"I don't think we can leave this here," said Will, "but I don't think you should wear it either. You take the scythe."

Susan struggled to her feet.

"Are you all right?" he asked.

"No."

Will put Grym on a counter. He stepped up and wrapped his arms around her. She started to cry.

"I'm sorry," she said between sobs.

"People are going to come any moment and find them," said Will. "We need to go."

"There's a soul on the main set. *It* told me so."

Susan couldn't look at Fran or Patty. Will held each woman's hand. He snapped Grym to his belt, clasping the band around the tether.

"It doesn't matter if we're seen," said Will, leading them to the set. "At this point, just get the soul."

"You're actual Deaths?" muttered Patty. "We're actually dead?"

"Yes," said Will.

They rounded the corner. A crowd of skeleton-faced men and women in robes waved scythes at a body lying on the ground. Smoke poured from a box to the side. Cardboard trees lined the set, and two microphones hung overhead.

Behind the onstage body, a glowing soul sat, staring at the crowd.

"There," said Susan.

"I see him."

The crowd of "Deaths" surged toward the body, waving their scythes. A woman in a red bikini jumped up from the other side of the room and they froze.

"Cut!" shouted the director. "No, no. Give them at least five extra seconds before you emerge. Re-set, and places."

"Stay here," whispered Susan. She wiped the tears and running makeup away, and joined the crowd.

"Action," said the director.

Susan pushed her way ahead, but kept bumping into actors. The crowd stopped when the woman appeared, and Susan disentangled herself, walking up to the body.

"Cut! What the hell are you doing?"

Susan let the blade fall. The soul stood, startled.

"This body is dead," she said.

"What?"

One of the actors reached down and looked, then shrieked.

"Oh my God, she's right!"

"Clear the set," shouted the director. "Emile, call 911. Good God, get Johnny down here—"

Susan joined a moving crowd. Then someone screamed from the direction of the makeup room.

She turned the other direction, followed by Will. She snapped the tether, adjusted her hands, and let the blade drop.

The scythe split her view apart, diving eagerly back to the World of Deaths. Colors, lights, sounds, smells, tastes, and the constant flow of her own tears all blurred into a single whirlpool.

The world spun in anger around her.

She angled the scythe as furious blasts of light accosted her, striking her from every direction.

One sun, two suns, one sun again. A waterfall of tears...

She stood on the narrow beach under the unending cliff. The reverse waterfall shot toward the sky on her right, parting at the Door to the Hereafter.

"Where are we?" asked Fran.

"Go over the bridge, and enter the Door," said Will.

The three souls started down the coast. The wall of rock on one side mirrored the wall of upward flowing water on the other; each shot for thousands of feet perpendicular into the sky. Fran walked several feet, then turned.

"I hope this is just a dream," she said to Susan.

Susan turned away, ashamed.

The three continued to the hundred foot steel door, vanishing into white light.

Her body trembled again. Susan fell to her knees, dropping the scythe.

Will knelt beside her, holding her gently. She rocked in his arms, sobbing.

Water continued to surge upward, toward the narrow strip of sky. The cliff and waterfall extended far beyond the horizon in either direction.

"We need to go back," said Will.

She nodded, struggling to her feet.

"We should throw Grym into the waterfall."

"Susan," he said. "We might be at war soon. What if the other Deaths need it?"

She stared at the bracelet hanging from his waist.

Standing, she lifted the scythe.

"Keep it away from me," she said.

"Agreed."

She swung.

CHAPTER TWENTY: WILL

Gathering Clouds

“She said it spoke to her.” Will frowned.

Erebus cocked an eyebrow, and gestured to the bracelet.

“It *spoke* to her?” he asked.

The two sat alone in his office, surrounded by photos of Erebus holding his scythe. Grym lay on Erebus’s long, mahogany desk. The teacher reached for a cup of coffee, and sipped slowly, eyeing Will over the cup. A smell of dust and lemon cleanser permeated the cramped room. A clump of flower lights on a bookcase behind Will provided the only light.

“Yes,” said Will. “The bracelet told her it’s Grym, or Caladbolg, the First Scythe.”

It also murdered two innocent people. Susan wanted to confess everything that’d happened, but both Will and Frank urged caution. *If she’s accused of murder, who knows what they’ll do. I refuse to place her in danger*.

Erebus took out a pad and pencil, and jotted something down. He peered at Will, smiling.

“I think I understand,” he said.

“Sir?”

“Let me review what you’ve told me.” He studied his notes, tapping his pencil while he spoke. “You and Susan set out to Reap a soul. You appeared in a crowd, which seemed to be filming some movie. They saw you, but you disguised yourselves by allowing them to paint your faces. Susan's bracelet…this bracelet here, *spoke* to her, so you hurried back."

"That's correct."

"And the two other souls?"

"Sir?" *How does he know? I didn't say a thing.*

Erebus rose, picking up the scythe. He turned the handle toward Will. "What do you see?" he asked.

"I don't see anything, just the scythe's handle, the snath."

"Look closer."

Will stared and saw three white dots, just above his teacher's finger, on the handle.

"You don't need to make excuses," continued Erebus. "I understand."

"What I told you—"

"Is a lovely story," interrupted the teacher, pulling back the scythe. "Yet I see the three marks. They'll vanish in a day, but they tell more than a painted face or a wondrous *talking* bracelet. Honestly, you could've told me. I'm proud, Will. I suspected someone might try this."

"You're proud?"

"The dots are soul markers. Every scythe records the number of successful Reapings. You and Susan left to Reap a single soul. You weren't satisfied, so collected three." He smiled, leaning the scythe against a wall.

"We only—"

"I don't know where you got the notion to invent such a *ludicrous* tale. I'm sure it was that cheating girl. I'm surprised you let her paint your face. Still, Reaping three souls instead of one is admirable work. I began my path toward a Silver Blade in much the same fashion, albeit without the theatrics."

He didn't believe a word of what I said.

"Take your bracelet back. They make more convincing baubles at the shops in Weston." He tossed Grym into Will's hand. "I'm leaving this out of your record. Next time, no face paint, no lies, and no excuses.

Reap extra, admit to it, and receive praise. Don't let your *girlfriend* tell you any different. Understand?"

"Professor, I really need you to listen. This bracelet, Grym—"

"Enough." Erebus's face grew dark. "I don't know what game you're playing, but it's done. Take your trinket and go."

Will rose, clutching the bracelet. He left the office and walked to an open courtyard. Twenty-foot walls of weathered rock surrounded cobblestones. Ribbons of red, blue, and black minerals weaved through beige sandstone, punctured by small windows. An hourglass inset in one wall showed the time.

He stared at the golden band with its emerald hourglass, reflecting the setting sun. He'd never heard the bracelet speak, but he saw its power. A shiver of fear crept up his spine.

Starting toward West Tower, he continued through the College.

"Will," shouted Mel. "What the hell happened to your face?"

"Never mind," grunted Will. He hurried on, trying to avoid making eye contact with anyone else. He needed to deal with this before going home.

"Yes?" came a voice, when he knocked on the door.

"Professor Domen?" asked Will. "Do you have a minute? It's Will Black, I had you last year for Scythology."

The chubby, rosy-cheeked Death opened his door.

"Will, your face—"

"I know, I need to talk."

"All right." He beckoned Will inside. The classroom was empty. Domen sat behind a paper-covered teacher's desk, waving at a chair. "Sit, sit. How are your classes going this year?"

Will put Grym on the desk. "I'm here about this."

"A bracelet?"

"Susan Sarnio and I just returned from a Reaping. We were spotted, and our faces painted. Susan became stressed, just like during the boskery final. She wore this bracelet then as well."

"When the boskery blade broke?"

"That's right," said Will. "Professor, I saw blue light cover her entire arm, like a blade formed from pure energy." Domen's eyes widened. "She said the bracelet spoke to her."

"It's an Elemental's bracelet?"

"No. It told Susan, this is Grym. This is Caladbolg."

Domen picked up the gold band, eying it warily. He turned it over, staring at the emerald hourglass.

"Where is Susan?" he asked.

"She's home," replied Will. "The Reaping frightened her. Especially when the bracelet came to life."

"It cannot be Grym," said Domen. "The First Scythe would be millions of years old."

"I only know what I saw."

"Where did you find this?"

Will swallowed. He knew Susan didn't want others learning about the library.

"I bought it," he lied, "in a shop outside Mors."

Domen shook his head, then rolled up his sleeve.

"Wait—" *It's dangerous.*

The teacher snapped the band onto his wrist. Will tensed, jumping to his feet.

Domen waved his arm, then swung it to the desk, slamming it on the top. "Ow," he muttered.

"What are you doing?" asked Will.

"You've piqued my interest, I admit. However, your claim's extraordinary. I believe this bracelet contains a 'Mental charm of some sort."

"There's no charm."

"I saw the boskery match," he said. "If she wore this, I don't doubt 'Mental powers were involved. Yet, I'm curious why an Elemental would encourage a bracelet to call itself Grym."

Domen opened his desk drawer and withdrew a dagger.

"What are you doing?" asked Will.

"Perhaps it responds to attack." He thrust the dagger down toward his wrist, just below Grym. Nothing happened. Frowning, he rose, walked to a mirror and smashed his fist into it. The mirror shattered, but the bracelet remained unchanged.

"Are you hurt, professor?"

"I'm fine." He grimaced, clutching a towel over his fist. Sitting at the desk, he unclasped the bracelet. "I'll keep this here, if you don't mind. I don't know its secret, but I'll find out."

"Thank you."

"Will, this voice you heard. What did it sound like?"

"I didn't hear it, Susan did."

"I see. Go home and wash your face. I'll tell Susan or you if I learn anything."

Will stared at the bracelet, then nodded and left.

Outside, pockets of white light dotted the campus. A haze of orange-red overhead lit the sky, where the setting sun vanished behind billowing clouds. *Domen doesn't believe it's the actual thing, but he kept the damned bracelet.*

West Tower shot toward the darkening sky behind him, a twisted mass of lights, shadows, and craggy stone. He looked up at the peak, then headed through the canyons toward Eagle Two.

When he opened the door, he found Frank in the kitchen.

"Where's the bracelet?"

"Professor Domen took it." Will poured himself a glass of water.

"Susan told me everything. What did you tell the teachers?"

Will put the glass down and splashed water and soap onto his face, washing the makeup away.

"Well?" asked Frank.

"I told them the bracelet spoke to Susan, and I saw it glow. I told them she heard it say that it's Grym." He dried off.

"What about the rest? She's devastated." He gestured to Susan's closed door.

"Erebus knew we'd Reaped three souls, but he believed it was intentional, and was proud. Domen thinks it's a 'Mental charm, but at least he kept it."

"So no one knows about the murders?"

"It wasn't Susan's fault," said Will, his voice sharp.

Frank held up his hands. "We told her not to wear it before talking to my mother. I'm leaving to visit Karis tomorrow, I'll speak with her then."

"We'll tell Kasumir, but no one else. They'd punish Susan if the Deaths discovered what happened."

"You won't be coming," said Frank. "That's why I came over tonight."

"What happened?"

"I returned from my Reaping early, but Michi and I hung around, waiting for you. She was still in insect form, talking to other bugs. When you went to Erebus's office, she listened, especially after you left."

"And?"

"He contacted Hann. They're planning to send a group of select Deaths to search for mortamant. He's volunteered you."

"Me?"

"Michi stayed with Hann. She's there now. Will, I don't think they're going to send Susan." He lowered his voice. "She's hurting a lot now, and needs you. This trip for mortamant might take *months*. You need to tell Hann you can't go."

"I'll go first thing in the morning. Can't you leave for Karis later?"

"I received a message," he replied. "Something's wrong. I leave at dawn, but I'll wait for you there."

"What happened?"

"I don't know yet." Frank stood. "Will, don't leave Susan now. I think something terrible is about to happen."

CHAPTER TWENTY-ONE: SUSAN

Echoes

Susan lay on her back, staring at the ceiling. She heard Will and Frank in the living room, but their words blurred into the background.

I'm a murderer. I killed two women.

She clutched her wrist, remembering the power surging through her arm. Fran and Patty's stares. Blood spilling from their chests.

Rising, she went to the sink, splashing water on her face. *It's not my fault.* Even in her mind, the sentence sounded hollow. She stared at the mirror. Splatters of blood covered her cheeks. She blinked and the blood vanished.

I'm going crazy.

She sat on the edge of her bed, trembling.

"Domen thinks it's a 'Mental charm, but at least he kept it." She overheard Will's voice through the door. *It's gone. Thank you, Will.*

At least the bracelet wouldn't trouble her anymore.

Susan lay down again, staring at the ceiling.

For two hours, her thoughts ran in circles. Patty and Fran's faces stared at her, blood on the ground, and the deep booming voice declaring *"I am Grym."* She tried to read, pulling out Lovethar's diary, but couldn't focus. Finally, she walked to the now empty kitchen and poured milk into a pot, switching the oven on.

It wasn't my fault.

She sipped the warm milk, allowing the liquid to sink gently down her throat.

It wasn't my fault.

Susan brought her mug back to the bedroom, where she changed into her nightgown. She turned to the page in Lovethar's diary she'd bookmarked.

"I met General Masrun today. A tall, brutish man, with a bracelet shaped like an hourglass," she read. *Why did Masrun have Grym? Is that how Deaths won the war?*

She lay down, forcing curiosity to supplant her guilt. If Domen used Caladbolg, they'd vanquish the Dragons again.

Again.

With Grym's appearance, history was repeating. A female Death, a war with Dragons, and the First Scythe. What does it mean?

She closed the book, letting herself sleep.

* * * *

Susan stood atop an endless expanse of sapphire blue. Ocean stretched beyond the horizons in every direction. Gentle waves lapped at the soles of her feet.

"Where am I?"

The gray sky above looked empty, like a blank canvas. Small purple clouds hung in the distance, melting their shade into the sea below.

She started forward, walking on the surface of the strange sea. A strawberry smell lingered in the air.

Something roared behind her, and the waves shuddered and foamed. She turned and watched an immense beast emerge from the ocean. Its thirty-foot wide snout broke the surface first, followed by rows of massive, gleaming teeth. She watched the underside of its throat, a hundred feet long and covered in every color she'd ever imagined, snake out of the water, arcing high above.

The Dragon roared again.

Its tail lashed the water, and it hovered, with transparent rainbow wings beating the air like gossamer prisms. The beautiful creature closed its mouth, and a noise resonated all around. The sound vibrated the water beneath her, echoing through every atom in Susan's body.

A song.

The Dragon lifted a single talon and pointed. The water frothed and bubbled. Susan stumbled backward as a mountain emerged from the sea. It pointed again, changing the sound in the air. The colors on its skin sharpened for a moment, before the entire mountain trembled.

Grass swept over its base, followed by flowers, and trees. Birds started to sing, and squirrels poked their heads out.

"Amazing." The Dragon didn't notice her. It turned in the sky, and spread its silky wings.

"Wait," she said. She ran forward and grabbed the Dragon's tail, wrapping both of her arms around its massive circumference. The Dragon flicked its tail, tossing her into the air.

She landed between its wings.

Scales covered its back, each a separate yet brilliant hue. The scales seemed soft, giving beneath her. The Dragon spread its wings again, wings so thin she saw the sea and island through them.

The creature sped skyward, flying at a dizzying speed. To her right, a second Dragon, even larger than the one she rode, emerged from the ocean, roaring. The other dragon was pitch black, darker than night. Its eyes glowed like red-hot coals. It snarled.

"A shadow Dragon?"

The rainbow Dragon flew faster, but the shadow Dragon pursued. They sped across the sea, past islands, over a landmass, and back to the open water. Susan's gargantuan mount veered around. She clung to its scales.

The Dragon sang.

The sound reverberated through the universe.

A sound so pure Susan's head swam.

Its rainbow scales quivered, amplifying the music, the harmonics of creation.

Two ribbons of water shot from the sea, looping toward the shadow Dragon's neck. The beast roared, but the water belted its neck, holding the dark creature captive.

The song altered.

White light climbed the chains of water, wrapping themselves around the shadow Dragon's head. They paused, shimmering, and the water vanished.

A man appeared on the shadow Dragon's back, holding long reins. He had short black hair, and wore a suit of rainbow scales. His green eyes burned like fierce emeralds. He stared at Susan.

He stared *through* Susan.

His eyes bored into her, and she cringed.

The shadow Dragon roared.

The emerald eyes bore deeper, and the world shattered.

She fell through a whirlwind of color and sound.

Shards of rainbow glass littered the floor, mixed with hay.

Susan stood in a dark stone chamber. Drops of weak sunlight crawled into the dismal room from a tiny slit ten feet above her head. An enormous door emblazoned with emerald hourglasses faced her.

The door opened and two men in black grabbed her, pulling Susan through a hall.

"What's going on?" she demanded.

They dragged Susan to a large roofless chamber, filled with onlookers. The sun shone above.

"Bow to the King of Donkar," said the men, pushing her down.

Raising her eyes, Susan saw a throne, under a flag with a bright green hourglass. An old man with long white hair sat reading a scroll. A band of gold crowned his head. Four enormous scythe blades, each thirty feet high stood beside the throne, mirrored by four on the opposite side.

One of the blades moved, and the entire wall shook.

She started. The shadow Dragon flexed its legs, and roared into the sky.

The white-haired king turned. His bright emerald eyes bore into her, and she trembled.

He opened his mouth to speak, but a sound interrupted him. The crowd screamed, running from the courtyard. Susan spun to see a rainbow Dragon perched in the distance. Bolts of fire and steel shot toward the creature, who cried in pain with each strike.

Her heart cried out to the Dragon. Its enormous sad eyes rolled forward, but a final song escaped its throat. The music swept over the courtyard, delighting Susan.

The men around her fell to the ground, clutching their ears in agony. Didn't they hear the glorious music? The king fell from his throne. The shadow Dragon rose and roared. Its inky form melted into a cloud of smoke, rushing at the white-haired king.

The emerald-eyed king screamed, tugged in opposite directions. The rainbow Dragon's song pulled him one way, while the enveloping smoke from the shadow Dragon wrestled him back. His body began to glow. The light brightened, until he shone white-hot.

The king shattered, vanishing. Both Dragons disappeared.

The song and roar both ended.

Silence followed.

A deafening silence.

The song would sing no more.

Men ran from the scene around her. Susan walked forward, waving the smoke away. On the throne, only the king's crown remained. The band had been stretched, and an emerald hourglass decorated its center.

She lifted the bracelet.

"*Use me. Use my power, and no one will ever stop you.*"

"Grym," she said.

The world around her spun, blurring into a whirlwind of color.

The ground beneath her rocked. She stood in another dark chamber.

Before her, stood a full-length mirror. She walked to it.

The emerald-eyed king with long white hair stared back from the mirror. The bracelet circled his wrist. Looking down, she saw it on her wrist as well.

"You are weak," he said. *"Just a girl."* He laughed.

"Leave me alone," shouted Susan. She walked forward but stopped as a sharp, shooting pain coursed through her.

"You need me. You need my power. Together, we are strong."

"You're a murderer."

"I will help."

The image of the king faded, and she saw herself in the mirror. Behind her, an enormous talon lifted.

The world in front of her shattered, splitting into fragments of glass. Shards flew forward, burying itself in her skin. So much pain. She looked down. The glass was gone, but she saw markings on her hands. They crawled upwards, toward the hourglass bracelet.

Susan gasped for air, struggling to breathe. Something clawed at her neck, something pulled her down, ripping her apart. Her arm burned from the inside.

She exploded into a burst of light.

* * * *

Susan sat up, covered in sweat. Every second of the dream remained in her mind, every sight, sound and smell. She could feel the rainbow scales of the Dragon, and hear its perfect song.

"It was only a dream," she whispered to the darkness.

"It was no dream," said a low voice.

Susan stared, an unreleased scream lingering on her lips.

In her lap, sitting atop the covers, she saw Caladbolg.

Reaching out a trembling hand, she touched the golden band.

I'm still dreaming. Domen has the bracelet.

"No, Susan. You never slept tonight."

Unable to contain it any longer, she screamed.

CHAPTER TWENTY-TWO: FRANK

Soldiers of Fear

Frank woke early, stuffing some clothes and food into a sack, which he slung over his shoulder. He grabbed a gorger, turning his thoughts to oleme, a dish enjoyed by other 'Mentals.

"You ready?" asked Michi.

"Yes."

They started through the canyons of the College. Stars still hung in the sky, next to a scythe-shaped crescent moon. A dull reddish glow on the eastern horizon hinted at the approaching dawn. The two Towers writhed upwards, massive pillars of shadow grasping like fingers, reaching for fading diamonds.

"Will and Susan want me to move in with them," he said, as they left the Ring of Scythes.

"Will you?"

"I think so, although the empty room they've had strikes me as odd."

"What do you mean?" asked Michi.

"Deaths aren't slow, they fill up things like rooms as soon as they can. Yet, the room's been vacant since this summer."

"Maybe they forgot?"

"Or maybe there *was* a Death there once."

"What do you mean?"

"Maybe someone lived there, and he died. I have no memory of any Death other than Susan or Will living at Eagle Two, but if a third Death was killed—"

"He'd cease to exist, and we'd never know."

"Exactly."

They continued past Silver Pond. Its glassy surface reflected the dim stars and the encroaching sunrise.

"You think that's what happened? Someone died?"

"I don't know," replied Frank. "Will's description of the Reaping concerns me. If Grym murdered two people, maybe it murdered a Death as well. I'm glad he got rid of the bracelet."

They lowered their voices when they entered the woods. Frank looked up, wary of anything moving. Their encounter with the Dragon lingered in his mind as they stepped through the foliage. Within the trees, darkness hung like a cloud, blanketing them from any thought of dawn.

"Do you worry about your power?" he asked.

"What do you mean?"

"You use the insects so much. Talking to them, or turning into one. If the cost is a sliver of your soul—"

Michi sighed. "My power works a bit differently from yours," she said. "The cost is the same, but since other beings are involved, it isn't always a sliver of *my* soul."

"I don't understand."

"Insects are good to me, but I know their use. Frank, I've killed them. The easiest way to take insect form is to trap my soul inside an already living creature, such as a fly. That fly doesn't survive the exchange."

"I'm sorry. I remember how upset you were whenever I'd smash a spider when we were kids."

"It's harder than that. I sense everything the creature feels. For a moment, I *am* that being, sharing their needs and desires. Yet, I then snuff them out. The first time I realized what I'd done, I was heartbroken. It bothers me less now, and that saddens me."

They continued through the dense trees. Michi led, with Frank close behind. To their right, shafts of reddish light crept through the branches.

His hand grew wet from dew on passing leaves. A gentle gray mist covered the floor, blanketing the thicket below. All around, a heavy smell of pine and damp earth filled the air.

Michi paused in a glade. Clinging the tree line, she sat on a stump.

"I'm asking friends to keep watch," she said.

"Do the insects know? About you taking their lives, I mean?"

"Frank, they're insects. They're not very intelligent. It's my thoughts that guide them." She sighed, looking away. "Still, I admit it pains me each time one loses a life. I'm connected to them, and they to me."

"I see."

She smiled, tossing her hair back. "I still have a much easier time using power than you. Does that make you jealous?"

"Jealous of using a few bugs? Get real."

He laughed. The mist ebbed, and the trees around them sharpened with the growing morning light. Frank kept a wary eye on the canopy above.

"We should get moving," said Michi. "What did the warning say?"

"Nothing specific. A feeling of worry and something else, something intense. Mother rarely touches my mind with pure emotion. Whatever it is, it's urgent."

Michi nodded, starting back into the trees.

"Did you learn anything else about this trip Hann's proposed?" he asked.

"They're taking Will and a few other Deaths. I don't know when they'll leave, but Hann's convinced they've found a new route to Donkar."

"Donkar? Where the Deaths originated? I thought it was just a myth."

"Real or not, he's sending a ship across the sea. Hann's very excited."

They reached a narrow creek and jumped to the other side. Frank watched deer eyeing them from behind a copse. His mind drifted to Susan. Perhaps he should use his power to assuage her guilt.

Michi stopped, holding up a hand.

"What's wrong—" Frank's voice caught in his throat as four white wolves leapt from the trees before them. They bared their fangs, growling.

The power reacted before Frank noticed. It snarled back, clawing its way forward toward his eyes, ready to spring forward and attack the creatures.

Darkness.

Like a tidal wave breaking against a beach, blackness swept through the forest, enveloping them. Frank waved his arms blindly, desperate to see. He floated in an inky void, opening his mouth to cry out, but no sound escaped.

Free me, the power snarled. Its eyes glowed red-hot as it paced behind his conscious mind.

He reached for the power, but recoiled.

Staring at his own power, he saw a white wolf, bleeding inky shadow in every direction. The wolf stood a hundred feet tall. Its mouth opened, revealing two-foot fangs, dripping blood.

My blood, thought Frank.

Free me, it demanded. It howled, sending shockwaves of terror through his soul. The eyes changed, turning to green flame.

The wolf vanished, replaced by a giant chained figure. Crimson blood pooled around its mouth.

Frank stared at himself, his arms in chains, and his bloodstained mouth.

Free me!

Frank pushed back with all his might and the image vanished.

His face hit something hard.

He opened his eyes next to a tree stump. He'd fallen into a pile of pine cones, and his hands and knees stung.

"Are you all right?" Michi touched his arm, her eyes wide with concern.

"What happened?"

A group of men approached with hands raised in apology.

"Training," said a voice in Frank's mind.

"They're fearmongers," said Michi.

He surveyed the seven albinos. He didn't know there were seven fearmongers living. Had his mother gathered them?

"What I saw in my mind—"

"Your deepest fear," replied the fearmonger.

Frank nodded. *My greatest fear is the power within me*.

"Wait until we've passed," he said, "and then continue. We'll need your powers soon."

The albino nodded.

Michi looked shaken. He wondered what she'd seen, but didn't ask. They continued through the forest.

CHAPTER TWENTY-THREE: SUSAN

Recommendations

"Susan, what's wrong?" asked Will, through the door.

She stared.

Grym, the First Scythe, sat on her lap atop the covers. The murderous tool glinted with an eerie gleam as if grinning.

She knocked the bracelet aside and stood, backing away.

"Susan? Are you all right? You screamed."

"You left that bracelet with Domen?" she asked, raising her voice.

"Yes, it's gone. Susan, open the door. What's going on?"

She pulled the bedspread aside, and then lifted the bracelet.

"*What are you?*"

"I am war personified. I am the King of Donkar, the Dragon's bane, and the First Scythe. I am the product of vicious hatred and beautiful love."

"I don't understand."

"Susan? Can you hear me?"

"*The visions I saw—*"

"My past."

She took a deep breath, staring at the gold band and the emerald hourglass. The green gem glowed with the ferocity of the king's eyes.

She paused.

Like Frank's eyes last year.

"Your Elemental friend possesses eyes of green flame? Interesting. He must be a direct descendant of the First Elementals. His power shall be great indeed."

"How did you get here? Will gave you—"

Grym's deep, booming voice laughed.

"You doubt my power, Susan?"

"I'm going to count to three, and then I'm kicking in the door."

Susan placed Grym on her bed, and opened the door. Will stumbled in, wearing a bathrobe. "What's happening?"

She pointed.

"No, that's not possible. I watched him lock it away, and besides, no one's been here—"

"It does what it wants. I'm going to Karis. Kasumir will know what to do."

"All right," said Will. "I'll get dressed. Susan, I'm sorry. I tried to get rid of it."

"I know."

He looked downcast as he left, but she turned back to Grym.

"*What do you want with me?"*

"You freed me, Susan. We need each other."

"I don't need a murderer for anything."

"I'm sorry you doubt me," said Grym's deep voice.

"Sorry you doubt me? What about Fran and Patty, the women you murdered? How do you feel about them?"

"They were nothing."

She threw Grym to the floor, disgusted.

"You need me," he insisted.

"*Shut up. I'm going to get dressed, and I don't want you to speak until we've reached Karis."*

"Susan, haven't you wondered why the Dragons are attacking now, *after the first female Death appears in the College?"*

"I said be quiet." She threw the covers over the bracelet, and moved the pile to the far side of the room. Turning her back, she pulled off the nightgown, and reached for her clothes.

"It's you they want, stupid girl," continued Grym. *"Everything's happening again, just as it did a million years ago. They want a Dragon Key."*

"What did you say?" Susan turned sharply. She'd spent months last year obsessing about the rumored Dragon Key.

Caladbolg remained silent. She pulled the bracelet out from the covers, staring into the emerald.

"What did you say about a Dragon Key?"

It sat lifeless in her hands. She finished dressing, then walked to the kitchen. She placed Grym on the counter and peeled a banana.

"Frank left before sunrise." Will sipped a mug of coffee. "We'll see him there. We should leave soon."

Will seemed distracted, but she wasn't sure. Heck, she was distracted herself. Grym's last assertion fit too perfectly with everything she'd suspected. The Dragon's wanted her, *but why?*

They left Eagle Two. Red and orange light warmed the morning sky behind the two towers, basking the campus in shades of flame. Susan tucked Grym into her bag. It remained silent as they passed through the canyons, walking toward the Ring of Scythes.

"Will Black," called a voice behind them. "Wait, I've been looking for you."

"No," she heard Will whisper.

Erebus hurried down a flight of steps.

"Come with me, Will," said Erebus.

"Sir, can this wait? I'm busy at the moment."

"Come with me this moment," he snapped.

Will gave Susan a pleading look. For a moment she considered continuing to Karis without him. However, Grym was unpredictable. Besides, on Frank's last trip he'd encountered a Dragon. This wasn't a time to travel alone.

They followed Erebus back through the campus. Hann stood in the classroom, waiting for them.

"Will, sit down," said Hann. "Susan, why don't you wait outside for a moment."

"No," said Will. "It's about the Reaping, isn't it? Well, Susan's my partner, and she's twice the Reaper I am. I won't talk unless she stays."

A slight smile flickered across Hann's lips. "Very well," he replied. "I'm sure anything told to you would reach her ears anyway. Both of you, sit."

Susan pulled a chair up, and placed her hands across the hidden bracelet.

"Erebus tells me you performed admirably on your Reaping. You Reaped three souls, instead of one."

Within the recesses of her mind, Susan heard Grym chuckle.

Will started to protest, but Hann raised his hand. "The circumstances don't matter. I don't care how you achieved the souls. Erebus recommended you for a special mission. He feels that you have skill with a scythe beyond a typical student."

"What sort of mission?"

"Several of my scouts have discovered a new mine across the sea, in the ancient land of Donkar, where Deaths began. It's a mine Sindril doesn't know about. I'm sending a small expedition there to collect mortamant and report on its viability as an alternate supply source. We want you to go with them."

"They're going to Donkar?" said Grym. *"Susan, we must travel with them."*

"You're not going anywhere."

"You want answers, don't you? You want the truth about who brought you here?"

She tightened her grip on her bag, but said nothing aloud. Struggling, she forced her mind clear.

Will shook his head. "Susan's my partner. She's twice the Reaper I am. She Reaped the extra souls, not me. I'm willing to go, but only if Susan goes as well."

"He loves you."

"Quiet."

"You can't want a *girl* along," said Erebus.

Someone knocked on the door. It opened and Eshue walked in.

"Excuse me, sir."

"Not now." Erebus stood, ushering him out.

"I wanted to talk about the Reaping," said Eshue. "My partner—"

"Wait outside. *Now*."

Eshue frowned but walked out. Erebus slammed the door shut.

"This is a private matter," said Hann. "The fewer who know, the better, and Susan already knows."

"She's not qualified," countered Erebus.

"Take Eshue." Will gestured. "He's as good as I am. Or take Frenchie. We'll stay."

"Enough of this." Hann stood. "Erebus, you brought this matter on yourself. I don't have enough senior Deaths to spare; our numbers are thin. Two Deaths from the Junior College must join the expedition."

"What do you propose?"

"We'll hold a Reapery," said Hann.

"There's never been a Reapery outside the Senior College," said Erebus, scratching his chin, "but it's a good idea."

"What's a Reapery?" asked Will.

"A contest," said Erebus. "All right, headmaster, we'll play it your way. Who shall participate?"

"Will and Susan of course, and Eshue, who's likely got his ear to the door. Will mentioned Francois, and he was a talent last year. Those four are enough."

Hann glared at them. "Not a word about what was discussed. You never know who's listening."

They nodded. Erebus opened the door, waving Eshue inside.

"If there's a contest, I don't want your help."

"Agreed," said Grym. *"You are strong."*

Susan shuddered. His words echoed Frank's from last year. Combined with the fiery green eyes, and the re-emergence of a voice in her head, she feared stepping backward a year.

No, I'm stronger now. I'm one of four Deaths chosen to possibly assist the entire war effort.

"Susan, are you coming?"

She snapped back to the moment. Will stood at the door with Hann and Erebus. She picked up the bag, slung it over her shoulder, and smiled.

"I'm ready for anything," she said.

CHAPTER TWENTY-FOUR: WILL

The Reapery

Will glanced at Susan's bag. He wished they could continue to Karis, or at least search for Domen and discuss Grym. *Did the professor even realize it was missing?*

They continued through the campus. No physical barrier separated the Senior College from the Junior College, but most of the older boys stayed on the eastern end. Under East Tower, the labyrinth of stone ravines and gullies looked no different from the maze of canyons on the western side of campus. The sky blushed in the late dawn light, a crimson tinge lit the clouds.

Will followed Hann past the arched pier where the Lethe Canal joined the college. Traces of salty sea air wafted from both boats and canal, a stark contrast to the strawberry smell of the college. Peering through rocky arches he noticed three badly damaged barges covered in burns and scorch marks.

Hann stopped at a mound of stone with a solid black door. To its right, Will observed a picture of a three-headed snake whose tail wrapped around a scythe.

Frenchie strode up, led by an older Death. The man nodded and walked away.

"What's going on?" asked Frenchie.

Hann opened the door, ushering Susan, Eshue, Frenchie, and himself inside. Erebus waited, closed the door, and followed. Inside, they passed through a long corridor, and then a long flight of stairs leading down, beneath the campus. The air grew damp and cool, like a cave.

At the end of the stairs, Hann waved them into a wide, narrow, well-lit chamber. A long series of stone arches faced them; beyond the arches Will observed only darkness.

"Welcome," said the headmaster. "This is the Reapery Room, part of the Senior College. You've each been selected to participate in a very special test. A contest, to determine who is the strongest Reaper. Two of you will be selected to join a special assignment, which will replace all duties for the remainder of the year."

"What sort of assignment?" asked Frenchie.

"Details will be discussed later," said Hann. "I place all of you under explicit orders not to discuss with *anyone* what you hear or see today. If this is a problem, you are free to leave now."

He paused, but none of the four young Deaths moved.

"Very well. Erebus and I shall stay here and observe. Shortly after the War, Elementals created training chambers such as this one. We use them for our older students. You'll find scythes inside, and the two students who Reap the greatest number of souls win the Reapery. Also, avoid obstacles."

"Is that it?" asked Eshue, laughing. "A race? When do we start?"

Hann smiled. "There is one final rule I must mention. Under no circumstance are you allowed to *help* each other. Inside, you are each alone. Take a few minutes to prepare. I will set the course. Remain here."

Hann passed through an arch and vanished. Erebus walked to a corner, leaning against the stone. Susan walked to Will and they moved away from the others.

"Are you ready for this?" he asked.

"Yes," she whispered. "I spoke to Grym. He's not going to assist or interfere. I think he wants to see how I perform on my own."

"We work best as a team, I don't like having to compete with you."

She shrugged. "It makes sense. They evaluate teamwork on the boskery field. I'm not surprised they have places like this. Will, you'd better do your best. I'm not going on an expedition with Eshue or Frenchie."

He smiled. "We could both lose intentionally. We'd be together."

"No," she said. "I'm a good Reaper and not ashamed of it. Besides, if we can help fight Sindril, I want to be there."

Will nodded, giving Susan's arm a gentle squeeze.

Hann stepped back through the arch. "We're ready. Leave everything against that wall. You need nothing inside the Reapery."

Susan placed her bag down. Will wondered if Grym was watching them somehow. The bracelet had found its way into Susan's locked bedroom. Maybe he'd been wrong not to throw it into the reverse waterfall bordering the Hereafter, as Susan suggested.

"Stand next to an archway. One Death per entrance." Hann pulled a whistle from his shirt and brought it to his lips. "When I signal, the Reapery begins."

Will stood at the archway next to Susan's. He peered through, but beyond the rock arc he saw only blackness.

Hann whistled and Will stepped forward. Blues, yellows, and violets came into focus, clouds of color hanging in an empty void. He felt stone beneath his feet, but looking down saw only open air and floating colors. To his right, a scythe stood. He grabbed it and continued forward.

The colors whirled and he stumbled as the landscape became a forest. He saw Susan to his left, holding a scythe. Turning, he saw Frenchie and Eshue on his right. Eshue ran forward.

Will started to run. A slight glow caught his attention. He let the scythe fall and Reaped a soul. It vanished. He started to move quicker. Two more souls sat nestled in the trees. He Reaped both and ran ahead, emerging in a wide clearing on the shores of a lake. The distant shore glowed with a strange light.

They're souls. Thousands of glowing souls huddled on the far shore.

Just then, a massive roar exploded. A shadow covered the lake. He looked up and saw a Dragon.

The beast's black, scaly body snaked for a hundred feet. Its two wings stretched farther than the width of the lake, each ending in razor-sharp claws. It blasted a jet of flames toward them.

Frenchie froze, but Will sprang to the left. He watched flames engulf the other boy, and tried to ignore his screams.

It's not real, he told himself. *It can't be.* His face scraped the ground as he rolled, and heat from the fire blast seared across his cheek.

The Dragon swooped lower, diving toward Susan.

"Look out!" he yelled.

Susan ran at the Dragon, lifted her scythe, and then ducked at the last minute. Its claw missed her, and her blade lodged into its ankle.

Will's breath caught as he watched the Dragon lift her off the ground and carry her across the water, shaking her. The scythe clung to the Dragon like a thorn. Susan dislodged and fell to the far side of the lake, in the middle of the glowing souls.

The Dragon vanished.

Will jumped to his feet. He had to get across. Eshue ran along the fringe to his right. He didn't see Frenchie. Jumping into the water, Will swam, struggling to hold the scythe. The water swirled around him, mingling with colors and the setting shifted.

Struggling to his feet, he heard cars whiz past. Skyscrapers and flashing lights surrounded him. Paying no attention the others, he ran. He saw a soul glinting on a corner, then another farther on, across the street. Car horns blasted as vehicles sped. At corners, the cars passed right through each other, not stopping at all.

"Argh," he heard Eshue yell, and saw a car strike the boy, knocking him backward.

Will turned his scythe upside down. Unsure if it'd work, he ran, using the scythe like a pole vault, and leaped into the air. He landed atop a speeding car. It rounded a corner, and continued barreling through the city. He felt himself falling, and jumped off.

A group of glowing souls surrounded him, and he swung the scythe.

The scene vanished again. His heart pumped with adrenaline. For the first time since the ordeal began, Will allowed himself to enjoy the contest.

Colors swirled and parted to reveal a cave of solid crystal. Sapphire and ruby stalactites hung from the shiny diamond ceiling like colored icicles. The walls were glassy quartz, and in their depths souls glowed.

He didn't see any of his competitors. He walked through the cave, unable to reach any of the trapped souls, buried in crystal.

Glancing at his scythe's snath, he noticed a long row of white dots. Was it enough?

He swung the blade at the wall. It entered the stone but stopped far short of the souls. He pushed, but the scythe was wedged. Placing one foot on either side, he yanked backward, freeing the blade.

What would Susan do?

He stared through the wall. The souls seemed trapped in an open chamber.

Closing his eyes, he concentrated on the tingle of power ebbing from the mortamant in the scythe.

Let the blade do the work.

He relaxed his hands, feeling the *hunger* of the blade. Pulses of energy bubbled across the snath.

Take me there.

The scythe fell through open air, and a portal opened, pulling Will into a whirlwind of color and sound. He opened his eyes inside the chamber filled with souls. He swung.

"Time," shouted Hann.

The room faded into blackness with colored clouds floating in the void. The arches emerged, and Will walked toward them. He leaned the scythe against one and stepped through.

"Congratulations," said Hann. "You are skilled, as Erebus suggested. You were the only Death to solve two of the three puzzles."

Susan stepped through an arch to his right.

"And congratulations to you as well, Susan," said Hann. "The first challenge is the most difficult, and you performed better than many Senior Deaths. You and Will are the winners."

Will nodded, relieved. No matter what the consequences, he'd remain with Susan.

CHAPTER TWENTY-FIVE: SUSAN

The Passage

"You did well, Susan," said Grym.

Breathing hard she picked up her bag. She wished he would stop speaking to her. The voice in her mind was an invasion, a violation of her privacy.

"Eshue and Francois," said Hann, "Please allow Erebus to escort you back to the Junior College. I remind both of you *not* to discuss this event with anyone. The boys nodded.

The Headmaster faced Susan and Will, clapping them on the shoulders. "Come with me."

Emerging into sunlight, Susan blinked. Hann walked straight to East Tower. The massive pillar of gnarled rock loomed over them, reaching beyond sight. She cringed, remembering the last time she'd entered. She'd gone to the headmaster's office then too, only as a ploy to defeat Sindril.

The elevator door closed and they sped toward the hundredth floor, traveling upwards for a full five minutes in silence.

Nothing had changed. The flower-filled chandelier overhead lit. The pair of crimson doors with ornate gold trim still stood at the end of the hallway. Only the nameplate beneath the skull door knocker had changed, it now read *Simon Hann, Headmaster of Deaths, Junior and Senior Colleges*.

"Come in and have a seat." He ushered them toward his desk. A pair of black curtains hung on the enormous circular window, and the telescopes were gone. At least he'd made some alterations.

"I remind you, this mission is secret." He folded his hands and sighed. "The mortamant shortage is the greatest threat our college has faced in generations. The rumors you've likely heard are true, Dragons attack our boats in broad daylight, and the supply route is untenable. For the first time in a million years, war lingers on the horizon, growing closer every day.

"My scouts scoured this world, searching for a new source of mortamant. They discovered an ancient mine in an area long abandoned, possibly even Donkar." He smiled. "You're going with a small group to the mine. You'll extract some mortamant and return, leaving a contingent there to continue mining.

"Of course, to keep this a secret, you won't be traveling by normal means. South of the college, the Acheron River snakes its way through wild forest toward the sea. So far, every Dragon attack has occurred to our north, along the Lethe supply route. By taking the Acheron, you should escape their detection. I've also enlisted two 'Mentals to help disguise your boat. You will meet them at the Acheron delta. A select group of Deaths chosen to stay at the mine will also join you there. Only you two and the 'Mentals will return. Do you understand your mission?"

"How long will this take?" she asked.

"The mine lies on the far side of the sea," replied Hann. "With fair sailing, and some luck, you'll return in two months. More importantly, you'll bring mortamant, and the promise of more to come."

He opened his desk drawer. Susan couldn't help remembering searching through Sindril's drawers, when she found the Dragoncall. The words lingered in her memory, Sindril's warning at their final encounter.

"You'll come yourself," he said, "and I'll be waiting. I want to go home, Susan. Surely, you can understand that. If you come to the Dragons, they will help both of us return."

Even as Sindril's words echoed in her mind, the deep voice of Grym replaced them.

"This mission strikes a blow at Sindril's plans," said the First Scythe. *"He's still out there, Susan, and he wants your strength even more than I do."*

She didn't feel reassured.

Hann handed Will a tightly wrapped parchment. "A map to the precise location of the mine," he said.

"What about food and water?" asked Will. "What about supplies? Two months is a long time."

"When you reach the boat, you'll find it laden with supplies. I've also prepared bags with gorgers and some spare clothes. I want you both to leave immediately." He paused, blushing. "I'll admit, I didn't expect Susan to go. The clothes aren't—"

"They're fine," said Susan. "Don't treat me differently. I'm the best Reaper for this job, and I'm proud to go."

"So be it," he replied. "However, there's a final detail. You can't leave by way of the College. I don't want *anyone* to know, no one at all. Until you meet the others at the rendezvous spot, tell no one where you're going. If you encounter another Death, tell them you're working for me, nothing more."

He stood and picked two bags up from a side table. Will slung one over his shoulder. Susan added her small bag to the heavier one, and put it on her back. They returned to the elevator, remaining silent for the descent.

The elevator squeaked and slowed. They reached the ground floor, but Hann held up a finger.

"What you're about to see is one of the greatest secrets of the College," he whispered.

He began pressing elevator keys in a rapid succession. He entered a long string of numbers, then held several keys at once. The carriage shuddered, then started to move downwards.

"What's below East Tower?" asked Will.

"Officially, nothing," said Hann. The door opened in a dark, dusty cave. A pair of flowers flickered to life.

"This passage hasn't been used regularly since the war," said Hann. "It's an escape route, leading to the Southern Forest. When you emerge, continue directly south until you reach the Acheron. Follow the river eastwards, avoiding the banks, until you reach the delta."

"We understand," said Will.

"It won't be easy. Our world, our very way of life, stands on the brink of destruction. I wish you Reapers the best of luck. Find me when you return."

"All right," said Susan.

Hann turned and entered the elevator. It shuddered and rose.

Alone in the dim passage, she turned to Will.

"What have we gotten ourselves into?" she asked. "Two months away from the campus!"

"At least. Yet, you heard him, the College needs us."

"I wish we could tell Frank," she said.

"He'll know," replied Will. "He warned me this might happen."

"Two months," she repeated. She touched his cheek, then leaned and kissed him on the lips. They lingered a moment, and she let his tongue touch hers.

"Come on," he said. "We'd better get moving."

They walked forward, then stopped. Beyond the two flower lights, the passageway was unlit. Susan picked up one of the small plants and held it in front of her like a flashlight. Its glow was scarcely enough to make out the walls, so they inched forward with caution.

The walls narrowed. In spots, sections had collapsed into piles of debris. At one point they set their packs down and crawled through a narrow opening on all fours. In another spot, dripping water formed a pool they had to wade through. On the other side, they removed their shoes and socks, waiting for their feet to dry.

"We've been walking for hours," said Will. "How long is this stupid passageway?"

"Let's have some food," she replied. She opened her bag. Inside, she saw two dozen gorgers. "We'll have to ration this. If we get lost it won't last long." She broke one of the gorgers in half and handed a piece to her boyfriend. Concentrating on the taste of mint chocolate chip, she felt the food cool in her hands. She bit into the bread-like food, and on her tongue tasted melting ice cream.

"Susan?"

"Yes?"

"I know *you* didn't hurt those women. You can't blame yourself."

She turned away. "Caladbolg acts on his own, but I chose to bring him in the first place."

"I notice it's a *him* now?"

"I had a vision," she replied. "He showed me his past. He was once King of the Donkari. I think the Dragons created him, and in their feud, he became…stretched."

"Twisted is a better word. He murdered two women."

"I haven't figured him out," she said. "Part of me wants to throw him into the sea, but I think he'd find his way back. For now, I'm going to just be careful."

"Sage advice," said the deep voice. *"After all, you need me."*

She ignored him, and continued. "Will, there's something more. He mentioned a *Dragon Key*."

"Like from last year? I thought Kasumir said it was a myth, a rumor started during the war to discredit Lovethar."

"She wasn't sure. She only knew the rumor of an object more powerful than scythes, something able to unlock the Hereafter itself. Will, what if the Dragons think *I* can help them find a Dragon Key?"

"You're getting warmer," said Grym. *"At least, if my suspicions are correct."*

"How would *you* help Dragons do anything?"

"I don't know," she continued, "but for the first time in a million years there's a female Death. Now, all of a sudden, the Dragons threaten war again. It can't be coincidence. Sindril insisted the Dragons wanted me. Maybe this is why."

Will held up a finger to his lips, gesturing her to quiet. In the distance, a faint white glow approached.

Stuffing the rest of her gorger down her mouth, Susan reached into the bag and withdrew the bracelet. She snapped the band to her wrist, and pulled her shirt sleeve over the emerald. Power surged through her arm: anticipating, ancient, and hungry. She put her arm behind her back, afraid it'd start glowing.

Will stood in front, taking the flower light.

Rayn emerged from the darkness. He started when he saw them.

"Will Black? What are you doing here?"

"We can't answer that," said Will. "We were sent by Hann."

The professor's eyes narrowed. "Really? Where are you going?"

"Again, we cannot answer. Speak to him if you must," said Will.

For a moment, the two stared at each other in the dim light.

"Why are you here, Professor?" asked Susan. "I thought the passage was abandoned."

"Susan, you're here too? Let me guess, for the same unnamed reason as your friend? I'm going to see the Headmaster. I know you're dating. If you two have snuck down here for some sort of *lewdness*, it will not be tolerated."

Even in the darkness, Susan felt her cheeks redden.

"It wasn't like that," said Will.

"Very well," said Rayn, adopting a different tone. "To answer your question, I was scouting a new project for Deaths and 'Mentals to collaborate on. Repairing this passageway seemed an ideal opportunity. What do you think, Susan? A chance for Deaths and 'Mentals to work together as equals."

"Sounds good," she said.

"Then I will continue. In this new era of 'Mental relations, your help continues to be appreciated."

"Right."

Rayn passed them, continuing into the darkness behind them. Susan pulled her arm from behind her back. The bracelet was strangely calm.

Will touched her arm, and they walked forward in silence for a while, until Rayn was far away.

"Did that strike you as weird?" asked Will.

"Yeah. I wonder if he's telling the truth."

"You think he's lying?"

"Maybe. It's hard to tell, since we're on edge. I don't know about you, but my nerves are shot."

"You're wearing Grym again, aren't you?"

Susan looked down, and quickly unclasped the bracelet, shoving it into the bag.

"Be careful," he warned.

They walked onward through the darkness until they saw sunlight in the distance.

CHAPTER TWENTY-SIX: FRANK

Lake of Sorrows

Frank entered the village, with Michi right behind. They walked past rows of neat clapboard homes with stone walls and gabled roofs. Four children ran by, hurling a boulder through midair with their minds.

Our version of boskery, he mused.

They passed the two-story hall in the center of town, and continued up a hill toward a stone house with a bright red door. Weeds overran much of the yard, and a cat emerged from under a bush, baring its teeth and hissing.

"Mother?" called Frank, knocking.

"Is anyone home?" asked Michi, behind him.

He couldn't sense beyond the door, and didn't want to call on his power. Yet, something troubled him. He knocked again. Father opened the door.

"Plamen," said Giri. "Please, come in."

Giri led Frank and Michi to a room in the back. Kasumir lay in bed, with a cloth over her forehead. Aunt Hinara stood behind the bed. She waved her hands over Kasumir, mumbling.

"What's happened?"

"Rayn came to discuss terms of our alliance with the Deaths," said Giri. "Shortly after he left, your mother became ill."

"Poison," said Hinara.

"Why would they do such a thing?" demanded Frank. "They need your help more than ever."

"We don't know who did this. She hasn't spoken for three days. A day before the fever took, she battled a Dragon. I believe that creature destroyed her mind."

Frank shuddered remembering his own encounter with one of the ancient beasts.

"Maybe I should wait outside," said Michi.

"No, stay," said Frank. "I need you here with me." He touched her shoulder, and Michi turned away.

Walking to Kasumir, Frank touched her face. It was hot. He knelt beside the bed.

"Mother, I'm here. Can you hear me?"

Mother's eyes were solid black pools from eyelid to eyelid; at least they should be. She stared at the ceiling now with eyes of gray cloud. *Lifeless eyes.*

He felt the power tugging at the back of his mind, baring its teeth in anger. Emotion surged through his limbs, struggling to break through to the surface.

He closed his eyes, reaching outward with his thoughts.

"Mother."

"I'm here, Plamen." Her voice sang in his head like a melody.

"What happened?"

"I'm dying."

"No."

"We all must come to our ends at some point. Mine has come, son. Tell your father I love him."

"No, there must be something we can do."

"Bring me to the lake."

"What lake?"

"The Lake of Sorrows."

"What are you talking about?"

Aloud, Kasumir groaned.

"I heard her thoughts," said Frank. "We don't have much time. She wants to go to a lake."

Hinara's hand shot to her mouth.

"You know what she means?"

"Yes," said Giri. "We must hurry." He closed his glowing green eyes and a tear fell down his cheek.

Frank stood.

"I will bring us," said Hinara. Aunt Hinara's eyes were the opposite of her sister Kasumir's. Between her eyelids, only solid white showed. Faint blue lines striped her skin. Frank realized he didn't know Aunt Hinara's power. He'd guessed she was a seer like his parents.

Hinara held her palms upwards and the blue stripes across her skin pulsed with vivid blue light. The house trembled, and rivulets of sapphire light shot from Hinara, circling them. The blue ribbons wrapped around Frank, Giri, Michi, and finally Kasumir.

In a flash of light, the house vanished. The five Elementals stood on the banks of a small lake nestled in the woods.

"Help me," said Giri. "We need to set her in the water."

Frank lifted his mother's legs, while his father held her back and arms. They carried Kasumir into the lake. Water lapped at his feet, and with the wet touch came something else: a feeling of unbelievable power.

"What is this place?" he asked.

Kasumir took a deep breath, and sat up in the water.

Startled, Frank fell backward, landing with a splash.

"Thank you," she said.

Crawling to shore, Frank shook the water off. The power behind his mind had grown. It surged through him. Shuddering, he fought it back.

"This is where we bury our dead," said Giri. "It is a secret place, one you must never speak of."

"There's something about the water," he said, shaking from head to toe.

"When war comes," said Kasumir. "Use this as a last resort. Our strongest are here."

"I don't understand."

"When an Elemental dies," said Aunt Hinara. "Their power is released. It can be stored, or even channeled. Deaths once used training sites built on the graves of Elementals, harnessing our power to suit their needs. We now keep our burial sites secret."

"Mother, you can't—"

"I'm not going yet, Plamen." She started to sink into the surface. Ripples of water glowed around her body. "You have given me extra time."

"Who did this to you?" demanded Frank. Anger surged through him. The power leaped forward, seizing his thoughts.

"Calm down," said Kasumir.

"Who?!"

Kasumir sighed. Stepping out of the water, she walked to him. Her eyes had darkened, and her body seemed stronger.

"Forgive me, Hinara and Giri, I must talk to my son alone."

She took Frank's hand, leading him around the lakeshore.

For several minutes neither spoke. He fought back tears.

"I don't want you to die," he said.

"I know."

"I'm sorry." He stopped, turning away. "I'm so sorry."

"Plamen, listen to me. You have nothing to apologize for."

"I should have stayed here, and spent more time with you. I'm a 'Mental, not a Death."

"You are my son, and I am proud of you. You've made difficult decisions, but they've bettered our world."

"Mother, I'm afraid."

"I know." She wrapped her arms around him, and the tears started falling.

"Plamen, I don't have much time. A darkness approaches, which will cover the world. If Dragons and Deaths collide, it is Elementals who must sway the balance."

She gasped, falling to her knees.

"Mother?"

She reached forward, dipping her hand into the lake. Again, ripples of glowing water formed around her skin.

"Plamen, do not fear your power. It is a part of you. However, you must be cautious. Emotions trigger and control it. Powerful emotions will unlock more than you desire."

She gasped again. He helped her stand, and they walked back to the others.

She motioned for Hinara, and whispered something in his aunt's ear. Then she took Giri's hand and walked into the lake.

The two faced each other, whispering something.

Kasumir's body glowed, growing brighter than the sun. The glowing form melted into the water, and the lake became a pool of light.

Michi wrapped her arms around him, and Frank wept.

CHAPTER TWENTY-SEVEN: SUSAN

Acheron

She clutched her throbbing arm.

"You are weak," said Caladbolg. "You're nothing at all." He laughed.

The world shattered. Glass flew toward her, burying itself below her skin. So much pain.

She exploded into a burst of light, melting into a glowing lake.

* * * *

Susan opened her eyes.

"You awake?" asked Will.

She nodded. "I must have drifted off for a second," she said, leaning against a pile of rubble. Trees surrounded them in every direction. A cluster of pines soared overhead, covering the ground in needles. In front, she saw narrow birches and gnarled oaks. No path cut through the dense foliage. High above the canopy, glimmers of daylight hinted at the approaching twilight.

"Was the Reapery really this morning?" asked Will. "This day feels endless. Maybe we should camp here?"

"No, I think we should try to find the river while it's daylight. We'll camp there."

She stood, lifting her bag from the rocks. Behind the pile of stone debris, a staircase, half-hidden by brush, led to the passageway.

They started through the forest, making their way slowly over roots and brambles. Branches swatted their faces as they forced a path.

"Are you sure we're heading south?" she asked.

"We're heading the same direction as the passage," replied Will. "I don't have a compass, but this should be right."

"Check your bag. He gave you a map, maybe there's a compass as well."

Will leaned against a tree and rummaged through his sack. "You're right," he said. "Good thinking." He checked the compass. "Yeah, it's the right direction."

He slung the bag over his shoulders again and they continued.

"Have you thought about what you'll do with Grym?" he asked.

"I'm taking him across the sea. If this mine really is in Donkar, it's where he belongs."

"You said he was a king in your vision. How could a bracelet be king?"

"He was once a man. Yet, in the vision, he wasn't *born*, a Dragon created him. I think they intended for Caladbolg to fight the Shadow Dragons. In a confrontation between two Dragons, he became the bracelet."

"I was imprisoned there," corrected Grym's voice.

"Let's talk about something else," she said.

Susan and Will looked up at a rustle in the trees. A flock of small birds flew overhead, veering to their left. Leaves danced in the birds' wake.

"When do you think they'll let us play boskery again?" asked Will.

"They melted the blades. Even if we find a new source of mortamant, the games won't resume until after the threat of a Dragon attack passes."

"Will it come to war?"

"I hope not, yet if Dragons started ferrying souls, what would that mean for us? Would the Deaths return to the Mortal World?"

"If you lose, you'll all be slain," said Grym.

"Why? Why kill us?"

"The Dragons don't want to ferry souls. They want to end the system, and form a new world. They were forged from the shadows of Earth Dragons. They will destroy everything until they supplant their counterparts."

She repeated Grym's words to Will.

"I don't buy it," he said. "They've been dormant for a million years. Why now? What's different."

"I am," said Susan. "Sindril said they wanted me. It's the only explanation that makes sense."

"Then I'm glad we're going across the Sea, far away from the Dragons."

"For your protection, you should leave me on."

"And risk murdering others?"

"Listen," said Will. "Do you hear that?"

She stopped. In the distance, a faint sound of flowing water murmured beneath the gentle whisper of the evening breeze.

"We're close."

They climbed over an overturned tree trunk and the underbrush grew thicker. Holding her hands in front of her, Susan cleared a path beside Will. Behind a bank of tall wild grasses, they reached a long clearing in the canopy. The Acheron stretched before them, a snake of silver sliding through the verdant forest. It twisted around a bend in either direction. The opposite shore was about twenty feet away. The water flowed in a calm but steady progression, moving from right to left.

"We made it to the river," said Will. "We'll make a camp here, then follow the bank tomorrow."

Above, the clouds glowed dim orange, gold and red. The darkening sky would soon fill with stars.

"Let's make a fire," said Susan. "Just like last year, when we went to see the 'Mentals."

"Last year we went in secret, now the Deaths want our help. Not a bad turnaround."

"Though it's still secret from most of the College," she added.

"It's still nice to be wanted. Hann chose us for the Reapery, when he could've selected anyone."

They gathered dead branches and dried leaves, heaping them into a pile.

"We don't have any matches," said Will. "I guess we could rub two sticks together."

Susan reached into her bag and pulled out Grym. She snapped the bracelet on.

"Start a fire, nothing more."

"Since when do you command—"

"Since now. You murdered two women in front of my eyes, striking from my hand. You will spend the rest of my life making it up to me. You do what I *say, and nothing else, or I'm throwing you in the river. If you want to see your precious Donkar, you'd better earn it."*

Grym said nothing. A blue spark jumped from the emerald and landed on the wood pile, setting it ablaze.

"Thank you. You once said we need each other." The bracelet remained silent. She went to unclasp it, then changed her mind and sat down.

"You're leaving that thing on?" asked Will.

"He won't bother us."

"I hope you're right." Using his sack as a pillow, he lay down beside the fire.

"We'll sleep in shifts," said Susan. "I've got the first watch. Since I'm the one who's armed, if you need to wake me during your shift, feel free."

"What are we watching for?"

"Anything. Forest animals, Deaths, and anyone else. Just hope no Dragons spot our fire."

"I couldn't believe you had the courage to attack a Dragon directly during the Reapery. You're amazing, Susan."

"That wasn't real, but thank you. Get some sleep, who knows how long it'll take to reach the ship."

He murmured something and shut his eyes.

Overhead, daylight faded, leaving a snaking band of silver stars over the Acheron. The forest loomed like a mass of twisted shadows on either bank. She sensed eyes amid the trees, as deer or some other animals watched her fire.

She ran a hand along the bracelet, thinking.

Soon, she heard a gentle buzzing from Will's snores. His features relaxed into a peaceful pose, facing the warmth of the fire. Sparks crackled from the lowering flames, vanishing into the evening overhead.

After a long period, she woke Will. She lay down, while he took watch. Staring into the fire, she wondered if Frank realized they were gone yet. What would Hann tell her teachers when she didn't return for months?

She closed her eyes, hoping she wouldn't dream about runes and shattering light.

CHAPTER TWENTY-EIGHT: WILL

The Delta

Stars hung across the river, disappearing into the ominous shadows of the forest. A slight tinge of golden-gray touched the sky where the river flowed. Dawn was close.

Will knelt down to wake Susan. She lay facing up, her long, black hair splayed wildly over her bag. Her angelic face moved gently with each breath. Leaning down, he kissed her cheek. She stirred.

"Good morning," he said.

"Morning? You let me sleep too long. I thought we'd change again."

"Don't worry about it. You have to wrestle with Grym every day, I'm sure you need your strength."

They breakfasted on gorgers, then spread the remains of the fire thin, kicking mud and dirt on top.

"You ready?" he asked.

She nodded, and they followed the river downstream. The Acheron twisted and turned, sometimes seeming to flow directly into the rising sun, other times arcing away. They paused at one bend, and Will dipped his hands into the water, splashing the cool liquid on his face.

The day brightened, and the forest took color. The shadows fled, revealing vivid greens, deep ambers, and gentle browns. A red-breasted robin perched on a branch nearby, flitting across the silver waves. The smell of damp moss, pine, and wild grasses permeated the air. Compared to the stone passages and mazelike canyons of the College, the banks of the Acheron felt alive.

They progressed for the remainder of the day, stopping once to eat. Animals abounded, but they saw no Deaths, Elementals, or Dragons. When Susan's sleeve moved, he caught the glint of the gold bracelet beneath.

"I'm going to climb that tree," said Susan after their dinner. "See if the delta's visible yet."

"All right."

He watched her lithe form find knots and branches, swinging high into a gnarled oak on the banks of the river.

"Hey, come up here. It's a great view."

Will reached for a low branch, and climbed slowly. He didn't have the climbing skill Susan possessed.

"Can you see the delta?" he asked.

"No, the river goes to the horizon. We'll need to camp again tonight."

Will reached a perch near Susan's feet and gazed out over the gently flowing river. It flowed beautifully between the lush forest banks. He turned his attention to Susan, who was watching him.

"What?" he asked.

"Two Deaths sitting in a tree," she joked.

He climbed higher, brushing her leg, and reached to take her hand.

"Careful," she warned, "that branch isn't—"

The branch underfoot snapped and Will lost his balance. He grasped for the trunk, but tumbled forward, splashing into the river.

Plunging beneath the cold waves, he saw a school of fish hurry away, startled. A moment later, a second splash sounded, as Susan jumped in after him.

She pulled him to the surface, treading water.

"I'm fine," he said, swimming toward the bank.

She laughed. "You klutz." She swam forward, grabbed his legs, and pulled him back under.

He wrestled with her, and then they both swam to the shore. Will laughed so hard his body shook.

"I guess we'll make camp here," she said, picking leaves from her hair. "We'll need to get out of these wet clothes. Turn your back."

"All right." He tossed Susan's pack to her, then opened his own, pulling out the spare clothes.

Facing away, he stripped his wet clothes off. Blood rushed to his cheeks as he realized they were both naked. He turned, sneaking a peek. Susan's body glistened from her damp clothes. He'd never seen a naked girl, even from the back.

"You'd better not be looking," she said.

Flushed, he turned away.

"We don't have towels," he said. "Do you just want to put dry clothes on, and get those wet too?"

"You may be my boyfriend, but I don't think it's time to see each other nude."

Will pulled on underwear and pants. He'd wait to dry more before adding a shirt or socks.

"Is it okay to turn around?"

"Yeah."

They faced each other. Will had never felt so aware of Susan's *femininity*. He wanted to kiss her, but didn't want to embarrass her further.

"Let's start a fire," he said.

* * * *

"Wake up," said Susan, touching his face.

Will woke from a dream about her. He blushed and turned away.

"It's dawn. We should leave now."

They hid evidence of their fire. The clothes from yesterday were still damp, but they rolled them and stuffed them into their packs. They walked for hours, following the curves and twists of the Acheron. The river widened and its flow quickened.

They talked for the length of the day, speaking about the College, their lives before, and their hopes for the future. Will had never felt so happy or so *alive*. He avoided asking more about Grym. She seemed determined to wear the bracelet.

The sky darkened in front of them. Rounding a bend, they saw a structure on the river bank. It stood taller than a tree, with narrow stone sides.

"What is that?" asked Susan.

"Some sort of tower ruin. I'm guessing that's where we're headed."

Susan touched her wrist. "Let's be cautious."

They crept toward the building. Twenty feet of solid stone banked the river. Fallen rocks poked through a web of encroaching trees and vines on the near side.

They walked forward, into the rubble.

"Looks deserted," said Will.

"Susan," said a woman's voice. The air shimmered, and a veil lifted. A tent and fire appeared. Behind the tent, Will glimpsed the edge of a ship in the water.

"Anil and Ilma," said Susan. "You're the Elementals we're sent to meet?"

"Yes," said Ilma. "We will hide your movements. I'm glad it's you, Susan. We didn't know which Deaths they'd send from the College. We already met the group from Mors."

Four men strode from the tent. Each stocky, muscular Death looked about twenty-five. Two of them carried scythes.

"My name is Sarmarin," said one. "This is Geraj, Henor, and Elkanah. You must be Susan Sarnio." He extended a hand. "And you are?"

"Will Black."

"I never thought Hann would send a *girl* and a kid. College must be in rough shape."

"Susan is one of the strongest Deaths we've seen," said Anil. His twin sister Ilma nodded.

"We'll see," said Sarmarin. A thin scar lined his face, stretching from eye to ear.

"When do we leave?" asked Will.

"Eat first," said Elkanah, "and we'll pack the camp. We leave tonight, letting darkness aid the 'Mentals' effort."

"How'd you like some real food?" asked Sarmarin. "We'll get plenty of gorgers on the ship, though I hope to fish as well."

"What do you have?" asked Will.

"Henor killed two deer," said Elkanah. "Come enjoy fresh venison. There's plenty left. It'll be the last decent meal you get for some time."

They sat down around the fire, and the older Deaths brought them each a plate and a slice of sizzling meat. It was tender and tasty, but Will didn't see the point of avoiding gorgers. Still, he accepted the dinner, watching Ilma and Anil organize the camp's breakdown.

Behind the tower ruin he saw their ship.

Two masts stretched from a narrow deck, probably a hundred feet long. Three triangular sails faced the schooner's bow, with a tall square sail behind them. Three more sails hung from the rear mast. A group of five Deaths stood on the boat hoisting sails and adjusting the rigging.

"If you're finished, we're almost ready," said Sarmarin. "I will show you to your cabin."

Will tossed the bones from his meat into the fire, which crackled and sparked.

"What is this tower?" asked Susan.

"Perhaps a lookout for the river," said Sarmarin. "I'm not sure."

He led them to the bank, where a long gangplank led to the ship. Will walked over, then turned and helped Susan board the ship.

The deck buzzed with activity. Nine older Deaths, plus the two Elementals scurried to ready the boat. Anil and Ilma each climbed into a crow's nest, one on each mast.

"They'll remain there until we reach the distant shore," explained Sarmarin. "We'll bring them food, but by raising them high, and using their abilities, the ship will never appear visible."

"What if they fall asleep?" asked Will.

"They'll sleep in turns if they need to, but the spell won't break. Keep in mind, nothing will mask our presence completely. If someone stared at the water, they'd see a disturbance. Your cabin's down below."

He led them to a wooden door, then a hallway. He opened a room. "I'm sorry it's cramped, and honestly I didn't expect Susan to be here. You'll be staying together."

Will walked into the small cabin. A bunk bed filled one wall, with a door to a private bathroom on the other. A large mirror stood beside the door, and to its left a porthole window faced the sea.

"It'll be fine," he said.

A single stool sat in front of the mirror, and Susan tossed her bag on the lower bunk, before sitting in the stool.

"Let's go," she said.

"You have the map?" asked Sarmarin. "The map to our destination? The Deaths aboard ship when we arrived from Mors said you'd have one."

"Yes," said Will. He pulled out the map and handed it over. "Take this too," he added, giving Sarmarin the compass.

The older Death nodded. "For now, there's nothing for you two to concern yourselves with. However, once we leave the coast, we'll assign you each chores. Kitchen duty, cleaning, things such as that."

"Hann never mentioned that," said Susan.

"On a ship, everyone must play a role," said Sarmarin. "For the remainder of the voyage, call me Captain. Elkanah will be my first mate. You can ask either him or me for help at any time. Hopefully, this will be an uneventful voyage. If you'll excuse me, we'll be sailing shortly."

He backed into the hall and closed their door.

Will climbed to the top bunk. "I never liked boats," he confessed.

"I've never been on one," said Susan, pressing her face against the porthole. "Other than the barge to Mors, I mean. As long as we're not spotted, this should be an enjoyable trip."

"Yeah," said Will, rolling his eyes, "a real dream come true."

He meant it jokingly, yet as he felt the boat lurch in the water, he wondered. He'd been alone until he met Susan. For nearly two years, he'd seen her every day, always growing closer to her. Now, they'd spend weeks together in a tiny boat, sharing a cramped cabin.

Will smiled.

CHAPTER TWENTY-NINE: SUSAN

Dream Come True

Susan walked to the deck, letting the sun warm her skin.

The first week aboard had passed without incident.

She spit up over the gunwale twice on the first day. Gunwale was a word she'd never heard before, until the older Deaths started laughing about "girly gagging over the gunwale." The Death able to say it the fastest had won some sort of stupid bet.

The second day went smoother. She enjoyed walking the deck, or even climbing up the rigging by the masts to talk with Anil or Ilma. The two 'Mentals seemed content to remain in their respective crow's nests. By the third day, Susan longed for land or birds. The ocean stretched infinitely in every direction, touching the horizon where blue met blue.

She'd received light chores such as mopping on the fourth day to sea, though the older Deaths seemed reluctant to give her work, or talk to her. She spent most days talking to Will. Occasionally she asked Grym a question, though he was moody at best. She rarely wore him, leaving the bracelet locked in her cabin.

"Susan," said Elkanah, approaching from behind. She stood by the starboard gunwale, gazing across the ocean. White crests stretched over the silvery surface, vanishing into the hazy distance.

"You and I haven't spoken much," continued the older Death. "How are you enjoying the trip?"

"It's been fine."

"Your stomach's settled?"

"Yes," she responded.

"You know, if you look hard enough you might see the edge of the Hereafter." He pointed ahead. "It lies to the south, just beyond the horizon."

"You mean the Door?" She strained her eyes, but saw nothing on the horizon.

"I sailed there once. From the ocean, it's a strange sight. A wall higher than the heavens, and on the other end, the sea jumps straight into the air. Watch the waves, they're pulled toward the Hereafter even now."

She watched the waves, which flowed away from the ship. Could they be flowing away from the world entirely?

Elkanah sighed, gazing with her across the water.

"Do you sail often?" she asked.

"I do. Not all Deaths Reap souls. Sarmarin and I are fishermen. We run a shop in Mors. It's called Mors Cod. A joke, after Morse code."

"I got it."

"I'll leave you," he said. "Remember to call if you need anything."

He left, and Susan resumed gazing at the sea. The unending flow of water soothed her soul. A curved cloud drifted overhead, shaped like a scythe. Time flowed on, like the ocean current, and the sun sailed past, dropping toward the horizon on her right. The open sky reddened into sunset orange, mirrored on the endless sea.

"Dinner," bellowed a voice behind her. She turned, following other Deaths into the narrow galley at the rear of the ship. They sat at long table, where plates with gorgers waited.

"Hey," said Will. "Haven't seen you much today. What have you been up to?"

"Just looking at the waves. You?"

"Sarmarin loaned me a book, a fairy tale about a sea captain who fought a Dragon."

"That's something I hope we *don't* see this trip," she said. She tried to remember the last time she'd had Chinese food. She took a bite and winced. The result wasn't what she'd expected.

"Is yours okay?"

"I'll take it to the cabin and eat later," she lied, doubting Sarmarin tolerated wasted food.

She rose, and Will followed.

"Excuse us," she said.

Most of the Deaths spoke little to her. One of them grunted, and another turned back to a game of cards.

"What's going on?" asked Will.

"I tried a new flavor, one I remember from before this world. At least I thought I remembered. She walked to the deck, looked around, then hurled the gorger overboard.

"Here," said Will, handing her what remained of his dinner. "I wasn't hungry."

* * * *

That night, Susan lay awake on the lower bunk. Will's breathing slowed and he started to snore.

On the boat, the strange dreams had stopped. She hadn't seen the glowing runes or shattering world in her sleep since leaving shore. Perhaps Frank really had been responsible, albeit unintentionally.

She rolled to the side, then onto her back again. She closed her eyes, letting the constant rock of the ship lull her into slumber.

A light flickered in the room. She opened her eyes and turned.

Nothing moved. She must've imagined it.

Closing her eyes again, she relaxed.

"Susan."

She opened her eyes again.

"Grym? Did you say something?"

Again the room was silent, save Will's gentle snores above.

She rose, walked to the bathroom and poured a glass of water. Tiptoeing back to her bunk, she saw a flicker again.

She sat on the stool in front of the mirror. Dim light from the porthole silhouetted her form in the glass. She peered into the dark.

"Susan." Spinning around, she walked to her sack and pulled out the bracelet.

"What do you want? Stop calling me."

"I haven't spoken in days," replied Grym's booming voice.

"Susan."

"Did you hear that?"

"Yes."

She snapped the bracelet to her wrist, sitting on the stool by the mirror. She glanced at Will's bunk, but didn't want to wake him yet.

"Is this a dream? Or a vision like you showed before?"

"No," he replied. Her arm started to glow blue.

"Susan," repeated the voice, louder.

She spun on the stool, and raised her wrist, letting the glow from Caladbolg light the mirror.

Her reflection vanished.

Sindril stared at her from the other side.

She screamed and he laughed.

"At last," he said. "After what you did to me."

"Susan?" asked Will behind her. "What's—"

Sindril waved his scythe and the world around her froze.

"No one will bother us now," he said.

Susan struggled to turn, but her body wouldn't move. Panic rose in her throat. Beneath her, the stool shuddered.

Behind Sindril, something moved.

"No," said Grym. *"It cannot be."*

A Dragon's claw twitched behind the former Headmaster. The Shadow Dragon roared. Darkness melted off its leg, seeping into Sindril.

"You are weak," said the Death. "You're nothing at all, Suzie. Just a girl." He laughed again.

"Leave me alone!"

A sharp, shooting pain coursed through her.

Runes appeared around the mirror's edge, glowing white-hot. Sindril mouthed something, closing his eyes in concentration.

The glowing runes moved, spinning in a circle.

"Whatever happens, Susan," said Grym, *"you must trust me. I will protect you."*

She tried to move, tried to rise, but her body remained paralyzed.

The runes uncoiled like a snake, springing toward her.

Light wrapped itself around her body, seeping into her soul.

She couldn't breathe. The runes strangled her, pulling her into the mirror.

With a surge of power, Caladbolg appeared before her, not as a bracelet, but as a white-haired king.

He raised his arm, *her arm*, and the runes attacked him instead of her.

For a moment, the world spun into a strange vision: a green-eyed king wrestling a glowing snake.

The two wills battled, fighting over her.

The snake unattached from Grym, then sprang forward.

The king screamed, tumbling into Susan and vanishing.

Her wrist burned as if singed by molten rock.

The runes wrapped around Susan again.

The glowing snake bared its fangs, and plunged into her chest.

It tore out her heart.

Her heart was an emerald hourglass.

The snake bit into the emerald, spilling sand.

Time slipped away from her heart.

My time.

Her body writhed in pain.

My soul.

The hourglass vanished and runes sprang toward her again.

"Help me."

The bracelet clawed outwards, slicing the energy which enveloped her.

Sindril yelled, and she saw him topple backward.

Every atom in her body screamed in agony.

The mirror shattered and the cabin filled with light.

* * * *

"Susan, are you all right?"

Will held her in his arms. Shards of glass littered the room. The stool lay on its side to her right. Her shirt sleeves had burned off. On one arm she saw runic-shaped scars. On the other, where the bracelet had been, she saw an emerald shaped bruise.

"What happened?" She started, the voice was hers, yet different.

"There was a flash of light and I couldn't move. The mirror exploded, and now you're—"

"I'm what?"

"You're alive," said Grym, *"and so am I."*

"The bracelet's gone," she said aloud.

"We are fused. We shall never be free of each other."

"Grym says he's attached to me permanently."

"You're welcome. I saved our lives."

"Susan, you should look in a mirror," said Will. "Something else happened."

She looked down at herself, then picked up a shard of mirror.

Staring back from the reflection was an older face, a woman's face.

"Sindril stole four years from you," said Grym.

"I'm older," she said. "How is that possible?"

"Did Grym do this?" asked Will.

"It was Sindril," she replied. "Grym saved me."

She looked down. Her breasts had grown, and her hips seemed rounder, but otherwise she looked the same. She stood.

"What do we do?" he asked. "Is there a way to turn you back?"

"I don't know," she replied. She looked in the mirror shard again, then put it down and looked at the black hourglass shape on her arm.

Four years gone.

He'd been trying to steal even more.

"*You're going to help me."*

"Help you what?" asked Grym.

"We're going to kill Sindril."

CHAPTER THIRTY: FRANK

Fangs at the Funeral

Frank stared at the lake.

All traces of light, *of his mother*, had vanished. The still water reflected trees and sun above.

"We'll hold a service at the village," said Aunt Hinara. "You should speak."

"I don't know what to say."

"She was your mother," said Hinara. "Speak from your heart."

Father stood like stone, his face betraying no emotion.

"I will take us back," said Aunt Hinara.

"No," said Giri. "I will walk. Plamen, come with me. Hinara, take Michi back to the village."

She nodded, and her blue stripes shot outwards, enveloping Michi in sapphire ribbons. Both women vanished.

"Come," said his father. He started to leave.

Frank stared at the lake. Kasumir was gone. She'd been murdered.

Giri placed a hand on his shoulder. "It's a long walk back. I thought we could talk."

Frank turned and followed his father away from the lake. A narrow, ill-kept path emerged in the forest. They walked in silence for ten minutes.

The wolf of his power hungered for revenge. It paced restlessly behind every thought.

"Plamen, your mother and I were not always the most affectionate parents."

Frank remained silent.

"We did love you, son. We were always proud of what you accomplished."

"I accomplished nothing," Frank replied, snarling. "Mother's dead. Deaths and Dragons stand on the brink of war. And for what?" His power itched for release. The red eyes glowered behind his own.

"You helped free the 'Mentals from years of oppression. They came to negotiate a truce, and asked for our help against the Dragons."

"That's it," said Frank. "They came here. Rayn came. He pretended to want a truce, and killed mother."

"You don't know that," said Giri quickly. "She fought a Dragon before she died. You know what a struggle that is."

"She was murdered. Either by Deaths or Dragons, or both."

"Plamen, calm down. Your emotions are—"

"Shut up!" Frank retreated into his mind, and the wolf leaped forward. Pure power surged through his body.

Giri spun around, his eyes flashing with green flame.

"Control yourself," he said. Frank sensed a presence reaching out, grasping toward his thoughts.

The wolf howled, rejecting the invasion.

"I will kill them all," he said, his will pinned beneath the ferocity of the wolf. Its fury seeped into his soul, tearing through him.

Kill, fury, anger, rage...

Like an inferno, flames of power burned through his skin, tearing outwards.

Giri put one hand on each shoulder. Frank struggled, trying to break free.

"*You are strong, my son.*" The words poured over him like water on flame. A pair of glowing green eyes appeared. *"Fight this, and own it."*

Frank relaxed, letting his power flow away. With all his will, he pulled himself out from the wolf's fury.

"I'm okay," he said.

Father relaxed his grip, but continued to watch him. "Strong emotions trigger our abilities, even when we least desire it."

"I know."

"Sit and rest a moment. You've had a shock."

Frank sat on a tree stump. He put his head in his hands and wept.

Neither said a word when Frank rose, wiping tears away.

"I'm not strong if this affects me so much."

"She was your mother. Shedding tears for her loss is not weakness, it is strength. We should go, they'll not start the ceremony without us."

Frank nodded. They walked through the forest for another hour before emerging at Karis.

The village had a somber air. Two 'Mentals noted their arrival and walked forward with flowers. Each wore a white robe over their clothes.

Giri accepted the flowers and they walked to the central hall. A crowd of white-robed Elementals stood outside. Michi came to Frank, holding a robe, which he donned. She reached for his hand and squeezed.

Inside the hall, rows of white-robed Elementals faced the center. Frank and his father walked to the middle of the room, and placed their flowers on Kasumir's chair. Others followed, silently adding their flowers to the growing pile.

Frank watched the ceremony with detachment, standing behind mother's empty chair. One after another walked up with a flower. Each then murmured something to him, or touched his arm. They didn't really care. It was all a show.

Afterwards, everyone walked outside and raised their hands. Several 'Mentals shot beams of light high into the clouds. Others turned fingers to flame, raising their hands in salute. Michi released a dozen flies who buzzed straight up.

More empty gestures.

The wolf lurked behind every thought, filled with rage.

Then, everyone left. More muttered condolences as the crowd thinned, until only Giri, Michi, and Aunt Hinara remained.

"Michi, please stay with us tonight," said Aunt Hinara. "I'm sure Plamen would appreciate it."

"Of course," she replied.

They walked to his parents' house.

Giri sat at the table, and Hinara left to fetch food.

"How are you feeling?" she asked.

"Fine," Frank replied.

"Maybe I should help your aunt." Michi went to the kitchen.

Frank sat.

"It'll take time," his father said.

"Was it Rayn or the Dragon? What do you think?"

Giri shook his head. "I don't know."

"What kind of seer are you?" Both Frank and the wolf within leaped up, ready to pounce.

"My emotions are strong too. *She was my wife!* You think I can call upon my power now? You should understand. Look at yourself, Plamen."

Frank looked up. Michi cowered in the door to the kitchen. On the wall mirror he saw a beast-like figure with eyes of a raging green inferno. The creature's mouth hung open, and his hands grappled like claws.

That's me.

"Frank?" asked Michi.

He shoved down hard, forcing the wolf back, but his anger was too great.

Frank ran out of the house.

I'll kill them all.

CHAPTER THIRTY-ONE: SUSAN

The Sword

Susan got out of the shower, toweled herself dry, and studied her reflection. She looked good, attractive even, but it was still wrong.

Four years of my life.

Who knows what would've happened if Grym hadn't stopped the curse. She'd probably be dead now.

Not dead, she corrected, *erased. I'd never have existed.*

For months she'd obsessed about Sindril's motivations, and why he wanted her at all. Now, those thoughts were over. She didn't care. She had only one goal.

Sindril wants me dead. I'm going to kill him before he has the chance.

"You're not a killer," said a deep voice.

Instinctively, she covered her new breasts. Then she remembered. Susan looked at the mark on her forearm. It wasn't a bruise or a burn, but something different. The hourglass stained her skin like a tattoo, etched permanently onto her arm. Grym was a part of her now.

"I want Sindril dead."

"It'll pass. You and I have fused; our personalities are bleeding. For the next few days, we'll struggle to find balance."

"And then?"

The bathroom vanished, and Susan stood on the endless sea he'd shown her before. Purple clouds hung in an empty gray sky. Caladbolg faced her, not as an ancient king, but as a young man with stern features and blazing emerald eyes.

"This place exists within your mind," he said. "It is easiest for us to talk here."

She looked down. "Where are my clothes?"

"You weren't wearing any, but it's your mind. Imagine clothes."

She took a deep breath, and a dress materialized atop her body.

"How do you feel?" he asked.

"What happened to me?"

"Sindril's curse," replied Caladbolg. "I fought it as best I could, but in the end, he tore part of your soul away. I don't think it was his intent to age you at all, but the clash of wills had a terrible cost."

"Four years' worth?"

"Give or take. Your body might be older, but you're still a child."

"He tore away part of my soul? I'll kill him. I hate Sindril so much. I'll tear him apart."

"Those are my emotions. It's strange, I feel cool and analytic. I'm not used to this. You've given me an inadvertent gift, Susan."

"What's that?"

"I'm alive. For the first time I'm not a tool."

"You've been alive before, I saw the vision, you were a king."

"I was a tool. A tool to defeat the Shadow Dragons. A tool that *failed.* They were too strong for me, or the Earth Dragons. Not that it matters now."

"If we find Sindril, can he separate us?"

"I don't know," said Caladbolg. "When the Dragons wrestled over me, I was trapped in the twisted remains of my crown."

"The bracelet."

"Exactly. Now I'm trapped within your body. If anyone could free me, it's a Dragon."

Susan sat on the surface of the water, and Grym sat facing her.

"I want privacy," she said.

"How?"

"Find a corner and hide unless I call you. Stay there, and stay out of my business."

"Why would I do that?" he asked.

"Because this change is what you've wanted. You have a life. You're not trapped behind a wall, you can exercise your power through me, and together we'll take our vengeance on the Dragons."

Grym stood.

"This is what I wanted, but not for the reason you mentioned," he said.

"Oh?"

"It's not life I've craved, Susan, it's death. I've lived for over a million years, trapped in darkness, unable to pass on. I may be a creation of the Dragons, but I have a *soul*. You want to know why I killed those women? The truth? Because I knew you'd fear me, and would search for a way to destroy me. Now, I have a way. Whether you cease or fade, I will pass on."

"If you want to die, you're going to have to wait a long time. I don't plan on dying soon."

"You gave me this gift, Susan. I will repay you. I will remain *in the corner*, as you say. Yet, I will always be watching."

"One more question, before you go," she said.

"Yes?"

"During the attack, my heart, what I *thought* was my heart, came out."

"And?"

"It was an emerald hourglass, like the symbol I saw on the flag behind you."

"The hourglass is the seal of Donkar. I didn't see one leave your chest, but the curse struck us both." Grym paused. "I'm not sure why you saw one, but my latent powers must have protected you by giving Sindril some of your *time*. If I wasn't there, I believe he would have taken more, and perhaps even killed you."

"We'll talk again."

"I'm certain we shall."

The sea and man vanished. She stood naked in the bathroom, clutching a towel.

* * * *

"I've cleaned up the mirror shards," said Will, when she emerged, after dressing.

"Thank you."

"This'll be awful hard to explain," he said. "With you being…well, you know."

She pulled him into an embrace.

"Will, I'm okay."

They walked to the deck.

"What happened?" asked Sarmarin.

Will stepped aside.

"I've been cursed," she replied.

Sarmarin whistled, eyeing her new body. "Looks like a blessing to me."

"You treat her with respect," said Will.

Susan turned and walked back to their room. "I want to be alone for a while, Will."

He nodded and remained above deck, while she returned to their cabin.

Sitting on the edge of the bed, she sighed.

"You'll have a lot more of that to deal with soon," said Grym.

"When I first arrived, they hated me."

"You're the only female in a world of men. Now, they'll see a woman, not a girl."

"I have a boyfriend."

"Does that matter?"

Standing, she walked to the porthole. Drops of water hung from the thick glass. A wave crashed into the window, and then subsided. The ship swayed beneath her.

"Were you married, Grym?"

"I don't know."

"You don't know? What does that mean?"

"For a thousand millennia, darkness was my prison, and I have spent a long time thinking. I have no memory of a wife, or of ever being wed. Yet, I know that Deaths vanish from existence if they're killed."

"You think your wife was killed?"

"I lived in a turbulent era, but it's more than that. The hourglass, and the constant image of time used in Donkar, remind me of something. I suspect I used my powers to stop Deaths from remembering those who'd been killed."

"What?"

"I am the tool of Dragons, and had many gifts, especially in my youth. The conclusion I've reached is that Deaths cease when they're killed because of me."

"Why would you do that?"

"If I lost someone, such as a wife, in battle, it might be easier to pretend they never existed at all."

Susan paused, imagining a queen of Donkar, a queen that Grym had erased from history. No, it was worse than that, with his misguided command, Caladbolg had erased every killed Death from existence.

"You've condemned untold numbers to oblivion, so even their memories will be lost. If a second war erupts—"

"It will."

"Well when it does, any Deaths who perish will cease *because of* you! *There must be a way to undo that process."*

"My powers are less than they've ever been, now, especially since we've fused. Besides, it is a hypothesis, which has plausibility. I don't know if I'm responsible."

The porthole vanished, and Susan again stood on the endless surface of the sea.

"We're going after Sindril, and then I want you gone. I want you out of my body."

"You'll never be rid of me," replied Grym. *"I'm sorry."*

This is my mind. He might be ancient and powerful, but it's my *soul.*

Using her imagination, she dreamed of chains leaping from the water. As she pictured them, they sprang forth, wrapping around Grym's arms and legs.

"I said I'd stay in a corner," he protested. *"You started talking to me."*

She pulled downward, and he sank beneath the waves, vanishing into an abyss.

"You fool," came a distant voice. *"You need me."*

CHAPTER THIRTY-TWO: WILL

The Woman

Will listened to Susan's gentle breathing on the bunk below. His mind raced. She looked so different now, so mature, so beautiful.

So sexy.

He rolled onto his side, picturing his girlfriend. He'd been attracted to her before, but never like this. He closed his eyes, but her face swam into his mind, as did her body.

He climbed out of the bunk, careful not to wake her. Holding his breath while he opened the door, he crept out of their cabin and headed to the deck. The moon hung above the mast, a watchful eye of pearly white in a dark sea littered with stars.

"Trouble sleeping?" asked Elkanah.

"Yeah."

"Susan's all grown up. She's a beaut. It'll be hard to keep the boys here away."

"She's still my girlfriend."

"Sure, sure. I'm just teasing." He laughed and walked away.

Will walked to the gunwale, watching the endless flow of gentle waves. Thin clouds hung in the distance, silhouetted against the dim glow of distant stars. A swath of water glowed white beneath the moon's reflection. The boat felt motionless, with only a slight murmur of passing water. He remembered a poem from school days in the Mortal World.

Day after day, day after day,
We stuck, nor breath nor motion;
As idle as a painted ship
Upon a painted ocean.
Water, water, every where…

He couldn't remember the rest, and somehow the words disquieted him. Were they really sailing to Donkar?

He walked to the foremast and started to climb.

"Be careful," called a Death below, "don't need a fall at night."

Will grunted acknowledgement, and continued. Pulling his legs one at a time, he climbed to the crow's nest.

"Will?" asked Ilma. The 'Mental's yellow eyes glowed cat-like. Her pale skin shimmered with hints of gold. The crow's nest was small, yet Will had room to join her.

"Hi, Ilma. How's your trip been?"

"Uneventful. My brother and I keep the ship veiled, but we've seen no signs of Dragons."

"That's good."

"I heard about Susan. How is she?"

"She's asleep now. She seems well, but I don't know."

"The rumor is she's aged years all at once. No one knows how."

"Sindril," replied Will. He didn't mention Grym or any other details. Ilma didn't press the issue.

"You love her, don't you?"

"Yes."

"Make sure she knows." Ilma moved her hands in a strange, complex rhythm, focusing the ship's concealment. "I fear a storm approaches."

"A storm?"

"On the horizon. You should return to your cabin."

Will gazed in every direction, but saw only thin hints of clouds. The 'Mental's eyes must be sharper than his.

"Are you going to be okay up here?"

Ilma reached to her feet, lifted a hooded raincoat and pulled it over her head.

"I'll be fine."

Will climbed down the mast. "She said we've got a storm coming," he told Elkanah, before returning to their cabin.

He opened the door gently and slipped inside. Susan still slept.

Laying on the bed, he noticed the ship's rocking increase. It rolled over the waves, and the sound of water slapping the porthole window grew louder as well.

The storm struck soon after. Will grabbed the sides of his bunk as the ship pitched violently in the waves.

"What's happening?" asked Susan, waking.

"We've hit a storm. We should stay here."

Thunder pounded the ocean outside. The cabin tilted, and Will crashed into the wall.

"Should we help the crew?" asked Susan.

"We don't know anything about boats. Just stay in your bunk."

The ship pitched again, and Will tumbled to the edge of his bed. He grabbed for the side but slipped, falling to the ground.

"Are you all right?"

Will's back screamed in protest.

"I think I bruised my arm."

"Can you move?"

He sat up, rubbing his shoulder. "Yeah."

Susan got up and helped him into her bunk. She held him tight against her chest as the storm rolled past, crashing over the ship. He felt the bulges of her new breasts pressing into his back. Her skin was warm behind him, and despite the clamor of the storm, he felt her heartbeat behind him.

They stayed on her bunk until the storm passed. Releasing her hold, she massaged his shoulder.

"I'll be fine," he said, climbing to his bunk.

* * * *

The next morning, they walked to the deck.

"How bad was the storm?" Will asked Sarmarin.

"Two of the sails have torn, and the bowsprit's cracked. It'll take the rest of the day to mend. We'll need to do more repairs once we reach land."

"Can we help?" asked Susan.

"I admire your enthusiasm," said Sarmarin. "Help Henor in the galley. I'm sure he'll find something for you."

They started to leave when Sarmarin called back.

"Susan, I have to say, you're looking fine." Several of the other Deaths whistled at the comment.

She didn't turn, and continued. Will bristled, but followed her to the galley.

Shards of glass covered the floor. For a moment, Will thought the kitchen had been attacked by Sindril, but then he realized it was from the storm.

"Mess everywhere," muttered Henor. "You two here to work? Grab a mop."

They started to clean the floor.

"Susan, could you reach down there, there's something stuck in the corner."

Henor pointed, and Susan bent down. The Death eyed her from behind, then smacked her rear playfully.

Will stepped forward and punched Henor in the jaw.

"Lay off," said Will.

"What's your problem?" demanded Henor. He raised his hand to retaliate, then lowered it.

"We're done cleaning," said Susan. "Come on, Will, let's get back to the cabin."

As they left, Henor grabbed Will's arm and pulled him back.

"You're lucky the boss wants you two unharmed," he hissed into Will's ear.

"Get off," said Will.

They walked back to the cabin.

"Thanks," said Susan, as Will closed the door, "but I can handle myself."

"I was just trying to help."

She sat on her bunk, holding her wrist.

"I want to go back to the College," said Will. "This stupid trip's not worth it."

"Too late now."

He sat beside her, staring at the hourglass mark.

"Does it hurt?" he asked.

"Not at all. I've dealt with Grym for now. I don't think he'll bother me, at least for a while."

"What will you do about the men on this ship?"

"Avoid them if possible. They haven't seen a woman since they came to this world, I'm sure they're confused. Aren't you?"

"A little."

"Good," she said, taking his hand. "I am too. This change came so suddenly, and it's who I am now. I need you, Will. You're my best friend, and more."

"Susan, I…"

"Yes?"

"I love you."

She didn't respond, and Will thought his heart would explode.

Susan smiled, but then looked away.

CHAPTER THIRTY-THREE: SUSAN

Ghosts of Ice and Snow

The ship sailed on for another two weeks. Susan continued to suffer the crew's leers and advances. Sarmarin seemed especially keen on taunting her, and the others followed their captain's example. She spent most days alone in their cabin, or atop the masts with Anil or Ilma. They gazed across the endless expanse of waves talking.

By their twentieth day at sea, the air grew chill. Frost formed on the mast as they sailed north. Grym never spoke again. She wondered if she'd buried him so far that he'd vanished.

No, she surmised, *he's just biding his time.*

She stared out the porthole, thinking of Will. She remembered his words, but still hadn't responded. Some days he seemed eager to discuss their relationship, yet at other times he became distant. Today, he'd avoided her all morning.

I do love him, don't I?

A wave splashed the window, dripping off ice which rimmed the edges.

"Susan" said Will, opening the door behind her. "Come up to the deck. We've spotted land."

She grabbed a coat and hurried upstairs. Deaths ran in a frenzy, and she pushed her way to the side. A strip of bluish-gray emerged from the waves on the border of the horizon.

"To starboard," shouted Sarmarin. The ship turned to the right, toward the distant coast.

Will came from behind, wrapping his arms around her waist.

"It's cold," he said.

"It is." Her words escaped as a puff of warm steam.

Two peaks soon appeared in the distance, twin mountains draped in snow.

"Do you think it's Donkar?" asked Will.

She reached into the depths of her soul, to the buried presence she'd hidden away.

"*Grym.*"

"Yes?"

"Is that shore Donkar? Is this your home?"

"The mountains are Ereshkigal and Arali, the Twin Teeth. The city at their feet was called Mictlan. Any mines you seek here are long abandoned. Yes, we have reached Donkar, or at least its ghost."

"Grym says this is part of Donkar. He recognizes the mountains."

"They remind me of the Towers of the College," said Will. "Two narrow mountains standing watch over something."

"The mine beneath Ereshkigal is your destination. Watch the heavens. This was one of the hidden northern mines, kept secret from the Dragons. If they learn of its location now, your world will never know peace."

The boat sailed closer to the Teeth. Their craggy sides twisted upwards into two white pillars of snow and ice. Clouds covered their peaks. At their feet, piles of stone and snow formed a jumble.

"Furl the sails," shouted Sarmarin. He adjusted a heavy wool coat, pulling his hood over his head. "You two coming?" he asked.

"Of course," said Will.

Susan tightened her coat, waiting for the crew to anchor. Sarmarin, Elkanah, Will, and Susan got into a dinghy. Elkanah and Will grabbed the oars and pulled them away from the ship, rowing toward the snowy banks of Donkar.

Flurries and drifts of white blew overhead as the boat struck ground. Sarmarin tested the snow with his foot.

"Let's go," said Sarmarin, holding the map.

They climbed ashore and Susan's feet vanished beneath a snow bank. The cold seeped over her boots and she shivered.

"I can warm your limbs," said Grym.

"All right."

A gentle warmth seeped into her legs and arms, a flow of power she both welcomed and feared.

"This was once a great port, the northwestern edge of my kingdom."

While she surveyed the snow-covered ruins, Caladbolg's sense of nostalgia bled into her mind. For a moment she saw halls with ivory banners and emerald hourglasses emblazoned on silver flags. She saw two-story windows of iron-rimmed glass and great winged statues, painted in rainbow colors. She blinked and the vision vanished, replaced by a snow-covered ruinous waste-land.

They walked toward a nearby structure. Snow blanketed its collapsed walls.

"What a dump," said Sarmarin.

"This was once the city of Mictlan," she said.

"How do you know that?" asked Elkanah. "No Deaths have been here before, besides the scouts."

"Deaths stood here once, long ago," she replied. "Before they called themselves Deaths, this was a town, a mighty sea port."

Sarmarin turned to her. "What aren't you telling us? How do you possess such knowledge?"

"I excelled in history," she lied. "I recognize the mountains, they resemble Ereshkigal and Arali, the Twin Teeth."

He clearly didn't believe her, but shook his head and continued.

"We'll learn the truth soon enough," muttered Elkanah behind them.

They continued through the city. Will yelled and jumped back.

"What is it?"

"There's something there," he pointed.

Sarmarin stepped forward, brushing snow off an overturned claw.

"A Dragon?" asked Will.

"Just a statue," said Sarmarin. "Part of one, at any rate." He held the map up, then flipped it upside down. "I'm not sure where to go." He wiped steam off the compass with his sleeve.

"This way," said Susan. She took Will's gloved hand and turned left, skirting the city, and headed toward the base of Ereshkigal. Sarmarin scowled, but followed them. Trudging through the snow was difficult and slow. They paused several times.

"Should've brought some food." Elkanah rubbed a gloved hand over his belly.

"I didn't know it'd be this snowy," said Sarmarin. Neither seemed affected by the cold, yet both were clearly hungry.

Will, on the other hand, shivered constantly and spoke little.

"Are you going to be all right?" asked Susan, when they resumed their trek.

"I'll be fine," he said through chattering teeth. "Besides, I can't go back alone, and there's nowhere to stay out here."

"Just stay close to me."

They rounded a snowdrift and the ghostly giant Ereshkigal loomed overhead. Her hide was a gnarled mass of rock, armored beneath sheets of jagged crystal. Blankets of white snow encircled her body. Chunks of icy armor and towering spikes of stone poked out from her snowy sides. They stood at the mountain's feet, straining their eyes upwards.

"No way they found anything out here." Sarmarin scowled. "I don't care how many 'Mentals they coerced, I can't see a thing."

"It's here," said Susan, walking forward. She cleared away a pile of fresh-fallen snow, revealing a smooth marble rock face. "This is the entrance."

She pressed her hand to the stone, and Grym's power flowed outward through her fingers. The marble shuddered, then slid back, revealing a flight of stairs.

"I'll be damned," said Sarmarin. He reached into his pack and pulled out a lantern. He affixed the lantern to a small metal pole, and then lit something inside. A brilliant red light erupted from the lantern, so bright Susan turned away.

"It'll only last about two hours," said Elkanah. "Let's get the others."

"Is that a 'Mental flare?" she asked.

"Something like that," muttered Sarmarin. "Come on, we're going back to the ship."

They struggled back to Mictlan. Will's steps slowed with every pace. He shivered violently.

"Lean on me," she said.

"Aren't you cold?" he asked.

They reached the dinghy, and Will collapsed inside.

The others remained silent as Sarmarin and Elkanah rowed them to the ship.

Helping Will aboard, she started to pull him toward their cabin.

"We'll return soon," said Sarmarin behind her. Then someone grabbed her and spun her around.

"What are you—"

Sarmarin slapped her across the face, knocking her to the deck. Then he grabbed her wrist and slapped a handcuff around it.

"Stop!"

She felt Grym's power surging. If she reached out, she could kill this Death.

"Use my power."

"No, I can't."

"I don't know what game you're playing at, but I want to know how the hell you knew about that mine, and especially how you opened it." Sarmarin closed the other handcuff onto her right wrist, ignoring the hourglass mark. With a click he connected the handcuffs to a chain around the mast.

"Let me go," she demanded.

"Tell me what's going on," demanded Sarmarin. "Or I'll throw your boyfriend into the sea."

Out of the corner of her eye she saw them grab Will, dragging him to the gunwale. He didn't struggle, she couldn't even tell if he was conscious.

"Use my power," repeated Grym.

"I'll tell you everything," she begged. "Let him go."

CHAPTER THIRTY-FOUR: FRANK

Elemental Fury

Frank stared at his feet, resting under the waves of the lake.

So much power. So much wasted power floating beneath the surface.

Using his own power cost a sliver of soul. What about the power of deceased ancestors? What penalty would Frank face if he desecrated the most holy site known to all Elementals?

It's worth it, growled the wolf. *Avenge Kasumir. Use her power alongside your own. Rid this world of all who oppose you.*

Together we are invincible.

Reaching out with his mind, Frank sensed the presence of thousands of decaying souls. Their energy filled the lake, seeping through his toes with limitless potential.

He pictured his mother.

Dragons and Deaths murdered her.

Dragons and Deaths murder each other.

The time of Dragons and Deaths is over,

The time of Elementals has arrived.

Rage coursed through every fiber of his being. Rage so intense and so raw that he felt helpless in its wake.

Closing his eyes, he pulled in.

Like water through a straw, power flowed out of the lake, joining his.

The wolf grew larger, sprouting a second head.

He pulled power through his feet, drawing the power of dead Elementals into his soul.

Frank's breathing labored. The foreign power burned through him like acid, polluting his soul, and poisoning his mind.

Just a little more.

Power mixed with power, energies combined and expanded.

The two-headed wolf sprouted a pair of eagle wings.

He struggled to focus, but the pressure was too great. Pulling his feet out of the water, Frank staggered, grabbing a tree.

He stood before the monstrous two-headed wolf with eagle wings. A snake's tail emerged from the beast's behind, rattling. The hideous chimera secreted forbidden power.

My power.

The world blurred in and out of focus.

I have the power, mother, I'll avenge your death.

He stumbled and fell.

The chimera roared.

Frank spread his wings and jumped into the sky, then crashed to the ground.

I don't have wings. What's wrong with me?

Around him the trees dripped with blood. He got to his feet and ran.

Skirting the village, he reached a dense area of woodlands.

"Frank," said an albino, approaching. "I didn't hear you. Our training continues well." *Fearmongers use telepathy, don't they? Were those words in my mind?*

"Come with me," Frank said, finding it awkward to form words with his mouth. He wasn't certain he'd spoken aloud at all.

"We are training." The albino gestured to six other fearmongers.

"All of you, come with me. We are on the attack. Deaths and Dragons slew my mother, we must avenge her."

"Kasumir is dead?"

"Murdered." His fingers balled into tight, trembling fists.

All seven fearmongers approached, staring at him.

"Murdered?" asked one. "How?"

"I don't know." Frank shook his head. "She fought a Dragon. We'll attack them first. Is your company ready?"

One of the albinos walked to him and drew him aside. "We're not ready to fight Dragons or anyone. We should go to the village and seek guidance," he said.

The chimera paced, clawing at his mind. Each wolf's mouth grinned.

"I don't have time to return to the village," said Frank.

"We can't just rush off against the most powerful race in this world."

"*Elementals* are the most powerful race." Frank knocked the fearmonger's hand aside. "No one can defeat us."

"You're not yourself." The albino's mind touched his.

"*Get out!" roared the chimera.*

Frank's power surged forward. He dove into the fearmonger's mind, forcing his way through the other's consciousness.

"Help me claim vengeance," demanded Frank.

The fearmonger struggled, but the chimera pinned the albino's mind down.

The fearmonger nodded, waving to the others. "We're going with him."

Frank continued, leading the seven fearmongers.

Power. More power.

They trekked onward through the forest. The fearmongers said nothing.

Frank paused. If he turned west he could attack the Dragons, but he had no idea where the creatures lived. The Deaths huddled in the College, easy prey.

They rounded a bend, startling a herd of deer.

Frank thought of Kasumir, struggling in her final moments. The rage welled again.

He shot his mind forward. The chimera pounced on a deer, devouring it.

The creature dropped dead, and more power rushed into Frank's poisoned soul.

"Frank," gasped a voice behind him. "I found you at last, I've been so worried."

Without thinking, he turned, extending his power again. The chimera struck something down, opening its fanged mouth.

"Frank, please. It's me. It's Michi."

He paused, wrestling the beast, but the power continued to press.

Michi fell, an open gash emerging on her face.

One of the fearmongers raised his hand and terror spread across her features.

"Please," she whispered. "I love you, Frank."

Frank's anger evaporated. He released his mental hold on her, and waved the fearmongers away.

"Help me," he said, falling to the ground. "I can't control it."

"I'm here," she said.

The world faded into darkness.

* * * *

Frank stood on a desert, beneath an empty sky.

The chimera faced him, its two wolf-heads snarling. The eagle wings spread, and its serpent tail lashed the air.

In his hand he held a boskery blade.

"You betrayed me," said one wolf-head. Its voice was Will's. "You stole my girlfriend, tortured her with visions, and led her to madness. She carries a murderer on her wrist because of you."

"No," said Frank, backing up.

"You're horrid," added the other wolf-head, speaking with Susan's voice. "You claimed to be my friend, but you only care for yourself. You're a selfish child."

The chimera turned away, its wings flapping. The serpentine tail writhed in the air, extending twenty feet above him, then came slashing toward the ground.

He ducked and rolled, but the tail caught his foot, knocking him over.

The chimera spun and both sets of fangs bared over his head. He felt hot drool dripping from the twin mouths.

"I'm sorry," he said.

"Sorry?" said Will and Susan in unison. "Sorry isn't good enough."

The beast raised a clawed leg.

Frank grabbed his boskery blade and sliced upward, knocking the oversized lupine claws away. The serpent tail slithered under the chimera, rattling. Tiny spikes lined the tail, each sharp enough to impale him.

Frank got to his feet, running.

"Where will you run?" demanded the beast. "I live in you."

"I want to be free."

"Free? You created me! You did this yourself."

Frank put the blade down, turning to face the enormous chimera. Treacherous power leeched from its hide, seeping into the air like venomous vapor.

"I *am* you, Plamen," said the chimera. "I am your soul."

"My name is Frank."

The beast lurched forward.

Frank spun, and a wall emerged from the sand. A mirror.

Frank stared at himself.

"You see me now." The chimera roared, and the mirror shattered.

Frank stood alone, facing an image of himself.

The other Frank shifted and blurred. One head became two, arms became a tail. It was a beast once more, howling into the sky.

Where is there to run? I cannot run from my reflection.

With open fangs, the chimera's jaws clamped around him. He remained still, and the creature passed through him harmlessly.

I will not run from you.

I will deny you no longer.

You are a part of myself.

Frank opened his palms, and welcomed the beast. He accepted the darkness in his heart, the rage and the fury. He accepted the pain that would never leave.

The chimera faded, drawn back into Frank's body.

* * * *

"Where am I?" he asked.

"You're back home," said his father. "You've been sleeping for a week."

"Is Michi here? Is she all right?"

"She's fine, though the scar you gave her will never heal. I'll get her."

Frank rose, his body weak and hungry. He watched Michi enter the room. A red mark ran down her cheek, from nose to ear.

"I'm sorry," he said.

"I know what you did." Her eyes glistened with unshed tears. "I know you took power from the lake. What did you hope to accomplish, Frank?"

"Vengeance, I suppose."

"You don't even know for certain she was murdered."

His father returned with a bowl of steaming soup. "Eat," he said, placing the bowl beside Frank. "You'll need strength."

"What should I do?"

"About the soup?" asked Giri.

"About mother. About this anger."

"Worry about that later. Eat now."

He exchanged a glance with Michi, then left them alone.

Frank sipped on the kerec root soup, a warm blend of cinnamon, kerec, and wildflowers, mixed with a spoonful of nostalgia. He watched Michi. The mark on her cheek tore at his heart.

I did that. I hurt her.

"The fearmongers are outside," she said.

"Why?"

"They never left. You did something to one of them. I don't think they'll abandon you now."

"I was out of control."

"You've made a mess, and now you have to clean it. Treat the albinos well, Frank."

"And you?"

"Treat me well, too."

"What do you think I should do?"

She sighed. "I think you should finish recuperating, then return to the College. What you need isn't revenge, it's *answers*. If the Dragons killed your mother, then help the Deaths, as they've been asking. If the Deaths played a role, you'll only discover the truth at the College."

"I'll return, then."

"Frank, I'm not leaving your side."

"No, I'm too dangerous."

"That's why you need me there. You need to be reminded. You're a good person, and you're stronger than you think."

He remembered his own voice telling Susan similar words last year.

"I am strong," he said to himself.

Michi touched his face. "Don't forget it."

* * * *

Three weeks later, Frank sat in a classroom, annoyed. His thoughts drifted to Will and Susan.

Where are they? It's been weeks.

None of the teachers knew what had happened. They were alive, else he'd never realize they were missing. Hann knew something, but avoided him whenever he approached.

Frank rose from his seat and scratched his collar. Michi crawled near his neck as a tiny beetle. Her legs tickled.

Walking through the stone labyrinth of the College he gazed up at West Tower.

I can't use my power to search for them. I have to trust that they're all right.

Red clouds hung behind the mountain of stone. The giant loomed into the sky like a dark finger, pointing to the heavens.

“Frank!”

The voice called into his mind, like a whisper from far away.

“Susan?”

“Help us!”

The voice faded into wind. Had he imagined it?

No, something was wrong.

Susan was in danger.

CHAPTER THIRTY-FIVE: SUSAN

Mine

"Let him go," repeated Susan.

Sarmarin waved the others to pause.

"Have you heard of Grym, the First Scythe?" she asked.

"The myth?" asked Sarmarin. "What of it?"

"It's no myth. He's real, and he told me about the mine."

"You expect me to believe that your information comes from a fairy tale?"

She proceeded to explain how she'd discovered the bracelet. She omitted many of the key details, including the library and Grym's murder of two women in the mortal world.

"We're fused," she concluded. "You can see the mark on my wrist. Please, captain, just let us go, it's all been a misunderstanding."

Sarmarin paused, scratching his chin. Then he laughed.

The crew looked uneasy, then started laughing with him.

"Send Will down to the galley for some hot food," he called. He unlocked Susan's handcuffs.

"You believe me?" she asked.

"Why not? You turned into a woman overnight. Besides, I work in Mors, and have sailed around the Hereafter. I've seen wonders far less believable than a myth brought to life."

Susan rubbed her wrists, then pulled up her sleeve, showing the hourglass. "This is the mark," she said.

"You should eat something as well. Warm yourself and prepare to return to the mine in half an hour."

She nodded, then proceeded to the galley. Will sat at a table sipping tea from a mug.

"Tell me I'm not the only one who passed out from cold," he said.

"You were. Are you feeling all right now?"

"I dreamed the Deaths threatened to throw me overboard."

"It was no dream. Will, I opened the mine with Grym. They wanted an explanation, but I've cleared things up."

"Oh?"

"Eat, and warm up. We're heading back to the mine soon." She pulled a gorger from the counter and envisioned hot apple pie.

"I think I'll stay here," he said.

"I want to see the mine; it's what we came all this way for." She lowered her voice. "You've seen how they taunt me, Will. I don't want to go alone. Will you come?"

He frowned but nodded, taking his own gorger.

They ate, then returned to the cabin and changed into two layers of socks each. They pulled their heavy coats back on, and wrapped scarves around their necks.

"Come on," shouted Sarmarin. "We're leaving."

This time, the crew joined them on the mainland. It took two trips for the dinghy to transport Deaths from the ship to the snowy shore of Mictlan. Susan and Will joined the convoy, leaving only Anil and Ilma aboard.

A bitter wind howled through the ruins of the once mighty port. Like before, Susan's senses flashed between the modern snowy wasteland, and a thriving city teeming with life. The Twin Teeth towered over the icy vestiges of Mictlan. Snow whipped down from the mountains, billowing over the huddled Deaths.

"Let's get moving," shouted Sarmarin. "We'll be safe inside the mine."

With a gust of wind, Susan saw the green emerald hourglass fluttering on a banner high behind the central hall. Donkari milled about town, carrying goods to and from a fleet of massive ships. Mictlan buzzed with activity.

She brushed snow off her face, again staring at the icy graveyard.

"What happened here?"

"I do not know," replied Grym. *"I was sealed before the War, and Masrun never crossed the Sea. Perhaps the city was abandoned when the Donkari sailed west. They took me with them, of course. This is the first time I've returned to my kingdom."*

The frigid wind whistled through the remains of a structure with a dome.

"The Temple of Dragons," noted Grym. *"This was a beautiful palace of stone and glass."* Through his eyes, Susan saw the soaring structure. Atop the marble cupola, a golden Dragon spread its wings, facing the dawn. Red stone formed the base of the three-story structure, trimmed with silver cornices and marble columns.

"You worshipped the Dragons?"

"Yes. Not just Earth Dragons, either. Both Earth and Shadow Dragons were sacred to the Donkari. They created us, after all."

Will shivered beside her. A pile of snow collapsed from one of the falling walls of the ruined temple. They continued.

At the base of Ereshkigal, Sarmarin held up a hand. "Susan," he called.

"Yes?"

"You opened this mine. Whether you possess Grym or not, you've earned the right to take the lead." He handed her a lantern.

"Thank you."

Will grabbed her hand as she started down the stairway. Away from the wind, the air calmed and grew warm. They walked down and down. The winding staircase descended a hundred feet before leveling off into a narrow passageway.

The flower-filled lantern cast a faint light ahead of her as Susan stepped over broken rocks and dust-covered rubble. She stopped at a wall of stone.

"This shouldn't be here," said Grym. His power flowed into her arm, and blue light extended from her wrist, arcing toward the stones.

"Be careful," warned Will.

Cutting her way through the stones, Susan opened a passage to the other side, then crawled through. She turned to see the other Deaths close behind. They continued until she reached a cramped room with two passageways. Metal hooks descended from the ceiling, affixed to chains. A smell of sulfur filled the chamber. She stopped.

"We're here," said Sarmarin. "By the looks of these passages, half the mountain must be solid mortamant. This will alter the future." He passed out two more lanterns. "You three, down that passage. You two, explore there."

Sarmarin and the three other Deaths from Mors: Elkanah, Henor, and Geraj remained in the central area with Will and Susan. The two other groups disappeared from view. At the base of one passageway, a metal crate stood on the cavern floor. Sarmarin extended his arms, and climbed to the top of the crate, standing over them, looking away.

"I hope this helps," said Susan. "Ever since we saw that boat burned by Dragons, I've feared for the College."

Sarmarin snapped his head around, a wild look in his eye. "I remember that day. The first burning." He glowered from above, clutching one of the metal hooks.

"It was terrible," said Will.

"Now," whispered Sarmarin.

Henor grabbed Susan from behind, clamping his hand over her mouth. She squirmed, but couldn't break free. She watched Elkanah and Geraj reach for Will. He spun, punching Elkanah in the face, but Geraj wrapped his arms around Will, holding her boyfriend still. Elkanah stroked his chin, then punched Will, leaving a black eye.

Sarmarin's eyes narrowed, turning bright yellow in the darkness. He opened his mouth and his teeth melted into fangs.

"Grym!"

The power surged through her arm, knocking Henor back. It sliced into the Death, leaving a slice of green blood across his body.

"He's not a Death!"

Henor's body trembled and writhed, dissolving and growing. His skin melted off, revealing bright violet scales. His neck extended, and his arms flailed until they became wings. A small Dragon lay dead behind her. Its neck extended, expanding even in death, until the two passageways vanished from sight behind the wall of undulating purple. The Dragon's body blocked both corridors, and filled much of the chamber they stood in.

There are Deaths back there, she thought for a moment.

There was no time, though. Sarmarin's face contorted above her. His teeth extended into fangs. Henor's body continued to grow, pressing against her, with scales sharp as blades. Susan's path was blocked. The only way out was to return towards the mine's entrance.

Too shocked to speak, she started forward. Geraj and Elkanah pulled Will out of sight, disappearing down the corridor they'd entered. She sprinted towards them, but Sarmarin leaped down. She screamed as he opened his fanged mouth. A bolt of flame erupted, encasing her.

"Susan!" Will yelled in the distance.

Flames surrounded her, but she felt no heat. She stared as the blue-gold inferno vanished, then touched her face. There were no burns or pain. Only her arm hurt. She glanced down, noticing a thin white film over the skin on her right forearm.

"It's over," said Sarmarin, his voice filled with hisses.

He stepped closer, the veins on his face bulging. A piece of skin fell from his cheek, revealing pulsing black scales.

"Grym!" She shouted in her mind, or perhaps aloud, but he didn't answer. The smell of sulfur filled the chamber, suffocating her.

Sarmarin struck Susan across the face with a violent blow. She collapsed backwards, her face stinging. Rocks dug into her back as she slammed into the cavern floor.

She lifted her arm, trying to fend him off.

"Grym, please!"

For a moment she sensed the ancient power deep within her, but it felt muted and buried. A chunk of flesh fell to the ground beside her, and she recoiled, realizing it was a hand. Sarmarin approached again, with long white claws like daggers where his fingers had been.

He held one of his claws against her throat, kneeling over her. Its razor edge cut into her skin.

"Don't worry," he said. "You're no good to me dead."

He smiled, but then backed up, his face contorted. Another chunk of skin fell off his face. Sarmarin clutched his belly, which grew. His entire body writhed, and he seemed to forget her for a moment, as his face squirmed in agony.

"No, not here," she heard the Dragon mutter.

Susan's head spun but she struggled to her feet and ran for the corridor. She sprinted after Will, running as fast as her sore feet would move. Behind her, the cave shook. Boulders loosed from the ceiling, crashing around her in clouds of dust. Susan dared to look back.

Sarmarin's skin and clothes were gone. A black Dragon with fierce yellow eyes clawed its way behind her. He shot a bolt of flames.

She jumped through the hole in the wall she'd cut, and dove for cover. Fire rushed past like a flaming hose, blasting through the hole above. The Dragon roared, trapped. She ran again, sprinting toward the stairs, and climbed two at a time. The mountain shuddered.

"Grym! Help me!"

The First Scythe didn't answer. White gossamer gauze covered her arm, blanketing the hourglass mark like a layer of film. She tore at it as she ran, but the fibers still wouldn't come off. She banged her arm on the wall, but it bounced off unscathed.

Ereshkigal thundered and moaned when she ran out of the mine. Sarmarin burst out of the rubble, roaring. His force and anger shook Ereshkigal's snow-covered mountain sides. An avalanche of white cascaded into Sarmarin's eyes, and he shot flame in all directions, tearing the mine's foundation with his claws. Rock exploded like debris erupting from a volcano. A boulder flew through the frigid air, slamming into Geraj's face. Geraj collapsed to the ground, his body dissolving into scales.

Elkanah clutched Will in enormous talons. His face stretched and melted, revealing a white Dragon with sapphire eyes. A row of black spikes ran down Elkanah's back, ending at a jagged tail. He took off, clutching Will.

"Susan, help me!" he screamed.

"You fool," shouted Elkanah, in the same voice she'd heard so many times on their voyage. "You've killed Geraj. Couldn't you control yourself?"

"Henor's gone as well," said Sarmarin, his voice familiar and yet filled with hisses. He dove forward and scooped Susan into his claws. She struggled but the ground dropped away beneath her.

"We have them both, and the mine's destroyed," said Elkanah. "Let us return."

"Agreed," said Sarmarin. "Though there's something to do first." He spread his bat-like wings, each over thirty feet long, and turned in mid-air. Susan fought for breath. The mountain blurred beneath her, crumbling into a mass of stone and snow. Sarmarin's claw felt like steel beneath her chest. The tips of the talon, where it met his black scales, were hot to the touch.

Sarmarin flew toward the ship and released a blast of flame. Even from his talons, she felt a wave of heat. Fire rocketed toward their ship, engulfing it in an inferno.

Anil and Ilma. No!

The ship burned in the icy sea. Susan raised her head, and saw Will, unconscious in the white Dragon's claws.

They sped away, then flew higher at an unbelievable speed. Clouds passed underneath, and she saw the curve of the horizon, and the darkness of space above. Stars twinkled in the distance.

The two Dragons soared without rest. Her belly writhed in agony, and her throat constricted, needing water. Elkanah and Sarmarin rarely spoke, and never to Susan. They chased the sunset three times. At night she tried to sleep, ignoring the pain that coursed through every joint.

During the day she stared between the distant clouds below, searching for any sign of rescue.

But who would come?

On the fourth day, the Dragons angled steeply, soaring lower. Too weak to move, Susan watched the descent with half-closed eyes. She saw land far below. A coastline and forests.And something beyond.

The College!

Her heart leaped when she recognized the two towers and the glint of the Ring of Scythes. They passed swiftly, on the edge of the horizon.

"If you can hear me, Grym, loan me whatever power you can. One message. One message is all I ask."

"Frank!"

She screamed his name with her mind, picturing his eyes of flaming emerald.

"Help us!"

* * * *

She lay on a soft bed, under a blanket. She rolled, grimacing at the pain in her limbs.

"You'll need some food and water," said a voice. "Drink this."

Susan opened her eyes.

Sindril stood above her, holding a pitcher. The man she'd fought last year, the man who'd brought her to this world, and then tried to kill her. The Death who'd betrayed them all.

"Sindril."

"Welcome, Susan."

She reached for Grym, but couldn't sense him at all.

"Help me."

"It's no use struggling," said Sindril. "You are mine."

Susan's story continues in the final volume of

The Scythe Wielder's Secret:
Daughter of Deaths.

ABOUT THE AUTHOR

Christopher Mannino's life is best described as an unending creative outlet. He teaches high school theatre in Greenbelt, Maryland. In addition to his daily drama classes, he runs several after-school performance/production drama groups. He spends his summers writing and singing. Mannino holds a Master of Arts in Theatre Education from Catholic University, and has studied mythology and literature both in America and at Oxford University. His work with young people helped inspire him to write young adult fantasy, although it was his love of reading that truly brought his writing to life.

Learn more about Mannino and the World of Deaths, and enjoy exciting free content at www.ChristopherMannino.com

Did you enjoy Sword of Deaths? If so, please help us spread the word about Christopher Mannino and MuseItUp Publishing. It's as easy as:

•Recommend the book to your family and friends
•Post a review
•Tweet and Facebook about it

Thank you
MuseItUp Publishing

CPSIA information can be obtained
at www.ICGtesting.com
Printed in the USA
FFOW04n1115240116